SUGAR CANDY COTTAGE

A perfect setting for a charming family—so
Folly Cottage seemed from the outside. But
Teresa's visit to her mysterious uncle and
the advent of a complete stranger made for
surprising revelations—about the family, and
about Teresa's own heart.

Also by the same author

The Fox From His Lair
Mixed Marriage
Letter To My Love
The Golden Collar
The Stratton Story
The Past Tense Of Love
The Friendly Air

and available in Coronet Books

Sugar Candy Cottage

Elizabeth Cadell

CORONET BOOKS
Hodder Paperbacks Ltd., London

Printed in Great Britain
for Coronet Books, Hodder Paperbacks Ltd.,
St Paul's House, Warwick Lane, London, E.C.4,
by Richard Clay (The Chaucer Press), Ltd.,
Bungay, Suffolk

ISBN 0 340 16073 X

Chapter One

THE man who stood before the house, hands thrust deep into pockets, had the air that men wear when they wait for a woman: a look half irritable, half resigned. Now and then he would stroll for a short distance along the gravel drive, turn and retrace his steps and then stand staring expectantly at the open front door.

A chauffeur came out of the house carrying two large suitcases, and put them in the luggage compartment of the waiting car. Following him came a maid, over her arm her mistress's fur coat, in her hand a smaller case. Round the side of the house came the daily woman with Lady Thurloe's silver-grey poodle in her arms, one paw upheld in preparation for waving good-bye. This momentary bustle over, there was a pause; all was in readiness.

A girl came out presently and walked down the steps leading to the drive. The man greeted her with a touch of impatience.

"Your mother's cutting it rather fine, Teresa. Any hitch?"

They both smiled; hitches had been known to occur even at this late stage in Lady Thurloe's arrangements. Then Teresa shook her head.

"No; no hitch," she said. "She's ready."

He looked down at her for some moments, studying her. He was a tall, powerfully built man in his early thirties, dark, good-looking, his manner serious and perhaps a little heavy. He had been engaged to Teresa for the past month; they were to marry three months from now—in September. Staring down at her now, he thought she looked tired; she had probably, he thought, stayed up late doing odd jobs for her mother.

His glance roamed over the waiting servants—the gardener now added to the number—and a smile, brief and puzzled, touched his lips. Here, he mused, was the familiar routine; here, assembled, grouped, ready for the send-off, was the chorus line; here was the cast, and only the principal was missing.

The setting, he realized, as his eyes roamed over it, had a theatricality all its own. In the background rose the Sussex

Downs, grey-green in the early June sun, black in the shadows. In the foreground was the long, low house, pink-washed, as pretty as a postcard, its lawns satin-smooth, its flower beds immaculate. Neville Morley, staring at it, remembered his own first impressions; it had brought to his mind the nostalgic descriptions of life-as-it-used-to-be, upon which the older generation were certain to embark unless one read the signs and escaped; descriptions of the days of ease and plenty, of gracious and leisurely living.

It was all, Neville decided with a sudden grin, a bit too good to be true. It was far too Home-and-Garden. But he acknowledged that it was a perfect setting for Lady Thurloe's grace and charm.

"What are you smiling at?" Teresa asked him.

"This." He waved a hand. "The usual. I always feel—when your mother's around—like a film extra getting five guineas for hanging about in the background."

"She's coming—she won't be a minute," said Teresa.

He looked at her.

"Sure you won't change your mind and come up to Town with me?" he asked.

She shook her head.

"No. It's wonderful to be at home—for a change."

"D'you miss your job?"

"No, not in the least. But——" she hesitated.

"But giving it up makes marriage seem much nearer—is that it?"

There was a hint of wounded pride behind the words, and she would have liked to reassure him, but honesty made her say instead:

"I think so. I feel . . . betwixt-and-between."

"Why won't you pack a few things when your mother's gone, and drive up to London with me? You can stay in my sister's flat while I'm over in Brussels. The business will only take me three days—then when I get back we can see a few shows and——"

"No." Again Teresa shook her head. "No. There's something I want to do today."

"What sort of something?"

"I'll tell you when Mother's gone."

"If she goes." Neveille's glance went briefly to the house. "Sure she hasn't changed her mind again? Wouldn't be the first time she's got as far as this and then backed out. I can't think why she goes travelling so much; she's really not keen on it."

Teresa let this inaccuracy go unchallenged. A lover of tranquillity, she had learned early in her life to disregard provocative openings. She was aware that her mother very much liked travelling and would, in fact, travel more if all could be made to proceed smoothly—but at the first hitch, the first uncertainty of sailing date or cabin or travelling companion, Lady Thurloe would announce that she would not, after all, go away. Two projects had fallen through earlier in the year; now, at last, the delicate parts had been assembled, the tricky operation carried through: she was to go on a fortnight's cruise in the Hebrides. She was to drive up to London and join her friends; her cabin was excellent, every comfort was assured. Teresa would be here to welcome her home.

Standing beside Neville, Teresa felt his impatience and slipped her hand into his. The gesture was made less from affection than from a sense of loyalty towards her mother. He looked down at her, and for a moment the scene faded and he saw only her grace and loveliness, her delicate, maddeningly remote beauty. She made no visible withdrawals, but he had never felt her really near to him; from the first moment of meeting, four years ago, she had had this quality of elusiveness. But she was going to be his; his ring was on her finger. When they were married, she would lose what he could only term for want of a better word, her shyness. She was twenty-three—almost twenty-four—and she was utterly unawakened. Sometimes, in moods of rare depression, he wondered whether she would ever melt in warm, glowing passion.

A stir brought him back abruptly to the present.

"Here she is," said Teresa.

"And about time," said Neville, and went forward to meet the woman who stood poised at the top of the steps.

Coralie Thurloe was tall and slender, and had retained much of the beauty of her youth. There was about her, however, no hint of any desire to appear younger than her years: her smooth skin was scarcely made up; her hair was a natural brown, her lips merely touched with colour. Her air was quiet, reposeful and prettily dignified, beautifully dressed, her whole appearance was that of a woman of means but also a woman of impeccable taste. Her manner was poised, but had a touch of hesitation that removed any hint of hardness.

She came slowly, gracefully down the steps and paused to pet the poodle; her voice, low and quiet, crooned over him for a few moments. She had an anxious word for the woman holding him, but her anxiety was not for the dog.

"You'll look after youself, Mrs. Piper, while I'm away? You need a good rest."

Mrs. Piper, flushing with pleasure, promised to rest. Lady Thurloe moved away to talk to the gardener, and left him to say a word of farewell to the maid. Then she turned to the chauffeur and with a smile got into the car, throwing, as she did so, a kind glance to the two errand boys who had paused at the gate and were viewing the proceedings with deep interest.

Neville, watching her, saw the magic working and once again marvelled. He had known her for over four years, and he had never seen it fail. A shrewd, even a cynical man, he had looked at first for flaws—and had found none. There had not, he admitted to himself, been a single sour note, a single crack in the amazingly smooth façade, and as time went on, a conviction had arisen in him that nobody could hold a pose—if it was a pose—so long and so untiringly. If it had been merely a performance, there would surely, he thought, have been times when she would have needed to relax. But she had remained what he was forced to call her own charming self: sweet, sympathetic and unselfish. She appeared to ask for nothing; if she cancelled her plans because they were not going well, she did so entirely without petulance, and with only a quiet intimation that she did not, after all, think that it would be amusing.

The real test, in Neville's eyes, had come when he expressed his wish to marry Teresa. Lady Thurloe had been for the past twenty years a widow; Teresa was her only child. If there were any selfishness in her mother, any possessiveness, it would surely, he thought, show now. But far from opposing or delaying the marriage, Lady Thurloe had expressed her delight and had even advised an early wedding. It was Teresa and not her mother who had raised difficulties; her mother had swept them away.

It had been almost the last time that Neville had questioned her sincerity—and the first time that he understood fully Teresa's affection for her mother. He knew that Teresa, despite her look of fragility, was sensible, humorous and intelligent; she would, he was convinced, have seen flaws in her mother if there had been any to see—but Teresa was devoted to her mother. She spoiled her, as everybody did; sometimes she laughed at her—but the laughter was gentle. It was proof enough; proof of what, Neville would have found it hard to say—but in his eyes now, as he watched Lady Thurloe making her farewells, there was not the touch of cynicism that had once showed in them when he looked at her.

She was in the car; all but the last good-byes had been said. Neville tucked the rug round her knees and she leaned forward, one slim, gloved hand detaining him.

"You'll look after Teresa?"

He laughed. "What do you think?"

Lady Thurloe was about to say something more; her hand was still on his arm; he was waiting—but no word was spoken. Instead, there came from the house a loud shout—and as all eyes turned towards the sound, there came out of the front door a woman brandishing a hat-box.

"Wait—wait!" she shouted.

She came awkwardly down the steps—short, almost squat, grey-haired, plain to ugliness—and with her appearance on the drive, every trace of artificiality was swept from the scene, and reality rushed in to take its place; in an instant, the atmosphere became that of the normal, the earthy and the everyday.

Lily Hyde, the woman ambling to the car, talking agitatedly as she went, was a distant cousin of Teresa's father. She had come some twenty years ago, at his request, to join the household. Her functions, as her status, were undefined; she was to be nanny to Teresa, she was to give a little help here and there in the house. She was then nearing forty, unmarried and with no means of her own; she had before her arrival been living with this and that aged cousin as companion, and she had little or no experience of children. But between her and Teresa there had sprung into being a mutual trust and affection which nothing had ever shaken. Between her and Coralie Thurloe was a link stronger than affection: Coralie needed her. Coralie needed a house that ran without her aid; Coralie needed freedom to pursue her own interests and amusements; above all, she needed someone who knew what she wanted and who would see that she got it if possible—and all this Lily Hyde provided.

She was, perhaps, the nearest thing to a machine ever made in human form. Square, solid, shabby and irredeemably awkward, she had the strength and tirelessness of an engine. She had few interests beyond the confines of Folly Cottage; from early morning to late at night she moved stolidly and unhurriedly from task to task, self-contained, contented and completely absorbed. She sat down only to meals and to do tasks which could be done better seated—for the rest of the time she padded round the house in stout black shoes with felt soles, a voluminous overall concealing her dress, her head swathed in a cotton scarf. She had no graces. She could not be called fat; her bulk was too solid to be termed obesity; she carried a good deal of flesh, but none of it looked superfluous.

Her manner was somewhat absent; she worked in silence, only muttering from time to time as thoughts or plans came into her head. She had grim humour and a ready tongue, but only Teresa enjoyed these, for only Teresa sought her out and spent happy hours in her company. It was Teresa who had renamed her Lolly, a name everybody but Coralie had adopted.

Lolly had her own sitting-room, and used it for the whole of her scant leisure; she had, she pointed out, given up her independence, but not her freedom. She had strong and unorthodox views on diet, religion and politics, and was prepared to air them if invited. She had no trace of meekness or humility; she was a penniless woman accepting a salary from Coralie, but she knew—and knew that Coralie knew—that money could not buy the service she gave; she knew that she was irreplaceable.

Once a year, in September, Lolly left Folly Cottage and went on a round of visits to her relations. She swept into the houses of her cousins, cleaned and polished and tidied with the same untiring zeal she showed at home, and swept out again at the end of two or three days, leaving her hostesses searching agitatedly for everything that she had put away in what she considered the right places. If this method of taking a holiday did not bring her rest, it brought her what she enjoyed far more: the latest titbits of family news. Drinking them in, she dealt them out again to Teresa in instalments until the following September came round.

Teresa was walking to meet her now; Lolly handed over the case and spoke in a breathless grunt.

"There. Good thing I spotted it." She went up to the car and put her head in to address Coralie. "Found it on the landing," she told her, "and if I hadn't yelled, then what? You'd have gone off without it and then you would have come back for it and lost the boat train." She banged the door, brushing aside Coralie's thanks. "You're late as it is," she said. "Boat trains don't wait. Enjoy yourself and keep warm and enjoy the scenery. Good-bye. See you in two weeks."

She signalled to the chauffeur; Lady Thurloe raised a hand in a last farewell, leaned back and was borne from sight.

"Lolly, you're an angel," said Teresa. "If mother'd discovered she hadn't got that, she——"

"——would have cancelled the trip." Lolly put up a thick arm and tucked a few whispy trails of hair into the bun at the back of her head. "Well, she's off now and I hope she'll enjoy herself.—You out to lunch, Teresa, or in?"

"Out," said Teresa. "I'm having lunch with Lawrence."

"When you gave up your job last week," Lolly reminded her, "you said you never wanted to see Brighton again."

"I forgot about Lawrence."

"You sure he's going to give you lunch?" Lolly asked. "What about that sour housekeeper of his? Won't she give notice?"

"I'll let you know when I come back," promised Teresa, and watched Lolly go with her awkward, rolling gait into the house.

"You didn't tell me you were lunching with your godfather," said Neville, as she vanished indoors.

"I rang him up this morning and asked if I could go in and have lunch with him. I want to see him specially," said Teresa. "I've got things I want to talk over with him."

"Such as?"

They were walking slowly towards the house; she did not answer the question until they were in the drawing-room and Neville had closed the door behind them. Then he repeated it and she looked at him with a thoughtful frown.

"Such as what we're going to do about Mother when we get married," she said slowly.

His expression was bewildered. "I don't understand," he said. "Is there a problem?"

"Yes. Lolly's leaving."

There was a pause. Neville was too surprised to speak. He had regarded Lolly—and he knew that Teresa had regarded her —as a permanent member of the household.

"Sure you've got it right?" he asked at last. "Why would she leave? Where would she go?"

"She could go to half a dozen places and she could earn twice as much as Mother gives her. I can't imagine her anywhere but here . . . but that isn't the point. Mother . . . You see, Neville, this means that Mother will be alone."

"Except for a gardener and a chauffeur and a maid, to say nothing of the daily woman or women," he said drily. "Don't get things out of proportion. Your mother's a very lucky woman."

"I know. And she knows. But when you and I arranged to marry in September, we both thought—I thought and I'm sure you thought too—that Lolly'd be here to—to——"

"Close the gap?"

"To make things seem more or less the same. But if I go, and if Lolly goes——"

"When did she tell your mother that she was going?"

"She hasn't told Mother yet. She told me—last night."

"And so you lay awake all night, worrying?"

"Not worrying. Thinking. Planning."

He looked at her. She had moved away and was sitting on a low window seat; she looked younger than her years, and more than ever remote—and for a moment he wondered whether she was about to ask him to put off their marriage. It had not been Teresa who had fixed the date; Lady Thurloe, he knew, had persuaded her to marry him at the end of the summer—and in his gratitude, he had been willing to put aside his own preference for living in London, and had agreed to Lady Thurloe's suggestion that he and Teresa should make their first home near Folly Cottage, in which Teresa had been born and in which she and her mother and Lolly had lived for so many years.

"Was this," he asked after a time, "what you were going in to see Lawrence about?"

"Yes."

"I don't see what he can do."

"He can advise me."

"Isn't a future husband's advice as good as a godfather's?"

"In this case, no." Teresa gave him a smile. "Because what I want to talk about is——" She hesitated and then brought out the name a little unwillingly—"my uncle Hubert."

Once more there was silence; Neville was searching his mind in order to assemble what facts he knew concerning Lady Thurloe's brother.

"Why drag Hubert out now?" he asked at length. "Twenty-two years is a long quarrel."

"Too long."

"You think he and your mother would make it up?"

Teresa rose and came to stand beside him, linking her arms in his.

"I think," she said gently, "that if a man wants to live in London after he's married, it's his wife's duty to see that he lives there."

"I'm perfectly willing to do as your mother suggested, and live down here for a few years. I could drive into Brighton every morning—it doesn't take more than twenty minutes—and I could get a train from there and be in London in less than an hour, non-stop. Your mother's a widow, and you're all she's got. I don't want to snatch you away."

"If I weren't all she's got? If her brother could be persuaded to live with her?"

"After twenty-two years of estrangement?"

"It's a long time, I admit—but quarrels have been made up after longer intervals than that."

"What was the row about?"

"I've never been able to find out." She corrected herself. "I've never really been interested enough, in the past, to—well, to press for information. But now and then, when it struck me that I seem to have fewer relations than any of my friends, I've remembered Mother's brother, and asked questions about him."

"And nobody's answered them?"

"Nobody said very much. Mother did hint once—before changing the subject—that the quarrel was in some way concerned with his wife, or his marriage. And that's all I know. But if his wife is dead——"

"If his wife's dead and your uncle wants a reconciliation, why hasn't he made the first move?"

"I don't know. But I think he was about ten years older than Mother, and——"

"And so you feel that he's of an age to need looking after?"

"You can laugh," she said, "but I don't see that there's any harm in following up the idea until I come across something that shows me it won't work."

"So you're going into Brighton to get some facts out of your godfather?"

"If I can. He knows everything about the old days; he and my father were friends long before my father married. Lawrence will know about the row, and what caused it—and so I'm going to see him and try to get all the details out of him."

"Has he ever spoken of your uncle?"

"Never. But then, I've never asked him to."

Neville lit a cigarette, inhaled and then spoke with an air of finality.

"All right. So you lunch with old Lawrence and fix up this reconciliation between your mother and the brother she hasn't seen for twenty-two years. Then you bring your Uncle Hubert down here to live with your mother, to fill the gap made by our marriage and Lolly's departure. Correct?"

She laughed and looked at him, and there was trust and affection in her eyes. He looked as solid as the furniture. She liked his looks and his manners, which were free from any kind of affectation. He had told her once that he had only one vanity: it would take a lot, he said, to throw him off his balance. He had sense, and used it. His life, he explained, had been conspicuous for its inconspicuousness, and he hoped it would remain so to the end. He admitted to being conventional, and to disliking most forms of unconventionality.

"It might sound a silly plan," said Teresa, "but there's no harm in trying to find out if it would work—is there?"

"You'd do much better if you persuaded Lolly to stay on for a year or two."

"I suggested that. She said that it would be much better for Mother to get used to both changes at once, instead of——"

"—hanging it out. There's something in that. Well, go and see Lawrence—and in the meantime don't give up hope of Lolly.

And when I come back from Brussels, I'll go and see the agents about that house out near Downstone and ask them how much they're hoping to get for it."

"You don't think my plan will succeed, and that you'll be able to take a house in London?"

"Frankly, no." He bent and kissed her. "But go and see Lawrence, by all means. He's a sensible fellow; he'll tell you that what's past is past, and is, as a rule, better left alone. And now I've got to go."

She went to the door to see him off; then she turned and walked slowly through the house, searching for Lolly. She found her at last in the little sitting-room she occupied on the first floor; a pile of mending lay on the table and Lolly was seated on a chair holding sheets and tablecloths up to the light and examining them for thin patches. She glanced up as Teresa came in, and then went on with what she was doing.

"Neville gone?" she asked absently.

"Yes. Can I talk to you, Lolly, for a minute?"

"Hm?"

Teresa studied her, and recognized the signs; Lolly was present in body, but absent in spirit.

"You're not listening," she said. "Is it . . . is it the book?"

Lolly's eyes came to rest on her, their expression gloomy.

"Yes," she said.

"It isn't . . . Oh Lolly, you haven't got stuck again?"

Teresa's voice was warm with sympathy; she knew too well what getting stuck would do to Lolly's spirits.

For Lolly, in her spare time, wrote books. In the odd moments between a thousand tasks, she wrote novels, using a chewed pencil and a paper-covered notebook with cash rulings. She wrote the first chapters of breathlessly exciting thrillers—and at Chapter six or seven or eight, came to a halt. The corpse was laid out; the handsome young detective-inspector was on the scene; suspects, young and old, smooth or sinister, waited to be interrogated. The murderer had but to be unmasked—but Lolly was unable to unmask him for the adequate reason that she did not know who he was. The evidence was too conflicting, too confusing; she could not point a finger at the real criminal.

"But Lolly"—Teresa spoke hesitatingly, for on this subject, and this only, Lolly could be touchy—"it was going so well."

"It was going too well," said Lolly. Her flat broad face was a picture of despair. "Any one of those ten people could have done it; any of them."

"But . . . but surely you must know who——"

"I tell you I don't know," said Lolly angrily. "It might be this one or that one; if I had the time, I'd sit down and decide which, but I haven't the time."

"But . . . but Lolly, when people write thrillers, I'm sure they write them backwards."

"Write them——" Lolly gave a snort. "Write a book backwards! Do you take me for a Chinaman?"

"What I meant was that the authors——"

"I don't want to do what other authors do, thank you. I know how to write. Those first chapters . . . they were going so well. The girl might have done it, but . . . I don't know. The hero . . . I thought he might turn out to have done it because he was weak——"

"But that girl you told me about——"

"She's a good, straightforward girl and she wouldn't have done a thing like that. And that's what's wrong all round; there isn't a single one of those suspects who would have done a wicked thing like that."

"Then it must be a perfect thriller and you've got to go on with it," said Teresa. "Don't you see? It means that the reader'll be absolutely foxed. Couldn't you do it as I said, Lolly? Couldn't you decide beforehand who did the murder, and then——"

"And if I decided beforehand, do you think I wouldn't give myself away in every line? Knowing who the villain was, do you suppose I could sit and give him a splendid character?" Scorn came into Lolly's voice. "You don't know much about writing, Teresa."

"Wouldn't you let me read it and——"

"No." Lolly's lips set in a firm line. "No. They're my people, and I'll go on with them until one or other of them gives himself away. I'll make the inspector pound away at them, and then one of them's bound to say something I can put a finger on. Don't you worry about it; see if I don't."

Teresa said no more. This, she knew, made the ninth book which had stopped for ever between Chapters seven and ten; it was a waste of good cash books.

She looked across at Lolly—and suddenly, for the first time, tried to imagine the house without her. It was as fantastic, she found, as trying to imagine the house without herself. They both belonged here. And Lolly . . . from the beginning there had been Lolly. Lolly in the nursery, on walks, at meals; Lolly in times of trouble or perplexity, Lolly in times of sickness. Lolly—Lolly everywhere. And now Lolly was going—where? And she, Teresa, was also going—where? To be married; to make a new home—but could any home anywhere ever be like this one? One had to marry; one wanted, in a way, to marry, but at this moment—Teresa faced the truth and acknowledged it with a sinking feeling—at this moment, marriage and a new home were merely names, merely prospects, and not alluring ones.

A sense of disloyalty towards Neville rose in her and steadied her. She raised her eyes to find Lolly's gaze on her, level and speculative.

"Don't go, Lolly," she begged impulsively.

Lolly pushed the sheets aside, took a cigarette from a box, lit it with jerky, awkward movements and turned herself round in her chair to face Teresa squarely.

" 'Don't go'," she repeated. "Well, why? Why don't go?"

"Because of Mother."

"Your mother, at this moment," pointed out Lolly, "places not one iota of dependence upon my——"

"Oh, but Lolly——"

"Yes, yes, yes, I know," said Lolly, "she adores me, she couldn't live without me, life when I leave her will be insupportable and so on and so on. Now, am I going to be allowed to say anything, or are you going to sit there and conduct an inquiry? If you are, I can get on with this work, which is very boring indeed but which has to be done. Now, shall I proceed?"

"Please," said Teresa meekly.

"Very well. I have been living here for twenty-three years. Your father wrote to me exactly twenty-three years and four months ago and said, 'Lily, you've no money and no home but you're fond of children and I'd rather trust you with this new Teresa of ours than half a dozen of these so-called Nannies. Come and try it,' he said. So I came. I came to keep an eye on you. But now you're going out into the world, and about time too. You've been sheltering in this house long enough and——"

"But——"

"Yes, yes, yes, I know; you went and got yourself a job. But it ought to have been a job in London, away from home and in a flat or a room of your own, instead of a job which allowed you to come home every evening. Well, now you're going to marry and I'm glad; Neville will take on where I'm leaving off. You're a gentle creature, I'm sorry to say; I wanted you to be tough because this present world is made for tough people—but you've been curled up in a nice warm nest all your life and Neville will see that you don't fall out of it with too great a bump. So I'm free."

"But Mother——"

"So I'm free. Your mother, at this moment, relies on you for company. If I stay, she'll begin to rely on me—and once that happens, I shall never get away, because once your mother wants anything, she——"

Lolly checked herself abruptly, and a wary look showed for a moment on her face, as though she were listening to what she had just said and wondering how much had been overheard. Then she pulled the mending towards her and began to busy herself with it; her next words were spoken without looking up.

"Hadn't you better get off if you're lunching with Lawrence?"

"There's no hurry. Well, yes, there is—but there's something I want to tell you first. I . . . I made up a plan."

"What sort of plan?"

"When you told me you were going, I got frightened about leaving Mother alone, and I suddenly thought of someone who might . . . well, come and live with her."

"Which someone?" asked Lolly, looking up in surprise. "Lawrence won't give up his house, if that's what you're after. It's big and cold and uncomfortable—but he won't leave it."

"Not Lawrence. I was thinking of Mother's brother, Uncle Hubert."

Lolly said nothing—but her hands suddenly became quite still. For a moment she remained motionless and then, with a slow gesture, she gathered the sheets together and put them back onto their pile. On it she rested her two huge fists—and then she raised her eyes to Teresa's.

"You won't get Hubert, either," she said slowly. "So you can put that out of your head."

"It was only an idea. But I knew that it would have to be discussed without Mother. Every time his name is mentioned . . ." She leaned forward. "Lolly, what *did* they quarrel about?"

Lolly rose and began to clear the table. "Money, mostly," she said. "But it was a grand quarrel; it wasn't one of those holes that you can put a patch over. It was a split like the Grand Canyon—that wide, and that deep."

"Were you here when the quarrel took place?"

"No. So you see, I don't know anything about it. Old Lawrence'll know; go and ask him. He was in the thick of it."

"Does anybody know where Uncle Hubert is living?"

"They know where he was living; he was living in the house in London."

"Which house in London?"

"The house he and your mother lived in all their lives."

Teresa waited, but no more was forthcoming. Lolly had obviously said all she was going to say.

But that she knew more, Teresa was convinced. One of Lolly's chief, and in Teresa's eyes, most endearing characteristics was her unquenchable interest in her fellow creatures. Though her sphere was not extensive, she had covered it thoroughly; there was not a man, woman or child in the district in whose concerns she did not have a benevolent and abiding interest. Without seeming to seek, she found out everything; there was no one with whom she came in contact who escaped her curiosity regarding all their affairs. It was not possible to suppose that she had made an exception of Teresa's uncle; Teresa guessed that she would have known exactly what the quarrel was about, how it had come about and when and where. But it was clear that she was not disposed to part with any of the information.

Teresa sighed.

"All right; keep it all to yourself," she said.

"Your mother's the person to go to for information."

"On the few occasions on which I've mentioned Uncle Hubert's name, Mother's gone quite pale and——"

"—and said, 'Never let that name be spoken in my presence.' Or something. Well, yes; it was quite a quarrel," said Lolly. "Haven't you ever asked Lawrence about it before?"

"No. Until now, I've . . . well, I've never been interested in Uncle Hubert. But last night, lying in bed, I began to think about him, and it struck me that . . . well, if his wife was dead, and if he was living alone like Lawrence, with nobody to look after him properly—well . . ."

"You'd take his hand, lead him from his lonely house to this one and persuade him to end his days with your mother?" Lolly smiled grimly. "Teresa Thurloe, I always told you you were a dreamer. But this isn't even a dream; it's just melodrama, and you'd do much better to put it right out of your mind."

"There's nothing melodramatic," pointed out Teresa, "in trying to patch up family quarrels. It's absurd to have Mother living alone here and her only brother—her only relation—living alone somewhere else. All I want to do is to find out what they quarrelled about, and try to make them see that it's all over and done with and that they're both too old to bear grudges. At this moment, nobody can tell me whether the plan's sensible or stupid. If someone tells me that Uncle Hubert isn't a widower, that he doesn't want to see Mother and that he wouldn't dream of making up the quarrel—then I'll drop the whole thing. But here and now, I don't see anything ridiculous about it—do you?"

"It's ill-advised, that's all. You might get your uncle to dig a hole and bury the hatchet, but your mother——" She stopped and shook her head. "Forget it," she said.

"You won't tell me anything about it?"

"I wasn't here, I told you. I came when it was all over. Go and ask Lawrence—and if you're going, you'd better go soon. If you keep that housekeeper of his waiting for lunch—even a cold lunch—she'll take it out of him. Cold bath water for the next two weeks, I shouldn't be surprised."

Teresa went slowly to the door.

"Why doesn't he get rid of her?"

"Because he's like all men, terrified out of his life that he won't get anybody else to look after him. I've offered and offered to get him somebody—in all these years, have you ever known me not able to put my hand on decent servants? But he's too frightened to go up to the old hag and say straight out: 'Look here, you old harridan, I've had enough of your bullying.' And so he goes on being bullied. Tell him from me he's a fool."

Teresa, going by bus into Brighton and making her way to her godfather's tall, cold, inconvenient house, felt under no necessity to deliver this message. She kissed the old man when he let her in, and followed him to the study in which he spent his days. The long open windows looked across to the sea; a cold wind blew in and did nothing to assist the small coal fire that burned in the grate. It was a man's room, thought Teresa; a room that would drive a tidy-minded woman mad; a room with an accumulation of books and papers and letters, the furniture arranged without plan or form, the desk littered, the large hide-covered chairs shabby and worn.

"Looks untidy," said old Sir Lawrence, turning and following her glance. "But I can put m'hand on anything I want. That's the only order old Mrs. Crofts obeys—to leave my things alone. None of this so-called tidying-up, I say to her, and she knows I mean it. But I suppose the place looks a bit of a shambles."

"It looks as it has always looked, and I can't imagine you in any other setting," Teresa told him.

"I can't imagine m'self in any other setting either." Sir Lawrence poured out two glasses of sherry, gave Teresa hers and then lowered himself carefully into a chair.

"Everybody's always told me that I was a fool to go on living in a big place like this after m'wife died, but I'm glad I didn't move out, even if it means putting up with a bit of discomfort. Mrs. Crofts is a damned sour old witch and makes out she's doing a monumental job in looking after me, but in fact all she has to look after is m'bedroom and this room; if I set foot anywhere else, she plays holy war. I wish I could get rid of her and find someone who knew how to smile—but I suppose I'm lucky to have her. Drink up that sherry and I'll get you another."

"Not yet, thank you. Lawrence——"

"Ah. Now it's coming," he said.

"What's coming?"

"Whatever it was you came to see me about. Said to m'self when I put down the phone: 'She wants to put off her wedding, and she's coming to ask me to speak to her mother.' Well, young woman, I won't."

"It's nothing about my wedding, and I don't want to put it off," Teresa told him. "It's about Uncle Hubert."

"About——" Sheer surprise stopped Sir Lawrence, and he stared across the room in bewilderment. "Hubert? Your mother's brother?"

"Yes."

"What in the world," he asked slowly, "put him into your head?"

"Lolly's leaving the cottage when I marry."

"Leaving?" He took some moments to digest this news, and then spoke with his eyes on the glass he was revolving slowly in his hands. "Well, I suppose that's no surprise, in a way."

"It surprised me—and it'll surprise Mother. Why doesn't it surprise you?"

"Because she's always considered herself there chiefly on your behalf. You think of her as someone who looks equally after yourself and your mother and the house—but she puts you first. With you out of the house, I don't think it's surprising that she should want to make a change. If she doesn't make it now, she'll never make it."

"That's what she says."

"And what has all that got to do with your Uncle Hubert?"

"Just . . . What was the quarrel about, Lawrence?" Teresa broke off to ask.

Her godfather rose without answering and, taking her glass, walked to the table and refilled it. Teresa, gazing at his spare, straight back, got the impression that he was playing for time, and a slight frown creased her brow. Nobody, she mused, seemed very anxious to answer her questions. Lolly dodged and Lawrence was taking twice the time necessary to refill the glasses; he was probably, she decided, preparing his script before reading it to her.

"Well?" she asked at last.

He turned and came back to his place and sat looking at her unhappily for a few moments.

"No point in digging up all that old history, is there?" he asked.

"I don't know. But if Mother's to be alone, why can't Uncle Hubert come and live with her? That is, if he's alone too."

"He's got a wife—or he had."

"Hasn't anybody heard of them during these twenty-two years?"

"Well, I haven't, and I don't suppose your mother has, either. If you want news of him, you'd have to go and see Walter Creed or his brother Hilary."

"Are they his lawyers as well as Mother's and mine?"

"Of course. They administer the Trust. They pay him his income. They'd know where your uncle was and whether his wife was still alive or not. But you won't get him to live with your mother; I can tell you that before you go wasting your time. And why this worry about your mother's future? She's got the most comfortable home in all Sussex, she's got servants and she's got plenty of money. When you've gone and Lolly's gone, she'll look round, find herself a congenial companion and charm her into going to live with her. What your mother wants, your mother will . . . Look, drink up that sherry and we'll have lunch."

"In a minute. You haven't told me what the quarrel was about."

He shifted uncomfortably in his chair.

"You've got your teeth into this, have you?"

"I think," answered Teresa, "that there's something to be said for finding out whether the idea could be made to work. Lolly said they quarrelled about money. Why? There couldn't have been a shortage."

"And that's where you're wrong, for a start," said Sir Lawrence. "There was a shortage. Not on your mother's side; on Hubert's."

"But——"

"Wait a minute. It's no use my telling you that this scheme of yours won't work. I suppose I've got to show you why it won't."

"All right, show me," invited Teresa.

Sir Lawrence leaned back and began slowly.

"Well . . . it was this way. Your mother and her brother inherited a fairly large house in London, and a comfortable income. Hubert was eleven years older than your mother, but they were good companions; they got on well, and they lived well while they were together. The point you've got to keep in mind is that your grandfather left all his money in Trust; your mother and Hubert couldn't touch the capital. When it comes to you, there won't be any strings and you'll be able to do as you like with it—but your mother and Hubert could only use the income, and the income wasn't left to them equally. Your grandfather was of the old school: he considered that a man can always make a living for himself, but not a woman. If a woman didn't marry, it was harder for her to provide for her old age. So your mother got eight hundred a year—and Hubert got four hundred a year and what he'd earn, presumably, in a job. But he preferred to live without a job; in those days twelve hundred a year—their pooled incomes—wasn't a princely sum, but it was a very comfortable one."

"Then Mother married?"

"Yes. Your mother married; she married a rich man, and Hubert seemed to feel that she'd let him go on using her share of the money and save him from having to find a job. But your mother had other ideas."

"That doesn't sound like Mother. She's very generous."

"I'm glad to hear you say so—but then, neither you nor I have ever tried to persuade her to part with several hundred pounds a year. Hubert's demands came down gradually; he——"

"Demands?"

"Well, he began by asking and then he went on to arguing and then he began demanding. He used to come down to the cottage and point out to your mother how badly off she'd left him. But he was wasting his time."

"She—refused?"

"Yes."

"And then they quarrelled?"

"Yes."

"You mean that because he asked her for money, she refused —and they parted for ever?"

"Well——" Sir Lawrence hesitated—"it wasn't only that. You see, Hubert did something—in pique or out of spite, or perhaps merely with a view to his own future comfort—I don't know— he did something which ruled him out for ever as far as your mother was concerned."

He paused; then rising, he walked to the window and stood with his back to the room, staring out at the sea.

"He stole?" prompted Teresa. "He embezzled? He forged?"

"No, no, no." Sir Lawrence turned. "Something far worse—in your mother's eyes."

"Well, what?"

"He married a—a woman he'd been living with."

"But you said he lived with Mother!"

"Yes, yes; so he did," said Sir Lawrence, his demeanour that of a man anxious to hurry past a dangerous corner. "But he had a—well, a——"

"A mistress?"

"Yes. I daresay if she'd been merely his mistress, it might have been all right. But she happened to be his cook, too. Your mother'd probably have been able to swallow one or the other, but the two together stuck in her throat. And . . . there was a row. An almighty row."

"It doesn't seem much," said Teresa slowly, "to have an almighty row about."

"No. But don't get out of period," Sir Lawrence reminded her. "Today, we look back at a fellow who married his cook, and feel he was a man of vision. Today, if a woman isn't a cook before she's married, she's a cook for ever afterwards. But twenty years ago, people had somewhat different ideas about cooks and about mistresses."

"But if she's dead——"

"Cooks never die. You'll find that she'll outlive your uncle by twenty years and more. But if you want news of them, you'll have to ask Walter Creed; he pays Hubert's income and he'll know all about him and his affairs. But if you take my advice, you'll forget all about Hubert and you'll marry Neville and go off and have good children, and you won't worry unnecessarily about your mother. She can't expect to have your companionship all her life."

"She hasn't had much of it so far," Teresa smiled. "Small school, big school, finishing school, Paris and Florence. I haven't been at home much. And then the job at Brighton."

"Well, you've been a dutiful daughter; now start being a dutiful wife. And now come and have some lunch." He held out a hand to Teresa. "It's all on the table here, and it's all cold; old Mrs. Crofts put it out and hinted strongly that she'd be obliged if we cleared it all away when we'd finished. Let's see: cold chicken, cold ham and the bare bones of a salad. Will you mix the dressing?"

"Yes." Teresa took the bowl, but her gaze remained on the old man's leathery cheeks, and she spoke slowly. "This morning . . . it's odd," she said, "but this morning I know for certain something that I've suspected for a long time. You and Mother . . . there's something, isn't there? You've never been quite——"

"Your mother and I are the best of friends."

"Good friends, yes. But . . . were you involved in this quarrel long ago?"

"Not in the slightest. I happened to be at the cottage when the top blew off everything—but that was all. Mere spectator. What you've felt, probably, since you grew up, is that there's a sort of minor conflict between your mother and myself. Well, you're right. And the conflict is—yourself. You see, it wasn't your mother who made me your godfather; it was your father. 'No,' I said to him, 'don't choose me, I'm much too old; choose a younger man; a man more your own age.' But he chose me— and he died when you were two, and I've survived him by over twenty years, which just shows you. But I always felt that you were—what's that silly phrase?—a sacred charge, and so everything your mother has arranged for you has been, so to speak, screened by me through my desire to see that it's something your father would have approved of. Mostly it was; sometimes it wasn't, and when it wasn't, I've gone to your mother and said so —frankly and with a lamentable lack of tact. And she hasn't liked it. The situation doesn't make for one of warm friendliness. Does that satisfy you?"

She smiled.

"Yes, thank you."

"Then come and mix the salad. Here y'are: oil, vinegar or lemon juice, whichever you prefer. And while you're doing that, I'll open a bottle of wine."

They sat down to eat. Teresa said nothing more about her uncle until the coffee was bubbling and they were back in their deep chairs. Then she raised the subject again.

"Where's the house?" she asked.

"Which house?"

"Uncle Hubert's."

Sir Lawrence looked at her for some moments, and a slow grin came over his face.

"My word, you're like your father," he said. "That's nothing to be surprised about—but you look a good deal like your mother, and so I always get a jolt when you behave like your father's daughter. He was a good man, Teresa—a fine man; you can't do better than be like him."

"Where's the house?"

"It's in Grosvenor Drive. Number 44—or was it 54; No; 54, that's it, 54. If it hasn't been bombed, or pulled down, I daresay it's still there. It used to be a good address, but I don't know what the district is like now. If I were you, Teresa my dear, I'd let the whole thing alone. If you try to put down a bridge between now and the past, you'll regret it. It never pays. If your uncle Hubert had wanted to see your mother, he could have done so any time in the past twenty or so years."

"I know. I promise that all I'll do is reconnoitre. Neville's gone to Brussels on business for three days; I've given up my job, and I'm free. All I'll do is take a look. There's no harm, is there, in walking up Grosvenor Drive and stopping to look at Number 54 and perhaps asking who lives there?"

"If you must do it, at least," implored Sir Lawrence, "do it discreetly. Don't let them know who you are. And if you don't like it, get out and get out fast."

"I will," promised Teresa. And meant it.

Chapter Two

TERESA spent a restless night. She would have liked to go to sleep and wake in the morning with her mind made up one way or the other: to act, or not to act. She lay awake, however, turning the matter over and over in her mind, and she found at last that to her original desire to make the future more comfortable for her mother, there was now added something that had not been there before: curiosity concerning her Uncle Hubert.

She tried to picture him with her mother as they had been when they were young, living together in the house in London. It was impossible, however, to imagine her mother anywhere but at Folly Cottage; she could not picture her in a great city, in a house standing alongside others in a busy street. Most difficult of all was to imagine her mother quarrelling violently. She was aware that her mother was what people called spoiled—by which they meant that she had been given too much of her own way—but Teresa felt that the term could not be applied to anybody as quiet, as gracious as her mother. Her mother liked things done in a certain way, and those round her knew that she could show swift irritation and displeasure at being denied what she wanted —but what she wanted was reasonable, and Teresa saw no reason why she should not be given it. To imagine a bitter quarrel was difficult. She wondered whether her uncle's resentment had lasted as long as her mother's.

Sir Lawrence had advised her against going to Grosvenor Drive; Lolly thought the scheme ill-advised. But curiosity, Teresa found in the morning, was stronger than reason, and she rose resolved to go. She would go and make her inquiries and by the time Neville returned from Brussels, she would be able to report success—or failure.

She met Lolly at breakfast. Teresa ate toast and drank coffee; Lolly, who was a strict vegetarian, ate small helpings from a collection of Health foods arrayed in their packages round her plate. In a bowl at her elbow, a chopped apple floated in olive oil; from time to time she took sips of whey from a tumbler.

She received without comment the news of Teresa's decision to go to London; she was busy mixing some food on her plate, and Teresa wondered whether she had heard. Then Lolly looked up.

"Well, don't get involved, that's all," she said. "There's no harm in looking at the house and asking a few questions in the neighbourhood—grocer's shops are the things to go to; everybody has to pop out some time or other and buy groceries, whether they deal regularly at the shop or not. Ask there, and you'll learn a lot—but keep away from your uncle until you're sure you want to see him. To be candid, I never thought much of him. He never did a stroke of honest work all the time I knew him—and he came cadging money off your mother. Why you want to drag him out of his hole is more than I can fathom. How much information did you get out of old Lawrence?"

Teresa smiled.

"Much more than I got out of you. Did you ever meet my aunt?"

"Your—Oh, your uncle's wife! Couldn't think who you meant for a moment. Yes, I met her. She was worth six of him and I can't understand why she married him. She'd have been far better off without him. In your mother's place, I'd have been grateful to any woman who took Hubert on. Come to think of it, you've got a poor set of relations; on your mother's side there's only Hubert, and on your father's side all those cousins your mother thinks are crazy, and I daresay she's right. I don't blame her for refusing to have them here."

"They can't all be out of their minds, can they?"

"They can all behave as though they were, and that comes to the same thing. Look at that Rosie Thurloe who came here when she was acting in that play at Brighton. Pink hair, and wearing a pair of long shorts, or short longs, I never discovered which, and rolling celebrities off her tongue in the hope of making us think she'd been intimate with them all, and I do mean intimate. And after all that, not even a free ticket for the show. If you've made up your mind to go round digging up odd relations, why not start on poor old Charlie Thurloe, down at Fowey? He's a widower, and he's all alone and he'd be the very thing to keep your mother company; she wouldn't have a dull moment. He'd bring home every barmaid within a radius of thirty miles—and that man's going on for seventy."

"It's only because Uncle Hubert's Mother's only relation that it seems to me so idiotic to let this silly quarrel go on."

"Well, have it your own way—but take my advice and don't get in too deep. Leave yourself an exit. And one more warning: don't bring your uncle or his wife anywhere near your mother. Not yet, anyway."

"I won't."

"Good. When are you going up to London?"

"Not until after lunch. And all I'm going to do is look at the house and try and find out something about who lives there. Uncle Hubert may have left long ago." She laughed. "This morning," she confessed, "it does sound a bit silly—but I'm going, just the same, Lolly."

"I know you are. And I know why. You want to get a look at this uncle of yours. Well, you'll be disappointed; your mother got all the beauty in that family."

"Well . . . I'll just take a look," said Teresa.

She timed her journey carefully; if she got to the house just after tea, she thought there would be a good chance of finding somebody at home. She considered taking the car, but decided after some thought that she would go by train.

She got to London, after all, later than she had intended; it was almost half past five when the train got in. She took a bus part of the way to Grosvenor Drive and walked the rest of the way.

Arriving at one end of the broad, busy street, she stood for some moments studying the surroundings. The district, which had once been residential was now, she saw, in process of being turned into a business sector. Tall new office buildings stood between the old Victorian houses; there were large gaps here and there with builders' signs displayed upon them. Crossing to the side of the street on which were the even numbers, Teresa saw that numbers forty-six to fifty had been swallowed up by the offices of an Insurance Company. Number 52 was hidden behind scaffolding and was having several feet added to its height.

She came to number 54 and, stopping, let her eyes roam as casually as possible over the house.

As with many London houses, the exterior gave nothing away. It was solidly built, square, ugly; five steps led up to the front door, and a few yards away were more steps, this time leading to the basement. At every window hung straight curtains screening the interior of the rooms. The curtains, she noted, were fresh, the steps newly-washed, the little yard below clean and uncluttered; having taken in these details, she found that they added nothing whatsoever to her hazy ideas about her uncle.

Doubts as to the wisdom of what she was doing came to her for the first time; she had had misgivings, but not this serious feeling that she was acting foolishly and even childishly. Her survey had taken no more than a few moments—but at the end of the time she found herself a good deal less eager to go on with her quest. Dreams dissolved fast in this atmosphere of solid reality, of grimy buildings and severe office structures and scaffolding and the hammering of workmen. Her normal good sense told her that coming to stare at a district or a building was not the sensible way to make contact with her uncle; if she had gone instead to the offices of Creed and Creed, either of the brothers—Walter or Hilary—would have been able to supply her with more information than the blank façade of the house at which she was gazing.

Disappointment flooded over her as she stood still for a last look at the house. It had been a childish scheme; impulsive, ill-advised—but it was a pity it hadn't proved workable. She acknowledged, as she let the last of her hopes die and allowed commonsense to regain its hold, that she was too much inclined to dream—but this time, she felt, the dream had had some backing of good, sound sense. If her uncle had been lonely, if he had needed her mother . . . there were a great many Ifs, but with some help from Lawrence or Lolly, her scheme might perhaps have been made to move a stage or two further before proving futile. As it was, she realized clearly that she had no desire to probe in grocers' shops for information about her uncle and aunt; she preferred to go to the lawyers and put her ideas before them and ask them for their advice on the matter.

Her uncle might be in the house—or he might not. Her aunt might be dead—or alive. She could still find out—if she wanted to—but she could not go up the steps and knock on the door and institute her inquiries. She would go home and she would think the matter over once more and then, if she still felt confident that the quarrel could be patched up, she would go to Creed and Creed.

She turned to go—but it was too late. A man had come down the street and had begun to mount the steps leading to the front door—and then he had paused and come down again, and Teresa realized that as he had approached, he had had plenty of time to note her intent survey of it.

He came down the steps; he reached the pavement, and they were face to face. Teresa saw that he was tall and rather thin, with a face whose plainness was redeemed by a pair of well-set, intelligent grey eyes. He looked about thirty.

He addressed her somewhat hesitatingly.

"You're . . . looking for somebody?"

"No." Teresa spoke hurriedly. "No, thank you. I'm not."

He said nothing, but his eyebrows went up. Half-turning, he let his gaze roam over the house, as she had been doing when he first saw her. His meaning was clear: there was nothing about it to cause a passer-by to stop and gaze at it for so long. Teresa felt herself colouring.

"I knew somebody who lived here . . . a very long time ago," she said. "Ages ago."

A smile twitched his mouth and lit the grey eyes.

"Ages?" His tone was quizzical. "Not more, shall we say, than twenty-two . . . twenty-four years?"

She made no answer, and the smile left his face. His tone became more formal.

"The house," he said, "belongs to a Mr. Hubert Towers. And has done, I understand, for the past forty or fifty years."

"Yes, I know," said Teresa.

"You know him?"

"I . . . No." She turned to go. "I was just . . . looking at the house. Good-bye."

He gave a slight bow.

"There's a taxi rank at the corner—may I call a taxi for you?" he asked.

Teresa, about to refuse, found herself, instead, walking beside him; he adjusted his long strides to her shorter steps, and for some moments they proceeded in silence. Then he halted.

"It's just struck me," he said, "that perhaps you didn't know that Mr. Towers still owns the house. He isn't in England at the moment, but his wife is here, and is in fact probably at home at this moment. If you wanted to see her . . ."

Teresa had stopped beside him; now she hurried on, and the man fell into step once more beside her.

"No," she said. "It's very kind of you to tell me, but I . . . As a matter of fact, I'm in rather a hurry. I'll . . . I'll come back at some other time."

"Mrs. Towers," said her companion, "will be sorry to have missed you. May I tell her that you'll be calling again?"

Teresa glanced at him swiftly; his eyes, frankly curious, speculative, held hers for a moment.

"My name is Tudor; Mark Tudor," he said. "I can tell you anything you want to know about the house. I happen to live there."

Surprise brought Teresa to a halt once more; for a wild moment, she had an idea that her uncle—unknown to her mother, to Lolly or Lawrence—might have had a son and that she might be confronting an unknown cousin. Then the man's age told her that she could not be right—but her momentary interest, frank and open, brought a smile to his lips.

"Sometimes," he said slowly, "impulses are odd things."

"Impulses?"

"Like the one you had today." His voice was calm, his tone detached. "You had an impulse—am I right?—to visit the house."

"I . . . Yes, I did."

"And you thought better of it—wisely, or unwisely."

"Wisely," said Teresa, before she could stop herself. Angry with herself, she let her gaze go somewhat pointedly to the taxi rank. Mark Tudor ignored the hint.

"You came looking for something, or somebody," he said. "and you're going away without finding out anything at all."

"I've already said"—Teresa's voice was cold—"that it was an impulse. Impulses can be extremely unwise."

"Perhaps. But I watched you as I walked up the street. Once, you almost went up the steps—didn't you?"

Teresa found herself smiling.

"Yes—but I thought better of it," she said. "And now will you call me a taxi?"

"Surely." He signalled, and the foremost taxi turned and came towards them. "All that's worrying me—just a little," he went on, "is that you're going away without knowing any more than when you came. Before you go, why don't you try to find out from me, if I can help you, anything you came to learn?"

She faced him, a slight frown on her brow.

"There's nothing you can tell me, thank you, Mr. Tudor."

"There's a good deal. I live in the top flat, and there are other tenants—but I know you didn't come to see them."

"How do you know?" Teresa ignored the taxi that had stopped beside them.

"In Mr. Towers' room there's a photograph of a woman—a girl; it was taken about twenty years ago. His wife told me that it was a photograph of Mr. Towers' sister. His sister—she also told me—had a daughter."

He stopped, but his smile was wide and so infectious that Teresa smiled in sympathy.

"All right," she said. "Mr. Towers is my uncle. And now may I go away."

"Most certainly." He walked forward and opened the door of the taxi. "But it's a pity, don't you think?" He handed her in and paused before closing the door. "As a total and intrusive stranger, may I give you a word of advice?"

"If you want to."

"I do want to. I want to beg you, next time you stand before a door, to push it open, and glance inside. You needn't go in; just glance. You see"—he was closing the door—"if you don't look, you don't . . . find out, do you? Good-bye."

His last words were soft, almost gentle. The door was closed; the taxi was moving, the driver sliding the partition open to hear her directions.

"Victoria Station," ordered Teresa, and sat back with a curious feeling of flatness.

Over. It was over. She had planned, she had come up to London to put her plan into operation—and she had thought better of it.

Better? Or worse?

Better, she told herself steadily. The past was her mother's; if there was to be any bridge, her mother should build it—or Hubert.

Uncle Hubert. In the house she had left behind her, her uncle lived with his wife and a number of tenants—and she knew nothing of any of them. Her uncle would return from his journeying and rejoin his wife and she would never meet him —them—never see them or learn what they were like.

In other words, Teresa told herself, she would be accepting other people's skeleton versions of an old, old quarrel—and her godfather's advice to leave well alone. She would think of Hubert Towers only as the man who married his mistress-cook and borrowed money and she would be careful to avoid any knowledge of him, and any contact with him.

And this course, which had seemed wise and sensible when she had decided upon it, looked now, after her meeting with the man called Mark Tudor, slightly shabby. She was running away, and he had guessed it—and thought her a coward. She was running away not because she had seen and decided for herself, but because Lolly and her godfather had decided for her. If she went home now, she would be going because she had accepted the opinions of others—opinions formed more than twenty-two years ago. Her uncle, from his house in London, had during all that time made no demands upon her mother; he had not importuned her—and she, his niece, was running away because she had accepted the judgment of those who had known him twenty-two years ago. She was running back to what she knew: the quietness, the orderliness, the graciousness of life as she had always known it. She had been afraid to mount the steps of Number 54 Grosvenor Drive because they might have led her to something that would have struck a jarring note in the pleasant music of her life. She was running back to shelter.

She sat staring out of one of the windows of the taxi. Buckingham Palace Road . . . Victoria Street. The station was in sight. She would get into the train and in just over an hour she would be at home.

She drew a deep breath and, leaning forward, tapped the glass partition. The driver opened it and inclined his head.

"Yes, Miss?"

"Will you turn, please?"

"Turn, Miss?"

"Yes. Turn back, please."

"You want to go back?"

"Yes, please."

"Back where yer came from, yer mean?"

"Yes, please."

"Just as yer like." The taxi driver's voice was heavy with sarcasm. "Anywhere yer say, Miss; 'syour money, not mine. You jes' say the word, and I'll take yer all rahnd London. I don't see enough of it, that's my trouble." He swung the taxi round in a wide circle. "Would yer like to go back the way yer came, or d'yer feel like a circular tour, kind of?"

"Straight back, please."

The partition shut with a bang. The taxi gathered speed, and Teresa sat back and felt a curious sense of relief—and then remembered that she had felt no relief at leaving Grosvenor Drive.

They came to the corner at which she had got into the taxi. She leaned forward and called to the driver.

"Number 54, please."

The taxi went on for a few yards and then drew up and she stepped out and paid the driver. Then she turned to mount the steps—and came to an abrupt halt.

On the bottom step, leaning negligently against the stone balustrade, his attitude one of calm expectation, was the man called Mark Tudor.

Chapter Three

"IF I'd been a man of tact," he remarked conversationally, as he came with leisurely steps to join her. "I would have gone into the house and peered out from behind a curtain, waiting for you to come back."

"You were so certain that I would?"

He smiled down at her in warm friendship.

"You looked so intelligent. And you were, after all, a woman, and curiosity had brought you here. And then your courage began to fail."

"Or my better sense began to prevail."

"You must learn to trust your instincts; they'll never lead you astray."

"How do you know?"

"Simply by looking at you." He led her up the steps. "You began to have doubts—and a word from a stranger can sometimes resolve doubts. And you came back, and I'm glad."

She walked up the steps beside him, her mind confused; she was thinking of the past, with her mother and her uncle and Lolly and Lawrence. She was imagining the future, with her uncle and his unknown wife. In between had come this man with the grey eyes and the low, musical voice. There was a smile on his lips, but there was an expression in his eyes which she could not read.

He went past her and inserted a key in the door; he pushed the door open and stepped aside.

"You don't know who I am, and you've only my word that your aunt lives here," he reminded her. "Shouldn't you ask for my credentials?"

"Didn't you tell me to trust my instincts?'"

He laughed, and gave her a slight bow.

"That puts me on my mettle," he said. "Shall we go in?"

He ushered her into a small outer hall and through it into a large inner one. Teresa saw that it was rather dark, and bare of furniture. But though there was nothing for the eye to rest on, there was a strong smell of cooking to assail her nostrils—and a

37

variety of sounds that came from all over the house to her ears.

From below came the sound of singing—a woman's voice. From the rooms above came the sound of hammering, of a violin playing waveringly, of a sewing machine whirring steadily—and of castanets playing a swift, expert, rhythmic rattle of sound.

She had barely time to take in these impressions—and then Mark Tudor had followed her in and closed the door sharply behind him.

And at its closing, all sounds ceased abruptly. The singing, the hammering, the violin and the castanets, the machine—all stopped so suddenly that Teresa was left wondering whether she had imagined them all.

Then footsteps sounded in the basement and on the stairs. A door off the hall opened and a woman entered and stood for a moment in the doorway.

Teresa saw before her a woman of about fifty, tall, with grey hair worn in plaits over her head. Her skin was smooth and dark, her eyes almost black; she was dressed in shabby clothes and wore an apron over her dress. Her hands were rough and work-stained. She looked unmistakably foreign, and Teresa, staring at her in amazement that she could not conceal, understood for the first time how little she had been told of the past. Nobody had told her that her uncle's wife was a foreigner; nobody had prepared her for this look of calm strength, this quiet air of dignity.

"But my goodness in Heaven!" came softly from the woman. "You are so like . . . yes, so like your mother. You are Lady Thurloe's daughter—isn't it so? I have forgotten your name, but it will . . . It is Teresa, no?"

She held out both her hands and took Teresa's in a brief clasp. Then she went on speaking in her quick, almost accentless English.

"Why have you come? Why have you come so suddenly like this? Your father is dead, I know that—but where is your mother? Is she well? It is so unexpected, so extraordinary that you should be here. Your uncle will be pleased that you have come—but he is not here, you know. He travels here, there, everywhere—all the time. He comes home, he stays a little while, he goes away. Here—there, like that. But how is it that you know Mark?"

"We met outside," said Mark. "She was looking for you, and I brought her inside."

"You were looking for me?" For a moment, Teresa thought there was a flicker in the dark eyes looking into her own. Then it was gone. "You were looking for me? I am glad; often I have wished to see you, to know how you looked. Your mother is well, and Miss Hyde?"

"Yes, thank you, Madame."

"Ah—not Madame! I am your aunt, is it not so? You must call me Tante—or better still, you must call me Zoë, which is my name. Yes, that will be better. Come"—she took Teresa's arm and led her across the hall—"we shall go to my room and we shall talk there. Come, Mark. But wait! First I shall have to arrange that the dinner does not spoil." She went to the foot of the stairs and shouted up at the still silent house. "Maxie! Maxie, come down; here is a lady you should see."

A door at the top of the house opened—and then another, and another. Over the railing of the landing there appeared cautiously the head of an old man with snow-white hair and whiskers. From behind his shoulder peered an old woman. They glanced down—and vanished. From the floor above there showed for an instant the face of a young girl, startlingly beautiful—and then it, too, was withdrawn. Then a man came down the stairs; he was short and sturdy, middle-aged. Teresa saw that one of his arms was amputated above the elbow.

"This is Maxie," said Zoë, as he reached the hall. "He stays here and he works for us. Maxie, have you guessed who this lady is?"

Maxie placed his hand on his stomach and gave a stiff bow.

"I have guessed," he said soberly. "She is the niece of Mr. Towers."

His English, like Zoë's, was fluent, but his accent was thick. Before he could say more, Zoë had waved him to the door leading to the kitchen. "The food, Maxie—please look after it while I am talking to Miss Thurloe." She took Teresa's arm. "Come; come, Mark. We shall go into my room."

A moment later, Teresa was glad that the pressure on her arm prevented any hesitation on her part—for at the first glimpse of the room her impression was that she had been ushered by mistake into a church. Crowded on every table, hanging on every inch of wall, arranged in niches or upon stands were holy objects; statuettes of the Virgin, large and small crucifixes, representations of the Passion, medallions of saints, countless replicas of holy relics. On every chair hung head-rests embroidered with holy themes; even on the folds of the window curtains were pinned holy pictures.

Zoë pushed a chair forward and turned to fetch another. As Mark went to her assistance, his eyes met those of Teresa, and she saw in them the same odd look of speculation that she had noticed before; he seemed to be trying to assess her reactions to the room, to her aunt, to the house, to Maxie.

They seated themselves and Zoë broke into rapid speech.

"It is so strange, so wonderful that you come so suddenly like this—and I know so little about you! You look like your mother, but you are not so . . . you are perhaps a little like your father too. Why did you come? Of course, to see your uncle—but it is long, no? Did your mother send you?"

"No. No, she didn't. I—I just came," said Teresa.

"Because you had curiosity about your uncle?" Zoë's questions were friendly, but frank.

"Yes."

"Miss Hyde lives with you still?"

"Yes."

"And Sir Lawrence—how is he?"

"You remember him?" asked Teresa with pleasure.

"Yes. He was a kind man," said Zoë. She paused. "So your mother does not know that you have come?"

"No. She—as a matter of fact, she's away."

"Ah." Zoë's voice was expressionless. "She would not like you to come, I think?"

"I don't know."

Teresa felt that her replies were scarcely satisfactory, but it was impossible to explain that she had come hoping to find that her uncle was a widower. More than ever she wondered at her stupidity; she had never seen anyone quite so alive as the woman seated in the chair opposite to hers, leaning forward and looking at her with a polite but scarcely warm expression.

"I am sorry that you should miss your uncle. But he travels, as I told you," said Zoë. "I do not know when he will go, and I do not know when he will return. I keep his room ready, always, in case he should come suddenly. He will come, he will be here for one month, two months, three—and then I will see that he is getting restless. He packs, he is off. France, Spain, Portugal; now it is Portugal, and he writes from Lisbon—but he does not say when he will come home. When he comes, will you like me to write to you?"

"That would be very kind," said Teresa.

She waited for more questions—but to her amazement, she saw that her aunt obviously considered the interview at an end. She had come to see her uncle. Her uncle was away. Her aunt would advise her when he returned.

A feeling of flatness swept over her. This, after all, was all it had amounted to. She had come out of the past—and far from wishing to keep her, her aunt was showing every sign of being anxious to escort her to the front door and close it behind her. Nobody in this house knew her—or wanted to know her. In the light of her anxiety to avoid becoming entangled in their affairs, their detachment, their indifference made her precautions seem more than childish. The embarrassed colour flooded her cheeks, and she rose. Mark Tudor spoke quickly.

"Oh—but you're not going?" he exclaimed. "Zoë, don't let her go. She hasn't seen Paloma, or the Baron, or the Baronne."

"How shall she be interested in those?" Zoë frowned. "They are strangers, and she did not come to see them. She does not know them."

"All the same, Paloma's worth looking at," said Mark.

Zoë's expression softened.

"That is true," she said. "It is true, Teresa. Would you believe, she is even more beautiful than you. She is Maxie's daughter. Wait, I will call her."

She went out of the room and once more shouted up the stairs.

"Paloma! Come downstairs! Here is somebody for you to meet!"

From above, the castanets sounded briefly but angrily. As clearly as if they had spoken, those downstairs understood that Paloma did not wish to come and meet the visitor.

"*Mais oui!*" begged Zoë. "Come, Paloma."

Clatter, clack. No, I won't.

"She is my niece. Her name is Teresa," shouted Zoë. "Come!"

Ripple, clatter, clack. Tell her to go to hell.

"Paloma, you are very wicked. Come, come and talk to us."

The answer was a cascade of sound, brilliantly executed, but so sustained that further exchange was impossible. In Zoë's room, Mark looked at Teresa, a slow grin over-spreading his face.

"No Paloma," he said. "Pity." And then, as Teresa said nothing, he added: "I hope you'll come back. But I don't think you're going to—am I right?"

Teresa hesitated. She would not come back with any hope of effecting a reconciliation between her mother and her uncle. There was something about her aunt—in spite of the obvious lack of welcome—that made her feel that she would like to see more of her and of her oddly-assorted household—but there was nothing here, she knew, that would interest her mother. It would not be possible to raise in her mother any spark of interest in Zoë or Maxie or Paloma; they belonged to a world into which she had no desire to penetrate.

Teresa wondered what Neville would think of them all, and decided that he, too, would think her newly-wakened interest inexplicable. Neville, though priding himself on being a good mixer, would be, Teresa knew, as uninterested as her mother; he might be persuaded to come and visit Zoë, but he would get little pleasure from the visit.

Zoë was coming back—but she was not coming alone. If Paloma had refused to come down, here was somebody, she explained, who was only too anxious to meet the niece of Mr. Towers. Teresa took the hand of the small, frail, white-haired old lady who accompanied her aunt, and listened to a silvery voice speaking in French.

"I have known your uncle for many, many years. You understand French?"

"Yes, Madame."

"He stayed in our home in France for many years. You have been to France?"

"Yes, Madame."

"I should like to see France again. But now," said the old lady, "this is our home, and your aunt looks after us very well. Very well indeed."

"But it is not like old times, eh?" put in Zoë.

"No." The Baronne smiled. "But you are good to us. Very, very good to us."

"That is nonsense," said Zoë. "And now I shall take you up the stairs. Come."

She led her out, and Teresa heard Mark's voice close beside her.

"She takes in sewing. The machine you heard—that's what she does all day. And her husband plays the violin every night in a French restaurant. He doesn't play well—but then it isn't a good restaurant. The proprietor knew him in the old days, and so he gives him a job. They're broke, poor old things."

"The Baron and his wife?" asked Teresa.

"Yes. I thought when I came here that the title was bogus—but it isn't. It's genuine. They wouldn't use it unless they had to. If the old man could really play the violin, for example—but he can't, and so he gets by playing half on his violin and half on his title."

Zoë, returning, looked at Teresa and seemed to speak with an effort.

"You will stay to dine with us?"

"No. Thank you very much," said Teresa. "It's very kind of you, but——"

Zoë did not press her.

"Well, you must come again when your uncle is here," she said. "And I would send my compliments to your mother, but I do not think that she would be pleased to have them. You live still in the house near Brighton?"

"Yes."

"I am glad that you came." Zoë was leading the way to the hall. "I am glad, but"—she turned and took Teresa's hand and spoke firmly—"but I do not think that you were wise to come again, my dear Teresa." She broke into rapid French. "What is past, is past. Your uncle and I lead one kind of life; you and your mother lead another. There is no bridge, and I do not think you would be wise to build one." She leaned forward and kissed Teresa, who for a moment was engulfed in a wave of garlic, gardenia and peppermints. "Good-bye. I am glad that I have seen you—just once."

As a dismissal, it was completely final, thought Teresa. For a moment, she thought of promising to return—and then felt that it was wiser to be silent. She had no more wish to build bridges.

"Mark will look after you," said Zoë. "Good-bye, my dear."

From above came once more the quavering sound of the violin and the whirr of the sewing machine. The castanets clacked; there was no hammering, but from the kitchen in the basement came the sound of chopping. A mixture of smells rose and filled Teresa's nostrils.

The front door was opened. Teresa and Mark were outside, walking down the steps to the pavement. She stopped at the bottom to give a last smile to Zoë, who stood at the door, waving. Then she turned and gave her hand to Mark.

"You've been very kind," she said, "but you musn't bother to come with me. I can get a taxi at the corner."

She saw that he was about to speak, but she gave him no opportunity. She had a feeling of having escaped from something —her own folly, perhaps. Her thoughts were confused, and she looked forward to being in the train, in a compartment by herself, alone and with leisure to sort out her impressions.

She smiled at Mark and walked away—and then turned to give one last salute to Zoë.

She saw Zoë looking down and smiling, and then she saw the smile vanish and a look of fear take its place. She even saw the mouth open—but she did not hear the cry of warning that issued from it. Mark's shout sounded dimly in her ears, and it was the last sound she heard, for, half-turning to see what had caused Zoë's change of expression, she was too late to save herself from stumbling against the poles that supported the scaffolding erected round the building next door. The impact threw her off balance; she made an attempt at recovery, and felt Mark's hand on her arm—then she knew that she was falling. A stabbing flash, and she knew no more.

Chapter Four

TERESA opened her eyes to find herself lying on a strange bed in a semi-darkened room. She waited without moving until the sense of unreality left her; then one by one, she fitted broken fragments of memory together: Grosvenor Drive, Mark Tudor, Zoë and the others. She had left the house and she had fallen and now she was lying here and someone was in the room . . .

"It's all right," came Mark's voice, low, steady, infinitely reassuring. "You hit your head, but not badly. We brought you into the house again, and you're on your uncle's bed in your uncle's room."

Teresa lay still. After a while she put a question.

"What time is it?"

"Just after seven. It looks like twilight, but that's because we drew the curtains."

"Where is——"

"Zoë? Down in the kitchen. She keeps coming in to see you and then going down again to prepare delicacies for you. She's waiting to give you a special preparation she makes with old brandy and——"

"I'd just like some water, please."

He brought it to her and held her shoulders as she drank.

"All right?" he asked, as she lay back, and she nodded.

"I . . . I've got to get home," she said.

"Yes. But if you're sensible, you'll stay where you are tonight and leave in the morning. We rang up your house."

"Oh . . . thank you. Who——"

"I did the telephoning. There isn't a telephone in the house, so I walked down to the kiosk at the end of the road. I spoke to Miss Hyde. I merely said that you were staying to dinner."

"Here?"

"Yes."

"Didn't she sound surprised?"

"She wanted to know why you hadn't telephoned yourself, and I said I'd offered to do it for you. I had to say something to explain why you hadn't returned, but if you can think of

45

anything better, I'll go down later and relay it. But I think you'd be wise to keep fairly quiet for a bit. You're not badly hurt, but a thing like this is a shock. For us," he added, "as well as for you."

Teresa lay thinking as well as she could; her head was throbbing, and she had a faint feeling of nausea. She wanted more than anything in the world to be at home in her own comfortable bedroom, but she knew that for the moment she would be wiser to stay where she was.

"If you'll tell her—Miss Hyde—that I've decided to stay the night . . ."

"Could you think of something I could say that would reassure her?"

"Yes. If you'd please say that I've got one of my school headaches——"

"School headaches?"

"Yes. I get bad headaches sometimes—about twice a year, and she calls them my school headaches because that's when they began."

"I'll tell her. She'll know I couldn't have made that up."

"Thank you."

She closed her eyes, and was grateful to him for staying in the chair by her bedside, unmoving and silent.

She fell after a time into a light doze; when she awoke, she saw that the door of the room was ajar, letting in a shaft of light from the passage; she could hear whispering. She stirred, and Mark moved from the doorway to admit Zoë.

"I'm so sorry"—Teresa managed a smile—"to have given you all this trouble."

"Trouble? What is the trouble?" asked Zoë, her voice, for sickroom purposes, pitched an octave lower. "There is no trouble. You must lie still and rest, that is all—and you must eat a little something. Something very, very light. Nobody in the whole world can cook like me, and I have something special for you. I think you should try to take it—isn't it so, Mark? She should eat."

"If you could," agreed Mark, addressing Teresa from the foot of the bed, "it would do you good."

"You shall try," decided Zoë. "Mark will look after you and I will go down and fetch something."

She went out and Mark closed the door after her. He stood for some moments looking down at Teresa.

"You look better," he said. "Feel better?"

"Much better, thank you." Her eyes were on a photograph in a silver frame standing on the dressing-table, and Mark nodded.

"Your mother," he said. "That's how it was I recognized you when I first saw you. Zoë brought me into this room and showed me your uncle's things; they're always kept ready for him, and he always keeps the photograph there." He paused. "Why did you come here?"

"It was a stupid idea," said Teresa, "and I'm ashamed of it."

"You wanted to see Zoë?"

"No. Not really. I was making up a little fantasy about finding my uncle and uniting him with my mother and patching up their quarrel so as he could be a companion for her."

"Where was Zoë to fit in?"

"I'd pictured him as a lonely widower," said Teresa, and heard Mark's delighted laughter.

"Well, well, well," he said, sobering. "It was a nice thought. But will your mother be left alone? A maid answered the telephone and put me on to a deep bass voice calling itself the housekeeper. Won't she be staying on?"

"Lolly? No. She thinks it's better to leave now and let my mother get used to the change all at once."

"Sounds wise. Do you want me to ring up your fiancé?"

"He's in Brussels, on business. How did you—— Oh, my ring."

"Yes. I observe, you observe," said Mark. "Did you tell him you were coming here?"

"Not exactly; I just told him about the plan."

"And he said it wouldn't work?"

"Everybody said it wouldn't work—and they were right. But my mother had gone off on a fortnight's cruise, and it seemed a good chance to—to——"

"Spy out the land. What do you think of Zoë?"

"I like her. But I don't think it would be any use . . ."

"Developing the acquaintance?"

"Yes. Is this a boarding house?"

"No. That is, I'm the only one here who's outside the circle. Zoë lives in two rooms on the ground floor. Your uncle lives in this room and, they tell me, keeps very much to himself. Zoë does the cooking and some of the housework; Maxie does what's known as the rough. The Baron, as I told you, goes out every evening to play his violin in a restaurant, and his wife makes a little money by sewing. Maxie's daughter Paloma has a room opposite theirs; she's one of the most alluring exponents of Spanish dancing I've ever had the pleasure of watching—but she can't keep jobs."

"Why?"

"Why? Because she's a virtuous girl, and this city is full of wicked men who chase her round the block after every performance. If the men in the audience don't pursue her, the management does. She leads, on the whole, a very active life dancing in and out of jobs. And there you have, so to speak, the family. I'm the only outsider, and I only got in after great difficulty. And here"—he turned at the sound of footsteps and threw open the door—"here's Zoë with something that smells very good."

"Come; eat," ordered Zoë briskly. She surrendered the tray to Mark, flicked open a napkin and spread it before Teresa. "Lean forward, my dear, and I will arrange your pillows—so. That is comfortable? Now you must drink this; it is very light, and very strong and it will make you feel better. Mark, your dinner is ready and you must go downstairs and eat it. I have had mine; I will stay here with Teresa."

"I'll be back," said Mark, and went out, closing the door behind him.

Zoë took the chair by the bed and her keen, dark, intelligent eyes rested on Teresa for some time before she spoke. Then:

"Do you feel well enough to talk?" she asked.

"Yes."

"How much," went on Zoë, "do you know about that quarrel long ago?"

"Nothing at all—except that it was about money," Teresa told her.

"That is true; it was about money. And also about me. Does your mother ever speak of her brother?"

"No."

"Ah." The sound was non-committal. "And now I am going to ask you to do something: when you go away from here, please do not speak of us all to your mother. Let it all be as it was. Do not tell her of Maxie, or Paloma, or the Baron and his wife. Forget us all, my dear, and do not try to mix people who cannot be mixed. Do you understand?"

"Yes."

"Your uncle will be sorry to have missed you, but . . ." She paused and sat for some time without speaking, her eyes fixed unseeingly on Coralie's photograph. "Yes," she said, rousing herself at last, "it is a pity that he did not see you, but"—she laid a hand on Teresa's—"I am glad that we met. I do not want you to come here again, because it would do no good—but I am glad, yes very glad that we met. Because when your mother speaks of me—if she ever speaks of me—you will know that I am not as bad as she thought. I was—you knew?—working for your uncle; I was his housekeeper, his laundress, his cook, his housemaid—everything. I was his servant—and I was his mistress. I would not have married him, but it seemed a sensible thing to do—he was alone, he was not any more very rich, he wanted to stay in this house and in those days things were more conventional, you understand? He married me; how much for his comfort, how much to hurt your mother, I never knew—but the arrangement suited me and I agreed to it and I kept always my share of the bargain; I looked after him well. There was no romance, but I am French and we are in these matters very sensible. I had been married before; I was a widow, without children, without money; I was glad to marry your uncle. But when he married me, he cut away the last strings between your mother and himself—that I knew. And for this evening, I am glad that you and I have been together; we do not know each other, but I like you and I think that you will never believe any stories about me which are not true."

She paused, and seemed once more lost in thought.

"Did you," asked Teresa after a time, "ever meet my father after the quarrel?"

"Yes. Once, he came here. He came with his cousin, Miss Hyde."

"Why? To patch it up?"

Zoë smiled—a slow smile without amusement. She shook her head.

"No. That they did not attempt. They told me that if I wanted them to help me at any time, they would do so." Her hand, still on Teresa's gave a small pressure, and then she was standing up. "Your father was a very good man, Teresa. I wish you could have known him. And now"—her voice was suddenly brisk—"now no more of the past. It is finished." She went to the door and looked back and spoke slowly. "What has come out of this," she said, "is my pleasure to have seen you. I hope that you have been happy to see me too, in a little way. I am glad that you will rest here tonight; tomorrow, Mark will drive you home, and we shall remember each other—but I think it will be wise that you do not come here again."

This was so much Teresa's own view that she found nothing to say. Even the suggestion of staying the night was welcome, for the thought of shaking off the pleasant drowsiness that had overtaken her, and making the journey back to the Cottage, had no great attraction.

Zoë obviously took her silence for agreement. She turned, took the tray and the napkin and prepared to go downstairs.

"I will come up again to make you comfortable," she promised.

Teresa, left alone, looked round the room, taking in its details for the first time. She saw that it was a bed-sittingroom, plainly and somewhat barely furnished, neat and—save for the photograph of her mother—bare of ornament. A man's dressing gown hung behind the door. On a shoe stand in a corner were arrayed several pairs of men's shoes, polished, shining. It looked like the room of a man of sparse, almost monk-like habit; it had none of the comfortable disorder that characterized her godfather's rooms.

She wondered suddenly if her uncle used the room as a refuge. She had a sudden clear picture of him sitting in the high-backed chair by the window. He would be withdrawn in here, but he would not be quiet, for the sounds from the other parts of the house penetrated only too clearly. It was easy to picture him in here, impossible to imagine him in the room full of holy relics into which Zoë had ushered her on her arrival.

She wished she knew more about him. Not a single person— Lolly, Sir Lawrence, Zoë—had said anything reassuring about his appearance or his character; he remained in the shadows of the past, her mother's brother, her mother's companion and her mother's adversary; very little emerged of the facts and nothing at all of the man. He quarrelled, he borrowed money—and he travelled. He had travelled far from his beginnings, Teresa thought, if he could make his home in this bare house with Maxie and Paloma and the frail old couple in the rooms opposite.

She heard a knock on the door, and at her call Mark entered. He closed the door behind him and stood smiling down at her. He looked lazy and relaxed and at ease, as she had come to know him, but she noted also that when the observer met his eyes, the impression of lethargy vanished abruptly. In the grey depths Teresa had seen lazy amusement, but she knew now that below this was watchfulness and even wariness.

"I rang up your house again," he said. "I spoke to Miss Hyde."

"Lolly? Oh, what did she say?" asked Teresa eagerly.

"She said she was sorry you had a headache and she sent you her love." He nodded towards the door, through which a medley of sounds was penetrating. "Does the noise disturb you?"

"No. Does it go on all the time?"

"The violin and the machine and the castanets? Most of the time."

"I suppose one would get used to it. How long have you lived here?"

"Two months."

"And my uncle hasn't been home all that time?"

"No. Zoë says that he keeps writing to assure her that he'll be back this week, next week, some time—but he stays where he is. But you're not coming back to see him when he returns?"

Teresa took her time.

"No," she said. "Everybody seems anxious to keep me from probing into the past."

"Who's everybody?"

"Lolly, my godfather—and now Zoë. Why do you——" She hesitated.

"Why do I—" prompted Mark, after a pause.

"Why do you live here? I can see that you like it now—but when you first came and were shown the place—didn't you . . . didn't you find them all a little odd?"

He smiled.

"Perhaps that's why I was so anxious to stay." He leaned on the rail at the foot of the bed. "Look at them all for a moment;

consider the set-up. Zoë cooks for them, mothers them, sends them off on their engagements and waits up for them to give them a hot meal. Maxie—strong, one-armed Maxie—is tied to the house because there aren't many jobs a one-armed man can do. Paloma the beautiful, practises her dancing and plays her castanets in her room and longs to be loved—in the purest sense. The old broken-down Baron and his wife . . . I stay here because I find them all interesting—and mysterious."

"Mysterious?"

"Why not? If people don't tell you about their lives, you find yourself weaving life stories round them. Then you probe a little —very gently—and you find that sometimes your stories weren't much off the beam. I made Maxie a hero of the Resistance—and found that he was."

"Is that where he——"

"—lost his arm? No. He lost his arm in an accident at the beginning of the War. It's all very interesting. Why, I ask myself, does every sound in the house stop instantly when the front door bell rings—or when strange voices are heard in the hall? Why does the Baron lock his door if a strange step sounds on the staircase? Paloma is so beautiful; why doesn't her father allow men—young men, decent men—into the house?"

"Aren't you imagining all this?"

"No. Nobody can be in the house for long without seeing it all—and so I ask myself: Is that why your uncle stays away so much? Or is he an insensitive, even a somewhat stupid man, who sees and hears nothing when he's at home? I shall know when he comes." He smiled. "You think I'm exaggerating?"

She looked at him for the first time with frank and undisguised interest; standing before her, he waited until her scrutiny was at an end.

"What's the verdict?" he asked.

"Perhaps I'm expecting too much when I try to form an opinion of a man I've only known for a couple of hours."

"Much too much," he agreed. "Besides, before you can make up your mind about a person, you've got to place them against some sort of background—and for some reason, you refuse to accept me as part of the family at Number 54."

"No, I don't. It just seemed—" She stopped. "What do you do?"

"I'm what's known as Something-in-the-City. On most mornings I go out punctually to work and don't get back until six—but there are days when I get out earlier. This, most fortunately, was one of those days."

Before she could decide how she should take this, he had turned to go. She saw his long, lean back and one of his hands —thin, rather bony—on the handle of the door; he opened it and looked back. "There's some arrangement about fixing you up for the night in Paloma's things; you're more or less of a size. I'll be back."

He went out and closed the door softly behind him, and Teresa settled back against the pillows and tried to assess how much had happened since she had stopped outside the house earlier in the evening and made what she hoped was a discreet and unobserved survey. Two hours ago, no more. If Mark Tudor had not come up, she would, she knew, have turned and gone away, probably for ever. Or if she had entered the house, she would have been met by Zoë—and sent away again. Now she was in her uncle's room and Mark Tudor had, in some strange way, brought the house and its inmates before her and made them real. In spite of herself her interest had been quickened; when she went away, she would take with her unsatisfied curiosity, certain regrets and—oddest of all—a feeling of having missed something important. Mark Tudor sensed something below the surface in this house and had tried to make her sense it too—and had succeeded.

A faint scratch came at the door—so soft that Teresa did not think it could be a knock. But it came again, and she called an invitation to enter.

The door opened slowly; the lovely face that had appeared for a moment over the banisters looked warily round the door. At Teresa's smile, Paloma entered and proved to have a body no less lovely than her face.

With her back against the still open door, she leaned her weight against the panels and walked backwards until the door closed; then she gave Teresa a slow, wide smile.

She wore a white cotton blouse with a round, low neckline. Her skirt was black, and voluminous—so wide, indeed, that it seemed to be worn over half a dozen stiff petticoats. Her arms and legs were bare; on her feet were the merest suggestion of shoes. Her hair was black and curling and hung over the rounded shoulders; her eyes were night-black and looked as soft as velvet.

She advanced to the foot of the bed, a half smile on her lips, and seemed to be waiting for Teresa to open the conversation. But Teresa, a lover of beauty, and no envier of beauty in other women, was content to watch the exquisite little face.

Paloma lifted an arm to show hanging from it a short, white cotton nightdress, gaily embroidered. With a gesture that was grace itself, she pointed to her own figure and then to Teresa.

"We're the same size," she said in French.

"It's very kind of you to lend it to me."

"Clean towel. Brush"—Paloma held up a new toothbrush and her small white teeth flashed in a brief little giggle. "Mark bought it for you. You have a comb?"

"Yes, thank you."

There was a knock, and Zoë put her head round the door.

"Ah—good," she said, coming in. "She has brought you the things. Paloma, go and tell everybody not to use the bathroom now; Teresa must get ready for bed. Go." She waited until the door closed behind Paloma, and then laid down the sheets and pillow cases she had brought in. "While you are in the bathroom, I shall make the bed." She went on in English: "You find it comfortable to lie on?"

"Yes, thank you."

"Your uncle likes a comfortable bed. That is his dressing gown hanging behind the door—please use it if you wish."

Teresa sat on a chair and watched her making the bed with swift, strong movements. When Zoë had gone, she sat lost in thought for a while. Then she shook her head in an attempt to clear it of the thousand confused impressions in her mind, and got to her feet experimentally. She found herself less shaky than she had anticipated. Her head still ached a little, but she had lost the feelings of giddiness and nausea. She undressed and put on Paloma's nightdress; then, taking her uncle's dressing gown from the peg on the door, she enveloped herself in it, took the towel and toothbrush and went out on to the landing.

Out there, the noises from all parts of the house, muffled behind the closed door, now sounded clearly enough for her to be able to distinguish them. From the kitchen came voices: Zoë's and Maxie's. From a room opposite the one Teresa had occupied, came more voices, one thin, one gruff—the Baron and the Baronne were talking. From upstairs, a new voice—Teresa would have said it was a child's, but nobody had said anything about a child.

She went into the bathroom; like the hall and like her uncle's room, it was barely furnished, clean, tidy, but showed signs of wear; the whole house, she thought, needed new paint, new fittings, new floor coverings. Everywhere needed brightening up —except, she added to herself, her aunt's room, which could do with some toning down. Religion was a great comfort, but did anyone need all those outward and visible signs? How could anyone sleep, as her aunt slept, among all those pictures, some of them almost terrifying?

She put speculation aside and applied herself to washing; she brushed her hair and her teeth. When she had done, she opened the door and walked out on to the landing, and the sound of voices came once more to her ears. Upstairs, a guitar began to twang softly. Then, over them, she heard the sound of the front door bell.

Instantly, all sounds ceased. The murmur from the kitchen came to an abrupt stop. The Baron and the Baronne no longer spoke. The guitar was silent. Over all the house was utter, absolute silence.

Teresa found that she, too, had become motionless and tense. Like the house, she was waiting. In spite of all her efforts, she found a sense of fear creeping over her.

There was a pause. Then footsteps were heard on the stairs leading from kitchen to hall. Leaning over the banisters, Teresa saw Zoë walking to the front door. A key turned—and Zoë's voice, loud and protesting, broke the silence.

"Mark! But how is this that you ring the bell? You have lost your key?"

And then Mark's voice, slow, laconic.

"Left it behind. Sorry to bother you, Zoë."

"Come in. You are very naughty." Was there relief in the voice, Teresa wondered, or was her imagination at work? "It is only Mark," Zoë shouted up the stairs. "He left his key behind."

The house—there was now, at least, no imagination—relaxed. The Baron and the Baronne resumed their talk; Zoë went down once more to the kitchen and was heard speaking to Maxie; the notes of the guitar sounded again, sad, lingering. Up the stairs came Mark's footsteps, light and swift. He reached the landing, and came face to face with Teresa.

For a moment she could have sworn that there was triumph in his look—and then the curtain had dropped, as she had already learned that it could drop, screening everything he wished to conceal.

"Sorry to give everybody a fright," he said.

Teresa stared at him, and suddenly a wave of discomfort, of unrest engulfed her. There was something below the surface—and he knew what it was, and would keep his own counsel for as long as it suited him.

"I'll drive you home tomorrow," he said, "if I may?"

A question hovered on her lips—and then a sound from the stairs above made them both turn. Teresa saw scrambling downstairs a small boy of about four—pyjama-clad, tousle-headed, dragging behind him a somewhat bald teddy bear.

No golden-haired cherub, this, decided Teresa after the first glance. He was almost the plainest child she had ever seen—and the most appealing. His hair was short and straight, and stuck up like a bottle brush. His face was freckled, his mouth too large, his nose scarcely there. His teeth, large square, and widely spaced, looked not unlike milestones.

He reached the landing and then, to Teresa's amazement, Mark Tudor had stopped and swung him up into his arms.

"Got you," he said. "On your way to the kitchen for snacks, eh?"

"No." The boy steadied himself by clutching a handful of the man's hair. "No. Came downstairs to find you."

"And now you'll go upstairs to find your bed. Say good night to the lovely lady," ordered Mark.

" 'Night."

"What's his name?" inquired Teresa.

"David."

"David and what else?" she asked.

"David Tudor, of course." Mark sounded surprised. "Didn't Paloma introduce you?"

A variety of sensations, all strange and most of them unsettling, rose in Teresa. Keeping a tight control over herself, she managed to check the amazed ejaculation that rose to her lips, and walked to the door of her uncle's room.

"Good night, David," she said—and then to Mark: "Is he yours?"

Mark bent his head and dug it affectionately into the small boy's stomach. Then he looked up and spoke with manifest pride.

"Naturally, he's mine," he said. "And when I say naturally, I don't want you to misunderstand me."

Teresa said good night and closed the door gently. Then she turned and stood staring thoughtfully across the room. The impressions of the past twenty-four hours had been confusing enough, but nothing had been as bewildering as the past few moments.

Mark Tudor—with or without a small boy called David. What did it matter to her? Nothing. Nothing whatsoever.

But with dismay creeping over her and bringing her close to panic, Teresa acknowledged to herself that it did matter. It mattered a great deal.

Chapter Five

SHE slept, to dream not of Zoë or of Maxie or Paloma; nor of the inscrutable Mark Tudor. It was Neville who filled her dreams. She walked up the steps of a strange dream house, and Neville—strong, solid, sensible Neville opened the door. She rushed down a dream street and fell headlong; it was Neville, infinitely comforting, who picked her up and reassured her.

When she awoke, her watch told her that it was eight o'clock. She felt well and strong and ready to rise and begin her preparations for going home. She thought of Mark Tudor, and decided that she would not allow him to drive her down to the cottage; she would insist upon being taken only to Victoria, and she would go home by train. He had been kind, but there was something about him that she did not understand and—this morning—did not want to understand. He was pleasant, she told herself, he was intelligent and he was amusing and—she hesitated—yes, he had undeniable charm, but there was also something about him that she found baffling.

She remembered the speculative look in his eyes as they had sometimes rested on her; he had almost, she thought, a watchful air. If he was looking to her to help him solve the mystery, real or imaginary, that lay over the house, he would look in vain; she was going home to resume her normal way of life with her mother, with Lolly and with Neville.

Neville. Getting out of bed, she found herself saying his name more than once aloud; the sound gave her a pleasant sense of security. Neville, she reflected with satisfaction, was a man who, when he spoke, spoke clearly and to the point; his lips never uttered something that his eyes contradicted. One knew exactly where one was with him—and knowing where one was, Teresa decided, was a very happy state of affairs.

She had, suddenly, a strange but strong feeling that she was not alone in the room. The door was closed, and had been closed since she wakened—but there were at intervals faint noises that she had scarcely noticed but for which she now found herself listening. A tiny scuffling sound, a scratching; perhaps a dog was in the room.

Then she saw a small hand come up and grasp the bed rail; from under the bed rose David Tudor, his mouth full of food, crumbs covering the coat of his pyjamas.

"How long have you been under there?" asked Teresa in astonishment.

He managed to smile at her, but he was some time in answering; after making one or two attempts to speak intelligently, he removed a large piece of toast from his mouth to clear the way for the sounds.

"I was eating my breakfast," he explained, and put back the toast.

Conversation would clearly be impossible until he had eaten it; Teresa sat on the bed and waited. His likeness to Mark at this moment was very strong; it showed in the rather long face, the long hands—and the calm, almost bland look.

"Where's your breakfast?" he inquired, at the end of the last mouthful.

"I suppose I'll go down and get it when I'm dressed."

"Zoë cooks it," he informed her. "Not our breakfast, though. We cook our own breakfast our own selves. We cook toast."

"I see. Well, hadn't you better go and dress?"

"It isn't time yet."

"Don't you go to school?"

"No. I'm too small for a proper school. I go to a nursery school," he said. "You're too big, aren't you," he decided after a short survey, "to go to school?"

"Yes. David, I shan't be able to get dressed until you go away."

"Why not?"

"Because—Well, I think they'll all be looking for you, won't they? Your . . . your mummy."

"I haven't got one. She went up to Heaven," explained David. "Long, long, *long* ago. Munfs and munfs and munfs ago. What's your name?"

"Teresa."

"Teresa who?"

"Teresa Thurloe."

"Have you come to live in this room?"

"No. I'm going home soon."

"Did Paloma give you that nightdress?"

Teresa laughed and stood up. "What you need," she said, "is a notebook and pencil." She put on the patched dressing gown and picked up her towel.

"Are you going to have a barf?"

"Yes." Teresa smiled down at the small, upturned face. "Hadn't you better run upstairs now?"

"Does your hair curl all by itself?"

"Yes. It—" She paused as a knock sounded on the door. "Come in."

Mark stood outside. He was fully dressed; his smile was warm and friendly.

"You haven't," he asked, "by any chance seen anything of —Ah! There he is! Has he been bothering you?"

"No." Teresa, to her own surprise and displeasure, heard the coolness in her voice.

"She wants a barf, and it's my time for a barf," said David.

"Well, you'll have to hang on and have a second bath, old fellow. Now say good-bye to the lady," said Mark, "and tell her you're sorry you invaded her sanctuary. Now move. Left, right. —Bath's yours, Miss Thurloe," he said over his shoulder, as they went up the stairs.

Before Teresa could shut the door, a call came from downstairs.

"Is that you Teresa, my dear?"

Teresa leaned over the banisters; at the foot of the stairs, dressed, aproned, looking neat and businesslike, stood Zoë.

"You slept well, Teresa?"

"Very well, thank you."

"Then when you are ready, come downstairs. Don't hurry; breakfast is at all times. You will not mind to eat . . . you will not mind eating in the kitchen?"

"Not at all, but I don't have much breakfast, thank you. Just coffee and——"

"Ah, always the same from you girls! Just like Paloma. Toast, toast, toast, coffee and nothing else. But come down when you are ready."

"I will, thank you."

A patter of light footsteps sounded; Paloma, with a brief

greeting, sped by on her way downstairs. She was wearing a shabby scarlet dressing gown and her hair was wild, but she looked as beautiful as she had done the night before.

She vanished, and Teresa was alone on the landing. In the morning light, the house looked bare and poor, and she wondered how her mother—her fastidious mother—had ever lived here. Where, she wondered, had all the furniture gone? There were things at the cottage which she knew her mother had brought from this house on her marriage—a beautiful spinet, now a sideboard; a set of Chippendale chairs, an inlaid desk and other valuable pieces; these Teresa had always understood to be her mother's share of the furniture. Since it was reasonable to suppose that her brother had possessed similarly good pieces, what had happened to them? How could he live, now, surrounded by the cheapest, the ugliest, the most thrown-together things? There was nothing she had seen in the house that could not have been picked up—that probably had been picked up in a cheap second-hand store. There was nothing but trash; there were no rugs, no good curtains, nothing whatsoever of value.

It was useless to try to guess. Teresa went into her uncle's room and finished dressing and then walked down the stairs and across the hall. Going to the head of the stairs leading to the basement, she stood still for a few moments, looking down at the colourful scene below.

A huge trestle table was covered with a vivid cloth; Zoë, at the old-fashioned stove, was working among shining copper pans; Maxie was seated beside Paloma at one end of the long table; at the other end sat the old Baron and his wife, he in a patched and faded dressing gown, she in a long white robe that might be a nightdress or a negligée. Swift chatter sounded in French; not the subdued and reluctant exchanges of the English breakfast table, but animated, even heated argument round the board.

And then Maxie looked up and saw Teresa, and at his low word making her presence known to the others, there fell the now familiar silence—sudden, inexplicable, complete.

Then Zoë had turned from the stove.

"Ah, Teresa. Come down, please. Come, come down and sit. Maxie, make a place—there, over there, by the Baron. A cup for Miss Thurloe, Maxie—and a napkin. Sit down, Teresa."

Teresa sat down—but there was no resumption of the careless

ease she had witnessed from the top of the stairway. Paloma gulped the last drops of her coffee, put down her cup and, with a smile toward Teresa, slipped away. The Baron bowed to acknowledge the introduction to Teresa, bowed again to take his leave, bowed yet again as he helped his wife to her feet and led her up the stairs. Maxie was clearing plates, knives and forks and carrying them to the sink; soon he, too, had gone, and nobody remained in the great, dim kitchen but Teresa and her aunt.

"They are shy," explained Zoë, placing fresh toast and newly-made coffee before Teresa. "They are good people, but they do not like to mix with strangers; they feel—they feel shy."

Teresa said nothing; she was wondering whether her uncle came down and took his meals here, or whether they were carried up to him. She would have liked to ask—this and other questions, but there seemed little to be gained by adding to her knowledge of a man she would probably never meet. There was one thing, however, that she felt she must know.

"When my uncle comes back,"—Zoë passed the sugar and she nodded in thanks—"will you tell him that I came?"

There was a pause. Zoë sat down on the chair that the Baronne had occupied, rested her elbows on the table and cupped her cheeks in her hands. Staring across the kitchen at the glowing flame of the stove, she spoke slowly at last.

"I shall not tell him," she said.

"Why?"

"Because it would not be any use. It would . . . it would accomplish nothing."

"But if he wanted to see me . . ."

Zoë raised her eyes and looked directly at the girl before her.

"So much I am sure of," she said. "He will never go to see you. Never."

There was complete finality in the words. Turning them over in her mind, Teresa saw no reason for regret; her uncle didn't want to see her and she—she now knew—had no great desire to see her uncle. The plan had collapsed; the scheme had been blown apart. The dream was over.

"If you're ready," came Mark's voice from above, "I'm ready to take you."

Both women looked up, startled; no sound had betrayed his

presence. Teresa wondered how long he had been standing at the head of the stairs.

Zoë's farewell was affectionate, but brief. Of the others in the house there was no sign. Drawn up outside the house was an aristocratic but shabby sports car which, Mark explained as he handed her into it, had been bought by him with more regard for performance than for appearance.

"She goes," he said. "What more can anyone ask?"

"Paint?" suggested Teresa.

"You're not ashamed to be seen in it?" he paused to ask.

"It depends on which of my friends we meet," said Teresa. She turned as they drove away, and gave a last look at the house. "Please," she said, turning back to Mark, "don't bother to take me home; if you'll drive me to the station, I can get a train and be home in just over an hour."

"But of course I'll drive you home. Suppose you collapsed in the train?"

"What would make me collapse?"

"Delayed shock. I've seen it happen. You had a nasty fall and you were out—unconscious, that is, for some time. I wouldn't have a moment's peace unless I delivered you personally to your home."

"It's a weekday, and you said you had a job in the City."

"A job, fortunately, which doesn't necessitate my clocking in and clocking out. So you see, I'm free and I'm at your service. —She goes beautifully, doesn't she?"

"She goes," admitted Teresa cautiously. "If David goes to a school, don't you have to——"

"I've just left him there. He'll be looked after and amused and handed back when I go to fetch him. Are there any other obstacles you can think of? There's your fiancé, of course, who probably wouldn't care to see you roaming the countryside with a strange man. When I say strange, I mean merely a man you haven't known for very long. But your fiancé is away and for the moment I can take his place. When I say take his place——"

"Why," asked Teresa, turning to study him curiously, "do you take such delight in creating situations which don't exist?"

"I never create situations which don't exist. Sometimes, I admit"—he threw her an extraordinarily attractive smile—"I may say things that other people would leave unsaid. Lack of tact, perhaps—heavyfootedness. But I don't—as you call it—create situations."

"Yes, you do. You want me to think that there's some secret —some sort of mystery at my uncle's house."

He stopped the car at a traffic light and stared across at the red signal across the street. He did not reply until they were once more on the move.

"There is some sort of secret at your uncle's house," he said calmly.

"The fact that they all listen every time someone comes to the house doesn't mean anything sinister. They might be merely curious."

"They might. Did you think that they were merely curious?"

She did not reply; she wanted to say that she was glad to be away from the house and that she was resolved not to let her mind dwell on anything that had occurred during the past sixteen hours. She was on her way home—and she was glad.

They did not speak for some time. Teresa was thinking of the cottage and contrasting it with the house in Grosvenor Drive. Mark was thinking of Teresa.

He stopped for petrol, and leaving the car, they strolled into the garden of an adjacent inn; Teresa sat on a deck chair in the sun and Mark brought out drinks; he propped himself against an insecure bench and looked down at her and raised his glass.

"To your future," he said. "May it be as sheltered as your past."

She looked up at him, the colour rising in her cheeks.

"Sheltered?"

"But yes. Would you say you hadn't been sheltered?"

"You made it sound as though . . . as though . . ."

"I didn't mean to make it sound as though," he said. "I merely wished it to go on, that's all."

"What's wrong with being sheltered?"

"It's a highly desirable state—for women, that is."

"But nowadays women aren't and so I've been a sort of parasite—is that what you meant?"

He looked down at her flushed face.

"We ought to get on well," he commented. "When I say something provocative, you stare at the scenery. When I propose an entirely harmless toast, you show your claws—which is interesting, because I wouldn't have suspected that you knew how to use them.—Drink up."

The order came so quietly that she had raised her glass to her lips and drunk before she realized that she was doing so. When she looked at him again, there was a new interest in her eyes. She saw for the first time that for all his apparent casualness of manner, all the lightness of his words, he was a man who would have no difficulty in making people take him seriously—if he wanted them to.

"What made you say that I was . . . sheltered?" she asked.

He smiled.

"That's easy. One has only to look. The world's a hard place, and most people have to push their way through it. Even gently-nurtured women. There are certain people, of course, who lack the ability to push; the weak ones; the meek ones. But I don't think you're meek and I'm certain you're not weak; therefore the reason you don't exhibit any sign of pushfulness is either (a) you don't need to push or (b) someone's doing it for you. Your mother in the past and your fiancé in the future."

"But I don't——"

"Wait a minute; don't interrupt. And don't be annoyed at my calling you sheltered; it was a conclusion I reached after recognizing in you certain signs which one very seldom sees nowadays. You're what I term—to myself—a dainty stepper. As a young man, I recognized that almost lost quality in my grandmother—since deceased. She was a dainty stepper. Shy, reserved, but with something I can only call style. She only had to enter a room to bring the most loutish man in it to his feet. If she expressed a wish, people fell over themselves to carry it out. She wasn't selfish or demanding; she was just—sheltered. And so are you, and I'm glad. I like your gentle expectation that life's doors will all open before you as you approach them. They will. I like your . . . your air. Did you know you had an air? You have. Half shyness, half a very, very charming dignity. I recognized it as I came towards you yesterday—while you were standing looking at the house. I recognized it because I've been waiting all my life to see it at some time—in some woman." He broke off. "I wonder if your fiancé would mind my laying myself at your feet in this way?"

His voice was utterly casual. Teresa stared at him and felt the colour burning in her cheeks. After a moment, he smiled. "You're angry?"

"No." Teresa heard her denial, and would have done much to recall it. She was not angry, but she felt that she ought to have been, and she struggled to put her feelings into words. "You're doing it again," she told him.

"Doing what?"

"Creating situations which don't exist."

He gave her a slow smile.

"No, I'm not. Your engagement—that exists. My seeing you —and discovering that you fitted perfectly into a frame that's never been filled until now; those things are real, too. There's no harm, is there, in putting them into words?"

"To a girl who's engaged?"

"If I'd known you before you were engaged, I would have told you then. But I see you now—and pay a man's homage to a lovely and gracious woman."

Teresa made another effort.

"You can't say that to me," she said soberly, "because I'm— because I——"

"Because you belong to somebody else?" Mark leaned forward and raised her left hand and looked at the ring on its third finger. "Until that," he said slowly, "is a wedding ring, you belong only to yourself."

He released her hand gently, and stood up. Teresa rose and without a word walked beside him to the car, her mind spinning. He opened the door for her and then put out a hand and stopped her as she was about to get in.

"Look back," he said. Teresa glanced over her shoulder, and he went on speaking quietly. "A chair, a bench, green grass, a shady tree. Nothing out of the way about any of them—but somehow, I have a feeling that it's a place we'll both remember —for ever."

She was in the car; he was beside her and now there was silence. The miles slipped by, and Teresa did not notice their passing; her eyes were on the two lean strong hands holding the wheel.

The sun went behind clouds as they neared the cottage and emerged again in time to light it and show it at its best. As Mark turned in at the gate, Teresa shook herself out of her abstraction and stared at it—and for the first time saw that its picturesqueness had a faintly unreal quality. After the drab, workaday look that characterized the house in Grosvenor Drive, this pink-and-white building looked not unlike a doll's house.

Mark stopped the car, but made no move to get out. Instead he leaned back and sat for some moments looking about him. Teresa waited with some interest for his comments.

"Well?" she said at last.

"Pretty much as I'd pictured it," he said. "House of the sugar-plum fairy. No wonder you keep running back here for shelter; I'd do the——"

"If you say that again, I shall be very angry," said Teresa, and found him twisting round in his seat to study her.

"Angry? Could you be? The gentle you?" He was not teasing; he sounded as though he really wanted to know.

She sat considering her reply—and as she did so, the front door opened and Lolly stood looking out at them. Neither Teresa nor Mark saw her, and slowly she took in their rapt interest, their complete absorption in one another. She could not see Mark's face, but she could see his head, bent over Teresa's—and she could see clearly enough Teresa's expression.

Her hand closed tightly on the side of the door, and depression, black and heavy, settled upon her. She had hoped, once, to see Teresa look at Neville with that still, intent, utterly charmed gaze—but had seen only friendliness and, at times, affection. Teresa had remained untouched by all Neville's efforts to please her. Four years—and in less than a day, this stranger had lit within her a lamp that nobody, up to now, had ever kindled. Teresa—with that soft gleam behind her eyes. Teresa, out there, her feelings written beautifully, movingly on her face; Teresa—and an unknown man.

Anger rose in Lolly and steadied her. She advanced firmly down the steps and, walking up to the car, stood staring down upon its occupants with a look compounded equally of astonishment and suspicion.

"Aren't you coming in?" she asked Teresa. "You live here, remember?"

They got out and Lolly stood stolidly, unsmilingly by, as Mark was presented to her. She gave him a stiff bow.

"Kind of you to bring Miss Thurloe home," she said. "Teresa, is your headache better?"

"It wasn't a headache, Lolly. I fell on the pavement as I left the house, and got a bit shaken up."

"I asked her to invent something that would calm your fears," explained Mark. "I didn't think you'd like to hear a strange man ringing up and telling you that she would be out all night. She's all right now."

"You mean you fainted or something?" demanded Lolly.

"Only for a little while."

"Did they call a doctor?"

"I didn't need a doctor," said Teresa. "Zoë looked after me."

"Zoë . . ." Lolly looked bewildered. "You call her Zoë?"

"Yes. She didn't seem like an aunt. Hadn't we better go inside and talk about it there?" suggested Teresa.

Lolly did not answer. She was staring up at Mark; it was a long way, for she came up to the middle button of his jacket. She was frowning thoughtfully.

"Seen you before somewhere—I'm sure of it," she said slowly. "Can't think where. Tudor . . . Tudor." She shook her head. "No. Never heard that name before, so I daresay I'm confusing you with somebody else." She turned and marched towards the house. "Let's go inside; we're keeping Mr. Tudor waiting and I daresay he's anxious to get back to London."

She led the way to the drawing-room; when Teresa and Mark were seated opposite to her, she looked across at them.

"Now," she said, "I'd like to hear exactly what happened last night. And then we won't detain Mr. Er."

"Tudor. Mark Tudor," said Mark gently.

Light broke on Lolly's face as she stared at him, but when she spoke again, there was an odd sound of disappointment in her voice. "Knew it," she said gloomily. "Knew I'd seen you before. But it wasn't you—it was your mother. Knew her as a girl. I met your father once or twice, but I'd forgotten the name. Where's your mother now?" she asked.

"She died very soon after I was born."

"Then I'm sorry," said Lolly. "She was a lovely girl—and she was a healthy girl, too, and she ought to have lived longer than that. I used to see her when I came down to stay at Brighton."

"Did Lawrence know her too?" asked Teresa.

"He knew her very well. In fact——" Lolly broke off. "Tell me what happened yesterday," she said. "Your uncle wasn't there, Mr. Tudor told me."

"He was abroad," said Teresa. "And"—she smiled at Mark —"I'll agree that it was a silly plan to go at all, but if it hadn't been for Mark, I would have given up the idea."

Lolly noted grimly the use of his Christian name, but said nothing. Her determined silence, however, made it clear that she could see no reason why he should have had any say in the matter.

"I saw her going away," said Mark, "and I did my best to make her see that——"

"—that I was running away," finished Teresa.

"And why," inquired Lolly of Mark, "should you have been interested in whether——"

"I'm deeply interested," said Mark. "I've been living there for the past two months and I've come to know them all very well."

"Who's all?" asked Lolly.

"There's"—Mark began to count on his fingers—"there's Mrs. Towers; there's the Baron and his wife and——"

"The who?"

"Title genuine. There's Maxie and his beautiful daughter Paloma."

"All living there?" said Lolly in a high voice of astonishment.

"Yes," said Teresa. "They're . . . they're sort of lodgers. And Mark and his son live there too."

"My *what?*" came from Mark in the utmost astonishment. Teresa looked at him, the colour coming into her cheeks.

"Isn't David——" she began.

"—my son? No. I rather wish he were. He's exactly what I'd want as a son. What made you think——"

"Well, you said his name was Tudor and"—Teresa, to her fury, found herself stammering—"and you said he was yours and——"

"He's my half-brother. My father," explained Mark, "was a widower for well over twenty years, and I would have said that he was entirely satisfied with me as his only child—but he married again. He was nearing sixty, and he was nearly thirty years older than his wife and it was rather a mistake—but David was the result." He looked at Lolly, who was following the account with avid interest, and shook his head apologetically. "I don't want to bore you with details of my family history."

Lolly shut her mouth, which had been open, drinking in details.

"Go on, go on," she snapped. "If you begin a thing for goodness sake finish it."

"It's rather harrowing," Mark warned her.

"Harrow or no harrow, let's have it," ordered Lolly.

"It's short, at all events," said Mark. "She found my father rather boring and left him—to his enormous relief—just before he died. She ran away with another man—and left David behind. And that"—his voice deepened—"that's the part I shall never understand. A woman might give up almost everything for a lover . . . but not a little child, surely? Not a child like David. How . . ."

His voice trailed away and he sat lost in thought until Lolly's voice recalled him to the present.

"And where is she now?" she demanded.

"At the bottom of the Atlantic Ocean." There was satisfaction in Mark's voice. "She was on her way to America with yet another gentleman friend, and she vanished. They said she'd been drinking, but I feel that some benevolent member of society took her up to the boat deck one dark night and pushed her overboard."

"Well, don't sound so pleased. The poor soul——" Lolly paused. "Well," she went on, "I daresay it was best that way. If she'd turned up after a few years and claimed her little boy—But I don't think a man's fit to bring up a child. How old is this boy?"

"Rising five," said Mark. "Healthy, with a splendid constitution, my own easy-going nature and my own high principles. Mrs. Towers is very fond of him."

"Zoë? Didn't she ever have any children of her own?" asked Lolly.

"Not as far as I know."

"Have you met Mr. Towers?"

"Not yet. He's expected home soon. But his wife has decided not to tell him anything about his niece's visit."

"I'm thankful for that, anyway. Teresa, hadn't you better go and rest? I'll ring up the doctor and ask him to come out and look at you."

"Good Heavens, I'm perfectly all right, Lolly!"

"You may think so, but a fall is a fall."

"Is a fall," conceded Mark. "But I really think she's all right."

"You may think so," said Lolly, "but her fiancé will want to make sure."

"Neville?" Teresa sat up and stared. "But Neville doesn't know I had an accident."

"He knows that you spent the night at your uncle's house," said Lolly. "He rang up last night from Brussels, and when you weren't here he wanted, naturally, to know where you were."

"And you told him? Oh Lolly—" There was a note of exasperation in Teresa's voice.

"Naturally I told him. Why shouldn't I tell him? I told him you'd gone to see your uncle and that you'd got a headache and were staying there for the night. He's coming home this morning and I daresay he'll drive straight down here from the airport. He'll probably be here quite soon."

The last sentence was addressed directly to Mark, who heard it unmoved.

"He must have been worried," he said calmly.

For a moment, Lolly looked nonplussed; she was so obviously waiting for him to rise and take his leave that this bland persistence took her unawares. Her irritation was so manifest that Teresa found herself laughing. She rose and went towards the cocktail cabinet.

"What'll you drink?" she asked Mark.

"Sherry, if you've got it, please."

He walked over and stood beside her; then he carried a glass of sherry to Lolly, who took it with no softening of her expression. They looked at one another, and Teresa, glancing over her shoulder, saw something pass between them—an appeal on Lolly's part, a denial on Mark's. She came to Lolly's rescue.

"When I've had my drink, I'll go upstairs and lie down till lunch time," she said, and saw relief in Lolly's eyes. "It was so kind of you," she went on, addressing Mark, "to bring me home —and I'm more than grateful for everything you've done."

This was dismissal indeed, and Mark bowed. But he drank slowly and talked with an ease and fluency that made Lolly forget how time was passing. When at last he put down his glass and began to take his leave, it was—for Lolly's purposes—too late. A crunching on the gravel, a peal on the doorbell announced the arrival of a visitor; as Teresa reached the door of the drawing-room, it opened to admit Neville.

They came face to face; over her head he gave a brief look at Lolly, and a more lingering one at Mark. Teresa presented her cheek, and found his hand turning her head so that he could bend and rest his lips on hers.

"Are you all right?" he asked, putting his arm round her shoulders as once more she faced the others. "How's the head?"

"Well, it wasn't really a headache," said Teresa. "Neville, this is Mr. Tudor. Mark, this is my fiancé, Neville Morley."

Neither man look enchanted. Neville studied the tall stranger who stood beside Lolly, looking at ease and at home; Mark gave him a swift, assessing glance and lost none of his calm demeanour.

"It was a fall," he explained. "Teresa fell over some scaffolding as she was leaving the house. I carried her in again and we persuaded her that it would be wiser to wait until the morning before going home." He smiled at Teresa—a brief, warm, intimate smile. "Never," he said gently, "would I have imagined that so slim a girl would make so strong a man so bereft of breath up so short a flight of stairs."

Nobody seemed to have any comment to make. Teresa freed herself from Neville's encircling arm. Neville gazed across the room at the other man and a frown of displeasure gathered on his brow. Lolly looked as though a bat had flown into the room and she was wondering how to get it out again and at the same time prevent it from flying into her face.

Mark broke the silence. With undisguised regret, he turned to Teresa.

"I'm afraid I must go," he said.

Lolly, with every appearance of relief, went to the door and opened it wide. Mark nodded to Neville, who barely nodded in return; then he held out his hand to Teresa.

"I shall come again, if I may," he said, "to see how you are."

"I think," said Neville swiftly, "that she'll be all right now. Thanks for being on the spot."

"There's always the chance," pointed out Mark, "of a little delayed shock. I'll look in tomorrow to see that everything's going on well."

He was gone. Lolly was leading him to the front door; opening it, she went out to the drive and walked beside him to his car. As they reached it, she turned and faced him squarely.

"Mr. Tudor," she began firmly, "I'm going to say something to you."

He bowed, and waited—but Lolly seemed to be at a loss for words. After groping for a time, she brought the next sentence out with a rush.

"Please don't come back," she said.

Mark's eyebrows went up.

"Merely to make polite inquiries?"

"You've been kind and we're all grateful, but don't tell me," said Lolly, "that you didn't enjoy yourself in there just now, doing your best to be as provocative as possible."

"Provocative?"

"Don't pretend you don't know what I'm talking about. A man who's engaged to a girl doesn't like to come back from somewhere and find another man in the drawing-room looking possessive."

"Possessive."

"That's what I said. Don't keep repeating my words. Lady Thurloe isn't here to say this, so I'll say it: you were doing your best to be annoying just now, and I don't understand why, but I think it would be better all round if you didn't come back any more. I hope I don't sound inhospitable, but there's no point in beating about the bush, and I think you saw quite clearly that Mr. Morley would rather you stayed away."

"Yes, I saw that quite clearly," said Mark.

"Good. I'm sorry, for your mother's sake, that we can't be friends, but——"

"Oh, but I hope we shall," said Mark.

"You mean"—she stared at him—"you mean that after all I've said, you're going to come back here—and stir up trouble?"

"Certainly not." Mark spoke quietly. "The moment Teresa tells me to stay away, I'll stay away."

There was a pause.

"She's—she's engaged," said Lolly abruptly at last.

"I saw the ring."

"And doesn't that mean anything to you?"

"Yes," said Mark. "It means that another man got there first and staked a claim. And now . . . he's got to fight to keep it."

"You mean you . . ." Lolly's voice died away. Then she took a deep breath. "You can't mean what you're saying," she ended incredulously.

Mark smiled; there was something, she thought, almost protective about his expression as he looked down at her.

"Of course I mean it," he said. "Do you think that having met her, I'm going to let her go again?"

"But . . ." Lolly made an effort to speak calmly. "She's engaged," she repeated. "You're too late."

"Not too late," corrected Mark.

"You mean to tell me that the fact of Teresa's engagement means nothing to you?"

"It means—as I see it—that she has engaged herself to meet a certain man at a certain church on a certain day in order to take certain vows. Until those vows are taken, the engagement remains an engagement."

"In other words, an engagement means nothing?"

"It means everything—if a woman is in love with the man. But"—his voice was gentle—"she isn't in love with him."

"She——"

"And you know it," ended Mark.

"Look," began Lolly desperately, "you're a complete stranger and——"

"Not to Teresa," he corrected. "Have you forgotten last night?"

She made no reply, and his gaze went beyond her to the green hedge surrounding them. His voice was slow and even.

"Extraordinary, isn't it?" he said. "One moment I was walking along the street, thinking of nothing. And then—I saw her. She was standing in front of the house, looking up at it. I waited for her to move on—my heart felt . . . pinched, as I waited. She would go—and I would remember that glimpse all my life and wonder who she was and where she had come from and why she had been snatched away from me after one brief look. But . . . she didn't go away. She stood there, and I came nearer, and nearer—and then I knew I'd seen her face before—or a face like hers. I remembered the photograph in her uncle's room—and I realized who she must be. And then I spoke to her, and I understood that if I couldn't do something, say something to prevent her, she would go away for ever."

He paused, and Lolly waited.

"And you—you stopped her," she said flatly at last. "How did you do it?"

"How? I don't know. When she drove away, I stood there and I realized that perhaps I was imagining that I had felt something pass between us. The world had changed for me—but for her? I didn't know. I could only stand there and say a prayer. She had gone—but if she felt anything, any slight part of what I had felt; if I had succeeded in communicating one small part of my feelings . . . she would come back."

"And she came back."

"Yes. She came back. I wanted to shout and to take her in my arms—but I didn't, of course. I had to behave as though my heart was beating normally, as though a wild hope hadn't been born in me." He looked down unseeingly at Lolly. "Who wrote those lines?" he asked.

> *"There is a garden in her face*
> *Where roses and white lilies grow*

I found myself saying them when I first saw her. Roses and white lilies . . ."

"Please—please go away," begged Lolly.

"Roses and white lilies," he repeated softly. "Yes, I'll go away —but I shall come back. She's wearing another man's ring—but she doesn't love him."

"She——"

"—doesn't love him. Haven't I got eyes? He came into the room—and I watched her, and what did I see? Affection. The kindest, the most gentle of welcomes—and more? No more. If I can see that, then you must see it too. And so must her mother.

And if you and her mother see only affection and still want her to marry him, then it must be because you feel that it will be the best thing for her. But I . . . I don't believe it for a moment."

"He's a good man," said Lolly. "He's decent, he's got a good background and she'll never want for anything. And her mother is set on the marriage."

"As mothers have been and will be for ever and ever." He looked down at Lolly. "Nothing I do," he said slowly, "will ever hurt Teresa."

"She's in good hands. He'll look after her all his life."

"If he gets her."

"Look,"—Lolly spoke urgently—"you don't understand. There are things you don't know—can't know. If you don't go away, you won't make her happy. You'll . . . you'll cause a lot of trouble. Her mother . . ."

"If Teresa is happy, her mother will be happy."

"No—yes." Lolly wrung her hands. "You must leave things as they are."

Mark got into his car and settled himself at the wheel and switched on the engine. Then he looked at her.

"If Teresa doesn't love me," he said slowly, "nothing I can do will make any difference—to anybody."

"You mean . . . you're going on with this?"

"To the end," said Mark.

The car moved, gathered speed and vanished into the roadway. Lolly stood staring after it, her eyes dark with foreboding.

Chapter Six

LOLLY'S religion was of an unorthodox kind. If asked, she would have said that she was a plain Christian; if pressed, she would have explained that this meant keeping in close touch with Christ and having as little as possible to do with the Church. As she vouchsafed no further explanation, only Teresa, who had watched the process, round-eyed, throughout her childhood, knew that keeping in close touch meant Lolly's flopping down on her knees at odd moments of the day, in her bedroom or in her sitting-room or in the linen cupboard, to remind God of His duty towards her.

"Oh God," she prayed in the bathroom on Mark's departure, "keep that man away. As soon as I looked at him, oh God, I thought: 'Now that should have been her man.' But You sent him too late, Lord, so don't send him any more, or there'll be trouble. There's nothing the matter with Neville, and we thank Thee for him; he'll make a good husband and if this Tudor doesn't have time to lay a spell on Teresa, all will be well, oh God. But if she begins to ask herself questions, if she begins to feel uncertain, if she decides that it won't be Neville after all, then her mother will . . . Oh God, something tells me there's trouble coming."

Getting to her feet, she found that she felt a good deal better. A trouble shared was a trouble halved; a Man who promised distinctly to refresh all those who were heavily laden, should do something now, for she was more than heavily laden and if Teresa's mother came back and found Mark Tudor hanging about, there would be more than travail. She had told God; now it was up to Him. If He knew what He was about, He would keep Mark Tudor away.

She was all the more dismayed, therefore, when two evenings later, the maid came to find her and told her that a Mr. Tudor was waiting in the drawing-room.

"Didn't you say Miss Teresa was out?"

"Yes, Miss. He said that if you weren't busy, he'd see you."

Lolly hesitated; then she marched with determination to the drawing-room, greeted Mark soberly and waved him to a chair.

"Sit down," she ordered. "We may as well have this out." Mark smiled at her.

"I quite agree. You begin," he invited.

"Very well. First, let me be frank: I have nothing against you, as far as anybody can judge by appearances. You look all right, and you sound all right and I don't mind admitting that if you'd presented yourself as a candidate a year or two ago, I wouldn't—subject to inquiries about you, of course—have minded your seeing something of Teresa. But you're too late."

"How late is too late?" inquired Mark.

"Too late is when everybody who loves a girl is convinced that she's acting in her own best interests. Mr. Morley is sound in every way, and they're in love with one another; if you're a man at all, you'll go away and leave well alone. There; I've been frank. Now say what you have to say."

"First of all, I have to thank you."

"Thank me?" Lolly's voice went up an octave in surprise. "Thank me what for?"

"For not wasting a thought on the fact that I might be a fortune hunter. I know that Teresa isn't penniless."

"I suppose her aunt told you that. Well, you needn't thank me. I don't think you'd go after any girl's money. But I do think that you enjoy stirring up trouble. You want to get Neville thoroughly stirred up."

"Stirred up." Mark repeated the words musingly. "If I'm any judge, nobody's ever really thrown him out of his stride. I'd be interested to see how he'd react to some competition."

"I've told you; it's too late for competition of any sort." She leaned forward, thrusting her plain, anxious face towards him and speaking with deep earnestness. "Mr. Tudor, will you please go away and leave things as they are? Teresa'll be happy, I promise you that. There isn't anybody in this world—except her godfather—who knows more about her and who wants to see her happy than I do. I've been with her since she was a baby, and I've protected her from . . . from a lot that you couldn't possibly know anything about. Leave it at that. There's more here than you can see."

"You mean that if anything—anybody—turns up to upset this eminently suitable match, Teresa's mother won't like it?"

"That's what I mean."

"Mothers are very necessary," said Mark, "but their influence doesn't extend beyond their daughters' years of discretion. I don't think Lady Thurloe's opinions would really influence me."

Lolly's face slowly whitened.

"If you won't take advice," she said slowly, "then take a warning: don't go on with this. If you go away now, and for ever, Teresa won't miss you. If you stay, and if you . . . if you succeed in getting between her and her fiancé, you'll be very wicked. And you'll pull her world down on top of her."

There was silence. Mark's eyebrows went up, and he met Lolly's eyes for a long moment, but he made no comment. Then, in a slow movement, he rose from his chair and stood looking down at her stout, square figure.

"What is Lady Thurloe like?" he asked.

"She's a very good-looking and a very charming woman. She's liked by her servants, admired by the village people, and copied by all her friends. She sits on Committees and subscribes to a great many charities. She has spent a great deal of care and thought—and money—on her daughter's upbringing. She met Neville Morley and asked him to the house and this match is mostly of her own making."

Mark did not appear to be listening; he was standing with his back to her, gazing out at the sunlit garden.

"Funny thing," he said musingly, without turning. "I get the feeling here that I get in Teresa's aunt's house: something"—he spun round slowly—"something below the surface."

"There's always something below the surface," said Lolly. "Every family has secrets of one kind or another, and they don't reveal them to strangers. And now will you go away, please? Teresa is dining out."

"That's not what the maid said when she let me in, but"—Mark gave her one of his wide, attractive smiles—"I'll take your word for it."

She let him out and watched him as he got into his car. She remained standing there when the car had gone; she was still standing there, brooding, when Teresa drove in with Neville ten minutes later.

Neville, she saw, was not coming in; he walked with Teresa to the door, said a word to Lolly, bent to kiss Teresa and then drove away.

The two women walked into the house together. Teresa, going into the drawing-room, settled herself on the sofa and put her hands behind her head.

"Tired?" asked Lolly.

"No. Just thinking."

"Why didn't Neville come in? You told me he was coming to dinner."

"I asked him not to. We had . . . a sort of argument."

"You didn't look to me as though you'd quarrelled. What was it about?"

"It wasn't a quarrel; it was just a difference of opinion. It was about Mark."

Mark. Always Mark. Lolly looked at her with a sinking heart. Mark. Teresa had not known him long—but they had met in unusual circumstances. And a man and a girl could learn a lot about one another when the man had held her in his arms, when he had laid her on a bed and waited for her to return to consciousness, when he had talked to her in Mark's low, lazy, pleasant voice and looked at her out of grey eyes fringed by lashes that ought to have belonged to a woman. Mark. He wanted her—and she was aware of him. The house, thought Lolly, fear creeping slowly over her, was swaying. The house, so carefully erected, so carefully built, so anxiously safeguarded—the house was in danger.

She thought of going up to the linen cupboard and reproaching God for turning a deaf ear to her appeal; He knew all the circumstances, and He had let this peril come near them all.

It was too much, she thought, for her to bear alone. If God didn't choose to do anything about it, she would go into Brighton and see Sir Lawrence and tell him what was happening. He would listen and he would act. It was too late to go this evening; she would go immediately after breakfast tomorrow. Sir Lawrence —in many ways he was as useless as all men, but on this matter he would know how to advise her.

She was so busy with her own thoughts that it was some time before she noticed Teresa's abstraction.

"You're very quiet," she told her at last. "I wouldn't worry too much about arguments, if I were you."

"I wasn't thinking about Neville. I was wondering," said Teresa, "why you hadn't told me that Mark had called."

Lolly took her time before answering.

"Who did tell you?" she asked at last.

"We passed him on the road. He wouldn't have come down here—or so I thought—unless he'd come to the house."

"Did Neville see him?"

"No. I know the car better than Neville does, and I recognized it. He did come here?"

"He did."

Teresa looked thoughtful.

"And you sent him away again?"

"I did."

"Why?" Teresa's tone was one of simple inquiry. "What are you afraid of?"

"Who said I was afraid of anything?" countered Lolly.

"Don't you like him?"

"I don't know him; how can I decide whether I like him or not? The only impression I formed is that he doesn't seem able to take a hint when it's handed to him, that's all."

"And did you give him more than a hint?"

"A decent man," said Lolly, "doesn't hang round girls who are engaged."

"Isn't that putting it a little strongly?"

"No, it isn't. If Neville were a bounder, there'd be some excuse —but he's a good man, plain for all to see."

"As long as I can see it, Lolly darling, is there really any need for you to worry?"

Lolly hesitated. To explain that she recognized in Mark Tudor an attraction that—if he cared to use it—few girls could resist, would not improve the position. To confess that she had seen in Teresa too much interest in him—interest, and more than interest —would make matters infinitely worse. It was better to say nothing—until tomorrow, when she would say it all to Sir Lawrence.

"I shan't worry any more," she said. "But somebody has to deal with these lately-come-Johnnies. Somebody has to put them in their place—and I think I've done just that."

Teresa looked at her speculatively.

"Lolly, are you getting secretive?"

"How so?"

"You didn't tell me you'd been to see Zoë."

"Do I have to remember every visit I made twenty-odd years ago?"

"Did you want to patch up the quarrel?"

"I did. But I found it was no good—so you see, I know what I was talking about when I advised you to keep away." She paused. "Does she still wear those plaits round her head?"

"Yes. She's very good-looking."

"She used to be. She reminded me of one of those pictures in the school story books—Rumanian peasant. I liked her."

"So did I. Lolly, the house is . . . well, the furniture's terrible and there aren't any decent pictures or ornaments—or anything. It couldn't have been like that when Mother lived there?"

"I daresay your uncle has been wearing a rut in the pavement between the house and the pawnshop. He can't go abroad as often as you say he does on four hundred a year. Does he still have the room over the drawing-room?"

"He has the room above Zoë's—but it's more like a Chapel than a drawing-room; it's crammed with holy things."

"I expect she's trying to convert him. You can see now, can't you, that there's not much left between your mother and that house?"

"Yes, I can see. There's something . . . something odd about them all."

"They sound more than odd." Lolly paused on the brink of adding that Mark had told her he sensed a secret in the house. It would be wise, she decided, to put herself out of reach of further discussion—and further questioning. She rose and went to the door.

"See you at dinner," she said.

Teresa watched the door close, and sighed. Lolly was acting watchdog—and growling menacingly. And Neville was growling —not menacingly, but uneasily. And they were both growling at Mark Tudor.

Teresa tried to bring her own feelings into the light and examine them—and found herself shrinking from the necessity of breaking the soft web of indecision in which she was caught. Mark . . . what had he said? A few words of regret that they had not met one another before. No more. That there would be more, she knew—and shrank from the knowledge. She was aware that she must search her heart, but she could not. Not yet. To search would be to find the answer to her present confusion. To search would be to find an answer that would change her life—and at this moment, she was afraid.

She met Lolly at dinner, and they spoke little. Parting from her after the meal, Teresa went up to her bedroom and undressing, got into bed and began to read. But the book did not hold her attention, and after a time she put it down and lay thinking of her visit to the house in Grosvenor Drive. From the colourful background of figures—Zoë, Maxie, the old couple, the glamorous Paloma—there emerged the single figure of Mark Tudor. He seemed to be before her, clear, near. She seemed to hear his voice; he seemed to be at her bedside, as he had been two nights before, quiet, unmoving—watching over her. She saw his smile and looked once more into his eyes.

With a sudden movement, she turned and put out her hand to switch off the light—and at that moment, the telephone by the bed rang.

As she picked up the receiver and heard Mark's voice, she knew that she had been waiting for his call. He spoke, and a little shiver of delight went through her.

"Are you up—or in bed?"

"I'm in bed."

"Am I disturbing you?"

"No."

"I was thinking of you—and some poetry came into my mind, and I wanted to say it to you. Are you listening?"

"Yes."

"Do you know your Byron?"

"No."

"He wrote some lines which describe how I feel. May I read them to you?"

"Please."

She heard his low voice.

> *"In the desert a fountain is springing*
> *In the wide waste there still is a tree*
> *And a bird in the solitude singing*
> *Which speaks to my spirit of thee.*

Did I read that well?"

"Yes. Very well?"

Mark went on softly:

> *"Thou art my life, my love, my heart*
> *The very eyes of me*
> *And hast command of every part*
> *To live and die for thee."*

There was silence.

"Did you listen?" he asked at last.

"Yes."

"Know who said that last bit?"

"Yes. Herrick."

"Good girl. Teresa——"

"Yes?"

"I tried to see you—but the lion at the gate slept not."

"I know. You passed us on the road."

"Us?"

"Neville and myself."

"I should have seen. Not him, but you. Teresa——"

"Yes?"

"David's in bed with a chill, and it isn't serious, but he'd like to see you."

"Did he say so?"

"He didn't like to put it into words; he felt it might be presumptuous. But it's lonely for him in bed all day, practically alone."

"Except for Zoë and Maxie and the rest?"

"They've all got foreign accents. He'd like to be read to in pure English. Will you come?"

"I . . . I think I will," said Teresa. "But I'm not sure."

"He's a very little boy," said Mark, "and he can't read to himself. And you have a lovely, lovely voice. Will you come?"

"I think so."

"Teresa——"

"Yes?"

"I want you to know something. I love you. I shall love you always. And I want you to know something else. I regard a husband as an absolutely insuperable barrier between myself and any woman. I respect his claims utterly. But . . . until he's a husband, I consider that he has to keep his weapons at hand to defend whatever title he lays claim to. Darling Teresa, you don't belong to anybody—yet. Sweet Teresa, good night."

Teresa laid the telephone softly on its stand, switched off the light and lay back and stared up into the darkness.

Chapter Seven

LOLLY left the house soon after breakfast on the following morning. The day was fine, and she decided that she would not, as Teresa had suggested last night, use the car; she would walk down to the village and order some things she needed, and then she would go into Brighton by bus.

Sir Lawrence let her in and led her upstairs to the study.

"You're earlier than you said you'd be," he told her, "but it's good to see you. How are you, Lolly?"

She sank into a chair and began to pull off her gloves, and he looked down at her and took in the details of her outfit and wished, whimsically, that he had worn his sun glasses. For Lolly, a lover of colour, saw no reason to follow the fashion of sober dressing for women of her age. She was wearing a vivid green skirt, a magenta blouse, a plum-coloured coat and a hat trimmed with brilliantly-coloured feathers. Her face, flushed with exertion, added the last touch to her patchwork appearance.

"How's the story going?" he asked.

"It's gone."

His eyebrows went up.

"Finished? You mean you got to the end of it?"

"I mean I didn't. How do you expect me," she asked, "to give my mind to murder when I've got all this worry creeping up on me?"

"Well, tell me about it. But first, would you like a drink of something?" he asked.

"I'd give a lot for a good, hot cup of coffee," said Lolly, "but that grudging old woman of yours might give notice if you asked for it."

"We can try." Sir Lawrence summoned his resolution, rang the bell, and to the tight-lipped woman who answered it, made his wishes known.

"It's early for coffee," was the surly response. "'Tisn't more than half ten. Black, or caffy o-lay?"

"With milk please."

The door banged, and Lolly gave a wide grin.

"The milk will turn sour," she prophesied. "Why don't you get rid of her?"

"I did try once, as you know. But the appalling creatures who answered my advertisement frightened me so much that I've never had the wish to try again. Half of them were harpies, and the rest were——"

"I know; were poor devils in search of an easy billet in which to end their days." She leaned back and stretched out her short, thick legs. "Lawrence, when I leave the cottage, why don't you let me come here and do for you?"

"Not a bit of it," he said. "When you leave Coralie, you'll buy yourself a little house somewhere and do for yourself. You've earned a rest." He clasped his hands behind his back and frowned down at her. "You've quite made up your mind, I suppose?"

"You didn't think I'd stay after Teresa married, did you?"

"No. To be frank, I didn't. But once or twice I wondered whether perhaps the years haven't made a difference."

"I won't bring out that old one about leopards not changing their spots," said Lolly, "but you can take it as read."

"You think she's just the same?"

"Just the same. And that's why I'm worried."

"But I thought it was Teresa you were worried about. What's been going on since she came to see me?"

"She went to see Hubert. She didn't see him because he was away. She met his wife. As far as I can make out, the visit didn't come to much; the place is run as a sort of boarding house and it's full of foreigners—but on the way out, Teresa fell; didn't hurt herself, but she stayed there the night."

There was a pause; Sir Lawrence, after waiting for more, prompted her.

"Well go on. You didn't come out here to see me just to tell me that. You said you were worried. If the visit wasn't a success, I suppose you mean that Teresa won't repeat it—and that's what you want, isn't it?"

"Yes. But it's this man," said Lolly slowly.

"Man?"

"You remember the Grants, who used to have that big house up on the Downs?"

"Of course I remember them. Three of the prettiest girls I ever knew—why should I forget them?"

"One of them married a man called Tudor."

"Yes. Nice feller; met him once after they were married."

"Well, this man is their son and if he hasn't got his mother's beauty he's got her eyes and he's got her charm. Yes, all her charm—and may the Lord help us, he knows how to use it."

"What's all this got to do with Hubert?" asked Sir Lawrence in bewilderment.

"Wait and see. The visit to Hubert brought him to light; he lives in Hubert's house. He met Teresa outside and persuaded her to go in. He was with her when she fell. He carried her in. He took charge: telephoned to me, watched by her bedside, brought her home. I heard the car when they arrived, but nothing more happened, no doors banging, no footsteps on the drive, nobody coming up the steps—so I went out to investigate. And there they were, the two of them, still in the car. He was talking to her, and I couldn't hear what he was saying and I daresay it was nothing very important, but there was a look on her face. . . . She was listening to him and when I went out to them and they got out of the car, she looked . . . Lawrence, she looked different: dreamy, quiet, sort of . . ." She stopped and looked up, her eyes full of misery. "I'm worried. What's more, I'm frightened."

Sir Lawrence said nothing; the door had opened and Mrs. Crofts, her face set in grim displeasure, was bringing in the coffee; setting it down on the table, she walked out of the room and shut the door sharply behind her. In silence, Sir Lawrence poured out two cups and brought one to Lolly.

"You're tired; you must be, or you wouldn't take this so seriously," he said. "Are you suggesting that Teresa is going to fall under the spell of every attractive fellow she meets? In the first place, she needn't see this man again; she——"

"Listen to me," broke in Lolly. "You know me. You've known me for forty years and more. Am I the kind of woman who makes a fuss about nothing?"

"No. I'll say that; you're not."

"Well, then. I tell you I smell trouble. I smell it here and I smell it there. It's coming. And this Tudor is going to bring most of it."

"Then there's no problem. Get rid of him. See that he doesn't get a chance to——"

"You haven't seen him—and you haven't heard it all. He says he's in love with Teresa."

Sir Lawrence, about to sip his coffee, put the cup back on to the saucer.

"Then the man's a fool—or worse," he said.

"He's no fool, and he's no knave, either," said Lolly. "If you're going to talk like one of the squires in an old melodrama, you'll make me angry. If he were a fool or worse, there'd be no problem. Teresa's got good judgment and a cool head—too cool, I've sometimes thought. The trouble is that we're dealing with a decent man."

"I presume he was told that Teresa's engaged?"

"That doesn't worry him in the least."

"Then he's a bounder."

"There you go again. I tell you, he isn't. He's clever, and——"

"Attractive, charming, decent and clever. Aren't you piling it on a bit?"

"I am not. You're only beginning to see what we're up against. He's clever enough, as I was going to tell you, to have got at the truth: namely, that Neville has had it too easy and that nobody has ever really laid siege to Teresa."

"Laid siege? A fellow asks a girl to marry him and——"

"—and with her mother pushing on one flank and myself shoving on the other, we manage to persuade her—because we're convinced of it ourselves—that he's the right man for her. Neville had it too easy—and now Mark Tudor has come into the picture and he's going to——"

"He's too late, I tell you. Teresa's engaged."

"An engagement," said Lolly, in a tone indicating that her patience was being strained to the utmost—"is simply, in his opinion, an engagement. He says that it's an engagement to meet on a certain day at a certain church in order to take certain vows. Until those vows are taken—he says—the arrangement remains merely an engagement. You and I might consider it binding, but then we're the old-fashioned sort—and we're not in love, as Mark Tudor is. He considers the field's wide open, and he's going in. And now you can tell me what to do. You've got your wish, that's one thing; you've told me over and over again that you thought Teresa should have had chances of meeting other men, knowing other men, falling in and out of love with other men before she settled down. Well, here's another man; now tell me what we do."

"There's no need to make too heavy weather of it," commented Sir Lawrence after some thought. "It's up to Neville, after all. In my opinion, he'll be able to look after his own; he's not a weak man."

"He's not a weak man—but he's not a charmer. And he's suffering from over-confidence; after all, Coralie made things easy for him, and so did I. And if he isn't a weak man, he's got, like everybody else, one or two weaknesses—and this Tudor will find them out. Neville will take a stand on his rights—and Mark Tudor will prove that he hasn't any rights. Neville will bank on Teresa's loyalty—but if she only feels affection for him, and something much stronger for the other man—then where will her loyalty lie?"

"She's given Neville a promise. She's promised to marry him."

"And if she can't follow that up by promising to love, honour and all the rest of it, do you think she won't hand him back his ring in all honesty? Of course she will. Neville is sound, but he doesn't really see much beyond his nose; he'll argue, as you do, that any man who goes after an engaged girl is an outsider—and while he's resting on that conclusion, Mark Tudor will be opening Teresa's eyes to the kind of courtship Neville never dreamed of and never troubled to make. Do you still think I'm exaggerating?"

"Yes."

"Very well. Then there's another angle which might penetrate your thick skull. Coralie will be back in just over a week. Mark Tudor will still be around. I sent him away—but he'll be back. Oh yes, he'll be back. Where, Coralie will ask, has this man come from? We shall have to tell her: from Hubert's house. And so she learns that Teresa went there. Do you dismiss that, too?"

"No." Sir Lawrence frowned. "I don't; I can see that things might be awkward if——"

"Awkward!" Lolly gave an exasperated snort. "Awkward! Do you think I've stayed for over twenty years in Coralie Thurloe's house in order to avoid an awkward situation?"

There was a long silence. Sir Lawrence, standing with his back to the fireplace, stared across the room at the ungainly woman in the big chair. His frown deepened; hands thrust deep in his pockets, he spoke at last slowly and almost unwillingly.

"That's something I've thought about a good deal in these last few years, Lolly," he said at last. "I've often wondered whether perhaps we weren't keeping siege outside a city that had been evacuated."

"In plain words, you mean that in the past twenty years, Coralie has changed?"

"Yes. After all, she's never shown any signs of——"

"That's simple. The reason she hasn't shown herself to be what you and I know she is, is because she's had her own way whenever I could give it to her—and when I couldn't, I've seen to it that she got enough to satisfy her. It hasn't always been easy, but that, after all, is what I went there for."

"But Lolly"—his voice was gentle—"twenty years is a long time. Are you sure——"

"Quite." Lolly was at her most abrupt. "Take a tigress: is she always dangerous? No. Only when she's threatened. How long did Teresa's father know Coralie? Six years—and it wasn't until nearly two years after their marriage that he really saw what she was. And it finished him. That, at least, you believe."

"Yes. But the position was different. He was a man in love, and he'd built her up into something half doll, half angel. What she destroyed wasn't a true picture of herself; it was the false one he'd had in his mind."

"It destroyed something in him—and it could destroy something in Teresa. She's like her father; she's gentle; she's—she's vulnerable. And she has the same blind spot: Coralie. Her mother. She knows her mother, of course, better than her father ever did. She knows that under that soft look there's something iron-hard. She knows that Coralie needs special treatment from the world and blows up—in the nicest way—if she doesn't get it. But she has never seen the spectacle of Coralie deprived of something on which she has really set her heart—of Coralie up against someone who will hold out to the end against her. She has never seen the kind of scene that her father saw—and it was to prevent her from ever seeing it that her father sent for me. It was to shield Teresa from the worst in Coralie that I promised to go and live there. I told him I'd stay until a sound man turned up to marry her and take over the job—and I've kept my promise. I've acted as a buffer and a shield—and a veil."

"You've done well, Lolly."

"I've done better than well. When Teresa was a child, it was easy; later, it wasn't so easy, because her ways often ran counter to her mother's. But I've managed to prevent a showdown. And because I've always hated Coralie, I was glad that Neville was going to free me. And now Mark Tudor has come into the picture, and I know that trouble is coming. Coralie is going to learn that Teresa has been to Hubert's house. Coralie is going to meet Mark Tudor, who lives there. Coralie, being quicker-witted than you, is going to realize that Mark Tudor won't make the docile son-in-law that Neville would. Neville would play along with her all his life—but Mark Tudor? No and no and no. And so she'll come up—once more—against an insurmountable obstacle. And then she'll come out in all her true and ugly colours. And she'll make another terrible, incredibly ugly scene. And this time, Teresa will be there to see it—and to see her mother as she really is."

Her voice trailed off, and she sat hunched in her chair. In the silence that followed, Sir Lawrence walked to and fro, his face drawn and unhappy. At last he paused by Lolly's chair and stood looking down at her soberly.

"Are you sure," he asked slowly, "that it hasn't been a mistake? I don't want to throw away all your devotion, all your self-sacrifice, but——"

"There was no sacrifice, and you know it. I adored Teresa's father and—in the end—he knew it too. This was all I could do for him and I did it, at first because I loved him—and then I went on doing it because I loved Teresa."

"But . . ." Sir Lawrence's words came hesitantly—"was it right to do it all? Was it right to let Teresa grow up thinking her mother was one thing, when her mother was in fact another? What is, is; if Teresa had learned early that her mother was, or could be, an utterly selfish and violent woman, then——"

"I've thought it all over," said Lolly, "countless times in the last twenty years. Let her know the truth, I've said to myself. Why shield her? She's a product of a tough age; she may be like her father, but she was born into a harsher world. But have you ever thought what Teresa's life would have been if I hadn't been there to stand between her and her mother? She would have had to give in to Coralie—once and for ever—or she would have had to oppose her. If she'd opposed her, their life . . . would it have been as smooth, as happy, as . . . as seemly as it has been? I thought of it in a hundred different ways, and I always came back to the same conclusion: that I was right to stay there and to keep Teresa's childhood and girlhood calm and unshadowed. I don't think she would have developed into the fine young woman she is if she'd been reared in a cat-and-dog atmosphere. The truth . . . sometimes the truth can be too ugly. And Coralie has many ugly sides. In the War, when she turned craven . . . I was there to hide the truth from Teresa. When she had intrigues with men—I was there to keep them from the house. A thousand lies and evasions and shifts—what was the use of letting Teresa see them? Could I say: Your mother is a cheat and a liar and worse but you must grow up fine and upright and good—could I? No. I could only be careful that she wasn't with her mother for too long periods—and I was careful. Boarding school, finishing school, travel abroad and then the job at Brighton—and in between, Coralie at her best, acting the pretty mother of a pretty daughter, and doing it, you'll admit, to perfection. No, Lawrence, it hasn't all been wasted."

"But she's a grown woman now; we can't go on holding up this . . . this shield, this umbrella for ever."

"Only till she's safely married. With a husband to look after her, it won't matter much what Coralie does. If Teresa is to learn at last what she is, let her learn it when she's safely away from Coralie, in a home of her own and with a man to lean on. But don't blame me for not letting her know the truth earlier. She was a little child and I promised to see that she had a happy upbringing—and I did. If that was wrong, I'm willing to take any blame that's coming to me in the hereafter."

"Perhaps," said Sir Lawrence slowly, "you got more help from Coralie than you know. I said just now that her husband had a wrong idea of her—but perhaps he didn't really paint the picture all by himself."

"You mean that Coralie was always acting?"

"Yes. When you come to think of it, there aren't more than two or three people in the world who really know what she's like. You know, and I know—and of course Hubert knows. And Hubert's wife."

"Hubert didn't care. Hubert knew his sister."

"Yes . . ." Sir Lawrence stared at her thoughtfully. "Yes,

Hubert knew her. Did it ever strike you, Lolly, thinking about that quarrel, that Hubert . . . stage-managed it?"

"Don't get you. What do you mean?" she asked.

"Hubert wanted money—Coralie's money. Coralie wouldn't let him have it. When he came down to the cottage for the last time, I suppose he realized, at last, that he wasn't going to get anything and I think he decided, as a little farewell present, to give a show."

"A show?"

"A performance—by his sister."

"I see," said Lolly slowly. "You mean that Hubert knew quite well what would happen if he worked Coralie up into a rage— and so he did it."

"Yes. He came down and announced that he'd married Zoë, and that touched Coralie on what he knew to be one of her softest spots. And she let go—and her husband saw her with the mask off." He jerked back his shoulders and stood upright. "We needn't talk about it, Lolly; it upsets me and it does no good. What do you want me to do about this fellow Tudor?"

"I want you to come to the house while he's there, and talk to him. You're a Trustee, you're Teresa's godfather and you're the only man qualified to take a protective stand on her behalf."

"Nonsense. Tell Neville to send the fellow to rightabouts."

"Neville can't do it on your level; he hasn't enough authority —yet. So this is what I'm going to do. Next time Mark Tudor calls at the cottage, I'll telephone to you and you've got to come at once. At once. Pretend you just dropped in casually, and I'll see that you get some time alone with him."

"And then what?" asked Sir Lawrence, his countenance full of foreboding.

"Then tell him he has no business to be hanging round Teresa. Tell him her mother's coming back, and wouldn't like it. Tell him . . . tell him what in Heaven you please," she burst out impatiently, "but get rid of him." She got to her feet and began to pull on her gloves. "And don't sit down when I've gone and think up ways of getting out of this," she warned. "It's your job and you've got to do it. Don't let's have any trouble at this stage. I've done my part; I've put up with Coralie for twenty years. I've staved off rows, I've kept her sweet and I've given Teresa what her father wanted her to have—a happy upbringing.

Now you can do a bit for a change. I'll ring you up—and you come. Understand?"

"Oh, I'll come, I'll come," mumbled Sir Lawrence, opening the door and accompanying her downstairs. "But what," he ended, as they stood on the front doorstep, "what in the Lord's name I'll say when I get there——"

"Don't rehearse it, for pity's sake." Lolly marched to the gate and turned to raise a hand in farewell. "Good-bye for now and ——" She saw a movement in one of the upper windows and caught a glimpse of a sour, peering face, and deliberately raised her voice—"get rid of that sour-faced old woman and find yourself somebody who knows how to make decent coffee."

She was gone. Sir Lawrence, who had also seen the curtain stir, stood fearfully in the hall listening for sounds. Then with a sigh he went cautiously upstairs.

Chapter Eight

". . . and so Smoochy ran and ran and ran," read Teresa, "and soon he reached the house of his friend Nobber and——"

"*Nobbler*," corrected David, from his listening post against the heaped pillows of his bed.

"I'm sorry. Nobbler. 'And Nobbler said "Why on earth are you panting, Smoocher? You——" ' "

"*Smoochy*." There was open reproach in David's voice. This was no way to read. Zoë did it much better, and Mark better still; even Maxie, though his accent was not equal to some of the harder words, didn't stumble as much as Teresa did.

Teresa sensed the criticism and stumbled even more. Her mind was elsewhere, and she wanted to put down the book and sort out her thoughts. But she was here in Mark's room visiting David, and she had to keep her mind on her reading.

She had asked him what he would like her to do and he had unhesitatingly chosen to be read to. The new and varied and colourful pile of books which Teresa had brought with her were inspected politely, gratefully—and put aside in favour of a small, battered work entitled *The Adventures of Smoochy*. Teresa sat in a low chair, opened it, began to read—and one part of her mind groped to find explanations for the incidents which had occurred on her arrival at the house that morning.

She had come up to London early, had visited a book shop and chosen some books for David; she had bought fruit and some long, curly sticks of barley sugar; then she had walked in the sunshine through busy streets until she reached Grosvenor Drive.

She was passing the scaffolding and picking her way through some rubble on the pavement when she glanced up and saw, at the other end of the street, a sight that made her pause.

Paloma was coming towards her with hurried footsteps that, even as Teresa looked, broke into a run. At her side was a policeman. He put out a hand and grasped her arm, and Paloma jerked it away and fled down the street. The man made no attempt to follow her—but he kept his eyes on her until she had run past Teresa, up the steps and into the house.

CORONET BOOKS

cordially invite you to join,
free of charge

THE CORONET ROMANCE CLUB

Do you enjoy novels of romance and romantic sus-pense? If so read this carefully.

All you have to do is complete and return this card, and you will receive from us a membership card plus the first edition of *Coronet Romance Club News*.

The first and subsequent issues of *Club News* (it will be published twice a year) will bring you not only news of the best romantic books available and forthcoming from Coronet Books; it will also include original short stories, news and gossip about authors and a letter to club members by our most famous romantic writer, Denise Robins. And it will come absolutely free.

Name _____

_____

Address _____

_____

_____

2

BUSINESS REPLY SERVICE
LICENCE NO. KE 2450

CORONET ROMANCE CLUB

St. Paul's House

Warwick Lane

LONDON

EC4B 4HB

Someone, Teresa saw, had been waiting to let the girl in. Someone else had seen the incident; someone had been poised, ready to open the door as Paloma reached it. It opened to admit her—and closed immediately.

The scene had been enacted so swiftly that only the sight of the policeman, still standing some distance away, convinced Teresa that she had not imagined it. She stood hesitating for a moment; the policeman's eyes, she saw, were on her. Then she went up the steps and rang the bell.

She heard the sound of its ringing inside the house, and waited. The minutes went by and then, puzzled, she pressed the bell again, this time more lingeringly.

There was no answer. After ringing the bell three times more, Teresa understood that there was not going to be any answer.

A mixture of feelings swept over her, the strongest of which, at first, was humiliation. There were people in there: Paloma, whom she had seen entering; the person who had admitted her. From her position on the top step, Teresa could see the windows of the basement, and she could see a large, horny hand—Maxie's—grasping the side of the curtain; he was without doubt watching her.

There was no use standing there any longer, Teresa decided at last; already some of the workmen from the scaffolding were glancing curiously at her. She turned and ran down the steps—and as she did so, came face to face with Zoë, who was on her way up.

"Oh!" Her aunt's exclamation held many emotions, but welcome was not among them. Zoë's eyes went from Teresa to the policeman who was still standing further down the street, and her face became so white that Teresa put out a hand to steady her.

"Are you . . . are you all right?" she asked anxiously.

"What?" Zoë's gaze came back to her, and she seemed to shake herself. "All right? Yes, of course I'm all right. Come; let us go in."

She inserted a key; a moment later they were standing in the hall.

"I rang several times," said Teresa, "but nobody seemed to hear."

"They are busy," said Zoë. "They do not hear. I am the one who always hears and who answers." She glanced at Teresa's packages. "You have come to see David?"

"Yes."

"He is better; it was nothing, you know. Mark did not alarm you?"

"No. But I felt that I'd like to come up and . . . and see if I could read to him . . . or something," said Teresa, and wondered why the words sounded so lame.

"I will take you up. Come." Zoë led the way upstairs, past the familiar first landing and up to a second which Teresa had not seen. She opened the door of a large room, and Teresa, entering, saw that it ran from the front right through to the back of the building; it had windows at both ends and was bright with sunshine. There were two beds in it, one at each end of the room, and several pieces of cheap furniture. The room was spotlessly clean and tidy.

In the smaller bed, propped against pillows, sat David. The bed was piled with books and toys.

"See who has come to see you," said Zoë.

David grinned happily; he looked well and was obviously enjoying being treated as an invalid. Teresa advanced with her gifts; turning as David was busy inspecting them, she saw Zoë leaning against the door, her eyes closed, her expression swept clean of every disguise, and showing a weariness so great that Teresa left the bedside and went towards her.

"Zoë . . ." She brought the name out for the first time and knew that it was thus she had thought of her; not as a relation, but as a stranger she had almost unwittingly come to like. "Zoë, please don't think I'm impertinent—or interfering. I don't know . . . I don't understand anything, but I feel you're worried and if I could do anything——"

She paused. Zoë had not moved but her eyes opened slowly.

"There is nothing," she said dully. "You are kind, but there is nothing that you can do. There is nothing anybody can do, I think."

"But I saw Paloma just now—outside—and there was a policeman with her and——"

Once more she stopped; Zoë's eyes had closed once more and she was standing there looking—Teresa found an amazing adjective—beaten. She looked tired and crushed and past pretence. Tears came slowly from her closed eyes and began to trickle down her cheeks—and then she had pulled out a handkerchief and was hastily wiping them away before David could see them. But David had not completed his inspection of the new books.

"It has been a long time," said Zoë, and now she was speaking in French. "I cannot tell you anything, for you would not understand. You are kind to wish to help—but there is nothing that you can do."

"How do you know?" urged Teresa. "I would so like to do something—anything. Why won't you let me?"

"Because"—Zoë put out a hand and gently touched the girl's arm for an instant—"because you are you. Because you are . . . who you are."

"I am your niece."

"Yes. You are the child of Hubert's sister—and so you, of all people, cannot help me."

"It is money?" said Teresa impulsively, and saw Zoë smile —a smile totally without mirth.

"Yes, it is money. It is money that has brought the trouble— but money cannot take the trouble away."

"But my uncle—can't he——"

"He can do nothing," said Zoë dully. She opened the door. "Stay with David; he will be glad to have you. Mark will not be home until lunch time."

And then Teresa was alone with the small boy, and the adventures of Smoochy were proceeding, but with far less zest, as David recognized, than the text deserved.

"Perhaps," he observed at last, weary of correcting the reader, "you're tired."

Teresa looked up.

"Well, yes—I am a little bit, David. And I'm not really a very good reader. I can play games, though; if you'd like Snakes and Ladders——"

She saw David hesitate, and understood the reason; she, too, had hesitated in years gone by before playing Snakes and Ladders with strangers. There were some who watched every move, who knew when the counter would come to halt right on the fatal open, yawning mouth of the reptile. There were others who could be trusted to look out of the window, or drop a handkerchief, or come out with a reassuring: "Why my goodness, you've just missed it by one" and who could even be trusted to declare roundly that one hadn't diced a five, but a four, thus missing disaster by one square inch.

"I'm not *awfully* good at it," she amended, and saw his face clear.

"That's the box, over there," he told her.

They were still playing—the score game all—when Teresa, who had heard no sound, looked up to see Mark standing in the doorway.

She wondered how long he had been there—but Mark could not have told her. He was standing taking in the picture, and he would remember it all his life; the sun slanting across the bed, the small boy, flushed with glee, the girl's fair head bent over the brightly-coloured board. David, who had held first place in his heart—and Teresa, who had come out of nowhere, unlooked-for, and who was now as dear in an entirely different way.

He came forward and sat on the bed and rumpled David's hair.

"How's everything?" he asked.

"I'm winning her," said David. "She won one and I won one and I'm nearly home and if I get a three, then I'll win her again."

"And if you get a two, you'll be down the drain.—And so you are," said Mark. "Go on—right down the serpent, even unto the tail."

David's mouth dropped.

"It's a . . . it's an awfully long snake," he pointed out. "It goes right down to number eleven, and I'll have to start pract'cly all over again."

"Well, that's the fun of it," explained Mark. "If you go home, the game's over, you chump; this way, you get it all over again. Go on—down you go."

"But if Teresa gets home . . ."

"Then she'll have won and you can both do it all over again. And there you are—she's gone down too. Go on, Teresa—no cheating. Watch her carefully, David."

They finished the game just as the door opened to admit Zoë with a tray on which was a light lunch and a glass of milk.

"This is all for David," she announced, and Teresa saw that she had recovered her self-possession. "For you others, there is food if you wish."

"No; I'm taking Teresa out to lunch," said Mark. "To that French place you recommended, Zoë."

"Tell them I sent you, and ask—remember specially to ask for Monsieur Laroule. He will take care of you very well. But I should go now, early, before the crowds of people go there. I will sit here and talk to David, and then Paloma will come and settle him down for his sleep."

They said good-bye, and Mark led Teresa out to his car. He drove silently; once, he put out a hand and touched hers briefly, as though to assure himself that she was really beside him.

On a table spread with a gay cloth, served by Monsieur Laroule himself, they ate specially-recommended food and drank delicious wine. The restaurant, small, was as yet uncrowded; they had a corner table, a little apart. Monsieur Laroule, an expert in these matters, noted that while both the man and the girl showed a certain intelligent interest in the food and the wine at the beginning of the meal, they grew more self-absorbed as it progressed. He made his report to his wife, who was in charge of the cash desk.

"He is in love," he told her in a swift exchange.

"And she?"

"I can't tell. Now if he were a Frenchman . . . But in his way," he conceded, "he has something. And he knows wine; that at least is a good sign."

"Do they talk of love?"

"No. But they are English, remember. It is all inside."

They were talking, not of love, but of nationalities. Mark, claiming with pride that Scotland came first and other nations several lengths behind, found Teresa's eyes resting on him in amazement.

"But—you're not Scottish!"

"Indeed I am."

"But . . . Tudor isn't a Scottish name."

"Nevertheless, we're a Scottish family. You don't," explained Mark, "have to be called Hamish MacTaggart in order to be a Scot. Or so my ancestor, Nathaniel Tudor, considered."

"Nathaniel isn't a Scottish name, either."

"That isn't surprising, because he was born on the wrong side of the Border. He was a man of Northumbria."

"Then how could he claim to be a Scot?"

"It's rather a long story—won't it bore you?"

"No."

"Well, he was a man who seemed to have a lot of time on his hands, and he spent a good deal of it taking part in those Border raids that used to go on during the fourteen and fifteen hundreds. Nathaniel Tudor used to join up with the Percys and go along just for the fun of it. But one day, he found himself separated from the main body. What's more, he was in enemy country. In other words, he was stranded in Scotland."

"But you said——"

"Chapter two. He was in a very awkward situation—you can see that, can't you? Remember that he was a man of Northumbria."

"But you said——"

"Chapter three. This is the exciting part. His situation was awkward for two reasons: one, he was being chased by wild and angry Scots and two, he had behind him on his horse the beautiful young Jeannie, who was the only daughter of one of the great Douglases. She'd given up trying to escape from Nathaniel and——"

"He'd run away with her?"

"He had. And she'd given up screeching, and was concentrating instead on giving the too-confident young Nathaniel directions which he thought would lead him back to England but which in fact led him slap into the midst of Jeannie's five hulking great Douglas brothers."

"Good for Jeannie. So then?"

"So then they wanted, naturally, to carve Nathaniel into five or six pieces—and Jeannie, naturally, said she wouldn't have him touched because she preferred him in one piece. 'Then what were you screeching for?' her brothers wanted to know. 'Because I don't want to go and live in that cold old England,' says Jeannie. 'In that case,' says Nathaniel, 'I'll stay over here; the soil's good and I can make a living.' 'But every one of our sons and daughters, and all their descendants,' insisted Jeannie, 'will have to be Scots.' And so they have been ever since." Mark looked across at her anxiously. "I hope you like the names Jean and Alistair and Ian and Bruce and Graham and Murdoch and Morag and Fiona?"

He did not wait for an answer. He had signalled to Monsieur Laroule and was ordering another bottle of wine—and then he looked across at Teresa and spoke on an entirely different subject.

"You said just now that you were worried about Zoë. Why?"

Teresa told him what had taken place when she reached the house that morning, and he sat for some time lost in thought.

"If, as she said, I'm concerned in the money part of it," asked Teresa at last, "why can't she explain exactly how? And why are policemen watching the house?"

"One policeman," corrected Mark.

"The police. What's the difference?" asked Teresa. "I saw what happened and you didn't. He tried to stop Paloma, and she pulled away from him and ran into the house. And someone was waiting to let her in—but when I rang, there wasn't a sound and nobody came. If Zoë hadn't come back just then——" She put her arms on the table and leaned on them and spoke urgently. "Mark——"

"Well?"

"When I was at the house that first evening, you tried to make me see that there was something . . . something odd about them all."

"And now you think there is?"

"Zoë's in some kind of trouble. Do you know what it is?"

"I think I know part of it. I don't know all of it—yet."

"Well, can't you tell me what you know?"

"I know—I think I know—why there's that dead silence whenever the front doorbell rings. They're frightened."

"Frightened of what?"

He hesitated.

"This and that," he said lightly at last.

Teresa frowned.

"Do you know something about them that you won't tell me?" she asked.

"No. I don't know anything. Guessing is easy—and interesting —but there's no point in my telling you my guesses. All I know, and all you know for certain is that they like to check up on everybody who comes into the house. There's a ringing on the front doorbell—and they all listen; they become tense, and they don't relax until Zoë has opened the door and told them that there's nothing to worry about."

"Could they be frightened . . . I mean, if the police wanted to stop Paloma and——"

"Paloma, I think, is the core of all the trouble."

"Paloma? Why?"

"Because she's beautiful, that's why. Every time she gets a job, some man or some men feel they'd like to see something of her —and how do you get to know a girl? You call on her. So they call on Paloma—and they don't get in. Maxie sees to that. For years they've kept out strangers. For years, Paloma was no problem because she was too young. Now she's not a child any more; she's a woman, and a disturbing one, as you saw. Paloma wants to open the door and let in her friends—and Zoë and Maxie won't let her do it. They're afraid. I think that for years they've kept themselves apart—apart, and safe from the curious. They want to go on that way—but they're beginning to understand that they can't. Or at any rate, not for much longer."

"But"— Teresa stared at him—"things can't be left like that! Can't my uncle——"

"He's not there."

"Could Zoë be frightened of——" Teresa hesitated. "If my uncle had got into debt, couldn't he have gone abroad and left Zoë to—to face his creditors?"

"He could. But the police wouldn't be interesting themselves in his debts, would they?"

"No . . . But Mark, if Zoë's in trouble, something can be done. My godfather would do something—I'm sure he would. He's one of those people who've got a lot of influence in what they call the highest places. He could help Zoë. I could ask him—at least, I could go to him and explain that she's in trouble. But"—her eagerness faded—"there's nothing I can tell him—nothing definite. It's all guess-work. It's all mystery."

"All mystery. Yes." He looked across at her thoughtfully. "Odd, isn't it, how you—of all people—should suddenly have become involved in mysteries?"

"I don't think I'm involved."

"In spite of what Zoë said?"

"I . . . I think she meant that I was involved because money was involved. My uncle's income will go, on his death, to my mother, and on her death it comes to me. That may be why Zoë feels that I'm in some way mixed up in her difficulties. But . . . but why can't she tell me enough to make it possible for me to help her?"

"Aren't you," Mark asked her, "going back on your first sensible resolution?"

"What was that?"

"To have nothing to do with any of it."

She studied him soberly for a few moments.

"Our positions seem to have changed," she remarked. "You began by wanting to draw me in; I was anxious to stay outside. Now I want to help, and you're beginning to sound discouraging. Why?"

"Because——" He smiled. "Well, perhaps because I know you a little better now, and feel that you don't really fit into the background."

"You accused me once of running away."

"Yes." He frowned. "And if you'd run away, perhaps you would have been right. Teresa, I think there's trouble ahead."

"For Zoë?"

"Perhaps for you too. I didn't want to bring you trouble."

Their eyes met in a long, deep searching look. At the end of it, Teresa smiled gently.

"You didn't," she told him.

"I shouldn't have asked you to come and see David this morning. What did Lolly say to that?"

"Nothing. I went looking for her to tell her, and I found she'd gone to Brighton to see my godfather."

"Then she went to call him in as reinforcements. May I prophesy that next time I call at your house, your godfather will appear—mysteriously. And he and I will be left alone—carefully. And he will tell me never to darken the doors again—forcefully."

"But you will."

"Yes, I will. Let me go on. Lolly, returning, will wonder where you are."

"No, she won't; I left her a note telling her where I was going."

"Then the rest is too easy. Lolly will communicate the information to your fiancé. 'Teresa's in town,' she'll say: 'why don't you meet her and fix up something?' Your fiancé—if he's wise—

will leave his business to take care of itself, and he will drive speedily round to Number 54 Grosvenor Drive, arriving in time to take you out to lunch—he hopes. You have gone—where and with whom? Zoë will tell him. He will rush out to his car and come here; it'll take him some time because traffic is heavier than when we came. Don't," he hastened to add, "think that I look on myself as anybody meriting all this attention. I know I don't —but Lolly has made certain plans for your happiness, and if I don't constitute a threat, I serve as a warning: there's many a slip, she will decide, between the cup of betrothal and the lip of matrimony." He gave her a slow smile. "And on that point, at least, she's right."

"If I thought you meant that," said Teresa, "then——"

"Then?"

"Then I think I would decide not to see you again."

"Do you only think? Why don't you know for certain?"

"Because I don't share Lolly's fears."

"You do me too much honour," he murmured. "And speaking of honour, will you bear in mind that I told you from the first what my intentions were?"

"You said a lot of rather wild things."

"I said no more than the simple truth. And if it was true then, it's more than true now. What does my compatriot, Robert Burns, have to say on the subject?

> *To see her is to love her*
> *And love but her for ever.*

I saw you—and the rest will keep. For whatever you think of me as a wild speaker," he went on without a pause, "you must give me full credit as a prophet. For here"—his eyes were on the door —"here is your fiancé, standing in the doorway and looking dark in the brow. If he takes my advice, he'll come up to me, seize me by the collar, jerk me to my feet—it ought to be easy, he's stronger than I am—and throw me through the window. And I would make no resistance, because——"

"Because?"

"Because you have given me no sign, no token. And until you do, how do I know whether you've heard what I've said to you so clearly? How——"

"Mark——" she said suddenly.

"Hush!" he put out a hand and touched hers for an instant. "You can tell me on Sunday."

"Sunday?"

"Sunday is your birthday," he reminded her.

Then he had risen, and was nodding to Neville, who stood by the table and, giving no sign of having seen the other man, was speaking to Teresa.

"I see you're almost through lunch," he said. "Pity; I'd hoped to get here in time to take you somewhere."

"Sit down and have a drink," invited Mark.

"No. No thanks," said Neville with an effort. "I haven't much time, Teresa; could you come with me and finish your lunch with me?"

"I could—but why don't you stay and have a drink?" asked Teresa.

It was odd, thought Mark, his heart filling anew with love, that a girl could be so intelligent—and such a fool. He addressed her gently, and there was no doubt in the other man's mind of what lay behind the gentleness.

"Please don't hesitate to go," he said. "Your fiancé's right; lunch time can be short. I'll finish my coffee and get back to David." He gave her no time to reply; he had walked round and was holding out her coat, and she had no option but to put it on. "Thank you for going to see him," he said, "and thank you for the books and the fruit. It was very kind of you."

Nothing could have sounded more formal, more correct, but for one second Neville's eyes rested on the speaker with open hatred. Then he was walking out with Teresa's hand under his arm. It was what he had come to accomplish, but a sense of defeat flooded him. Then rage, blinding and shaking, gripped him for a moment, but by the time they were out of the building, he had regained his self-control and was assisting Teresa into his car.

They drove without speaking; he was thinking of what he was going to say; Teresa was absorbed in all that had happened that morning. A great deal had occurred, but she was still unwilling to look too closely at her own reactions. There would be time tonight, when she was in her room, Thoughts cleared in the quiet darkness, and she would be able to search her heart and decide at last what she was to do.

"That fellow," came savagely from Neville, "wants dealing with."

"Mark Tudor?"

"Who else? Why the devil, Teresa, do you allow him to take up your time?"

"I went to see David, and Mark came in and——"

"Naturally he came in. Do you think that wasn't his whole idea, to come in at the right moment for asking you out to lunch? Don't you see what he's after? He's after you. He saw you, and he liked you, and the fact that you're engaged to somebody else wouldn't mean a thing to a man of his sort. But if he doesn't understand the decencies, surely you do? What do you think I feel like when I think of you in the bedroom—yes, it was the bedroom—of a man, and in that house? You should never have entered the place. Anybody but you would have seen at once what a shady lot they are."

"How do you know?" Teresa's voice was cool, but he was too incensed to notice.

"How do I know? Because I went in and saw them, that's how. I rang the bell and a woman came to the door—a dark, foreign woman who——"

"My uncle's wife," came coldly from Teresa.

"Well, I suppose so. I didn't inquire. I told her who I was, and I found out where you were. And while she was telling me, there were footsteps, and somebody came rushing downstairs—a girl, a wild-looking sort of girl. She was crying, and she must have thought I was somebody else, because she came at me in a rush, and then stopped and looked at me as though I'd bitten her— and then she turned and went upstairs again and threw herself into the arms of a stocky fellow with one arm. Her lover, I shouldn't be surprised."

"Her father," said Teresa. "Please go on."

The iciness of her tone, however, had pulled him up. He gave a swift glance at her, and his next words were quieter.

"I'm sorry. I was angry. But I didn't like the set-up in the house and I didn't like to feel that you'd been there and got mixed up with them all. They're nothing to you and you ought to keep away. This Tudor—none of us knows the first thing about him, but a man who doesn't mind living in a place like that can't be called exactly fastidious. And for reasons best known to himself, he's doing his best to get under my skin." He shot another rapid glance at Teresa, this time from beneath angry brows. "And what I can't get over is the astounding fact that you actually went to that house again and——"

"I went to see a little boy who's been sick."

"Did you really think Tudor wasn't using him as an excuse to get you there?"

Teresa had no time to answer the question. They had reached Neville's club, and the next few minutes were occupied in the business of parking the car, entering the building and answering the civil inquiries of the hall porter. Then Neville went away to wash and make arrangements for lunch, and Teresa was left alone on an enormous sofa in the lounge to await his return.

The lounge was empty; it was also quiet. This was a good opportunity, she realized, for a calm and leisurely survey of all that had taken place since her first visit to the house in Grosvenor Drive. It was a good opportunity to search her mind for reasons for many strange things. It was a good opportunity—and a timely one—to examine her position.

Teresa examined it. She was engaged to marry Neville. She had accepted him with feelings divided almost equally between gratitude, apprehension and affection; she thought him a good man and she thought herself capable of making him a good wife. They had her mother's approval; more than approval, for Teresa, looking back with eyes whose focus seemed suddenly to have changed, saw for the first time how much her engagement owed to her mother's skilful handling of the preliminaries. Her mother, in whom she had the greatest faith, had believed she would be happy with Neville, and as she herself had never felt as affectionate towards any man as she did towards him, she had agreed to marry him—and had never had the slightest doubt that she was doing the right, the wise thing.

Until she met Mark Tudor.

And what, Teresa asked herself, fighting for honesty, what had happened then?

It was not, she told herself, that she had taken a foolish fancy to a passing stranger. All Mark Tudor had done at first was to open her eyes to the fact that she had never in her life met anybody with whom she felt so much at ease. She had never before known how pleasant the company of a man could be. Groping in the recesses of her mind, she pulled Neville forward for inspection and found that her feelings about him had not, after all, changed; she still thought him good, sound, reliable and the kind of man every mother would wish her daughter to marry—and the kind of man every sensible girl would be glad to marry. But she no longer wanted to marry him.

Seated on the too-large sofa, Teresa stared across the room and faced the fact that it would have been better for everybody if she had taken Lolly's advice and her godfather's advice, and gone about with a few more men before settling down with Neville. She had accepted too easily her mother's opinion that she would only be going farther in order to fare worse.

And now?

Neville had asked a question and he had a right to a reassuring answer. She had promised to marry him; she was waiting now for him to ask her—as he would without doubt ask her—to see no more of Mark Tudor.

A fog of depression settled on her. The large, comfortable, old-fashioned lounge whirled under a mist of regret and apprehension. She tried to think of Neville, but nothing came but a memory of Mark's gentle smiling face. He seemed to be in the room; he seemed to be on the sofa beside her. His eyes were, as always, faintly amused—he seemed to be waiting for her to make her decision.

Neville entered the lounge and spoke to her twice before she heard him. At last he touched her shoulder, and she started and stared at him in bewilderment.

"Dreaming?" he asked.

"Yes, dreaming," said Teresa.

They walked into the dining-room. Neville ordered coffee for Teresa and lunch for himself. Teresa waited and braced herself for what was coming.

But when he spoke at last, there was a note in his voice which she had never heard before, and which cleared her mind, suddenly, of all sensations except anger. She had expected reproaches, appeals, arguments—but she had not expected him to adopt a hectoring, almost bullying attitude.

"About this fellow," he said without preliminary. "This Tudor. I think we'd better put our cards on the table. You don't"—he stared at her across the table, anger in his eyes—

"you don't seem to feel the same aversion to him that Lolly and I do."

"I don't think anybody could feel . . . averse to him," said Teresa calmly. "You and Lolly are annoyed because he behaves——"

"——because he behaves as though that ring on your finger didn't exist. And it does exist; I put it there, and so I know. And when a man puts a ring on a girl's finger he expects to get some peace of mind about the relationship between them. He doesn't—and God knows I didn't—expect any stray clown to put a spell on her." He stared across at her. "What is it you like so much about this fellow? I would have thought that you, of all people, would have been proof against his type. He's a—a mountebank, a——"

"You're getting angry."

"I'm not getting angry. I've got angry. I've been angry ever since I first laid eyes on the fellow. I . . . All right, I'm jealous. No, damn it, I'm not jealous. Why the hell should I be jealous of a clown?"

"Then don't be," advised Teresa, in the same calm voice.

"Then don't give me cause to be."

"Have I given you cause?"

"Cause?" He laughed, a little too loudly. "Cause? Why don't you ask Lolly why she's worried? You can't accuse her of being jealous. What both of us are stumped over—Lolly and myself—is the fact that you . . ." He paused, looking at her under drawn brows. "It's so *unlike* you, Teresa. You didn't go to that house to read to that boy; you may have told yourself that that was the reason, but you know damned well you went to see Tudor."

Teresa waited to get her anger under control.

"There's a lot in the house to interest me," she pointed out, "apart from Mark or David Tudor. I——"

"I know what you're going to say: your uncle lives there. Well, from what I saw of the place, and from what I gather from you, he lives more out of it than in it. And even if they didn't all look a shady lot, they're not people who could possibly interest you. You admitted your plan had fallen down, and you'd made up your mind not to go back there. But you did go back. And it was that blasted Tudor who made you. And what I want to say is this: a man who butts in between an engaged couple is

an outsider and ought to be told so without delay. I can tell him
—or you can. Which is it to be?"

"You, obviously," said Teresa coldly, "because you think so,
and I don't."

"You mean you . . . you actually *like* him?"

"Yes. I like him." Teresa's voice was quiet; her hand played
with her empty coffee cup. "I think he's intelligent and I also
think he's honest. But I'm willing to agree that I shouldn't have
allowed him to make you uneasy."

"Well, that's something. Thank you for the crumbs. And are
you willing to agree that as my fiancée, you owe it to me to keep
other men at a distance?"

"Yes; I agree that——"

"Then I'll say no more." Neville sat back with a look of relief.
"Now we know where we are. You tell him to leave you alone,
and if he shows any disposition to go on bothering you, let me
deal with him."

"Neville, I——"

"If he annoys you again, let me handle him. But I think you'll
find that before your mother gets back, he'll get out of the way
—and fast."

She gave him a long, searching look, and saw his colour
darken. His own gaze shifted, and she knew that what she suspected was true: he was putting aside the matter until her
mother returned. He feared Mark, and he feared his own ability
to deal with him—and he was going to delay the crisis until he
could be certain that Coralie was present—to back him, to
strengthen him, to bolster him up.

She said no more. They rose at the conclusion of the meal, and
he drove her to the station and she took the first train home.

Arriving at the house, she found Lolly just about to walk
down to the village; they met in the hall and Teresa stood for
some moments looking down unseeingly at the letters that had
arrived by the midday post and now lay on the hall table.

"Tired?" asked Lolly, from the door.

"No. Will you be back to tea?"

"Don't think so; probably stay and have it at this bazaar.
Why don't you come along and buy something? It'll please
them."

"No." Teresa was on her way upstairs. "No, I don't think I'll come." She paused at the bend of the staircase and looked down. "Lolly."

"Well?"

"Did you tell Mark Tudor that my birthday was on Sunday?"

Lolly looked up in astonishment.

"I certainly did not."

"Then how could he have known?"

"Perhaps Zoë remembered it."

"Perhaps."

Teresa went slowly out of sight, and Lolly stood where she was, staring after her and noting the girl's dreamy, withdrawn air. She seemed, far, far away.

Where, Lolly wondered miserably, where had Teresa gone?

Chapter Nine

TERESA'S birthday began uneventfully. The sun shone, the weather seemed settled, the servants came with their modest gifts, the poodle wore a large bow, the gardener brought in a fragrant bunch of flowers, and Lolly produced a bulky parcel and stood apologizing as Teresa opened it.

"It won't fit you and it's the wrong colour and I daresay it's out of fashion—but I told them you would change it if you loathed it. And it's a bit too warm for this time of the year, but you can always put it by until the autumn. It might sag a bit when it's washed, but you'll just have to risk it."

"It's beautiful," said Teresa, holding up the pea green sweater and leaning over to kiss the donor. "I shall wear it next week to welcome Mother."

"Next week? This week. She's be home in six days."

"Oh." A startled look came into Teresa's eyes. "Has the time really gone so fast?"

"Well, it's gone; fast or slow, I wouldn't know," said Lolly. "What are you going to do today?"

"I thought I'd go into Brighton and give Lawrence a surprise, and thank him for his cheque."

"Neville will be coming, I suppose?"

"Yes; he's coming to dinner. He rang up last night. Didn't I tell you?"

"You didn't, but I took it that he would. Will you be home for lunch?"

"No. If Lawrence's housekeeper won't cook something extra for me, I'll persuade him to take me out."

"Well, look after yourself," said Lolly. "Are you taking the car?"

"No; the bus."

"Why don't you get yourself driven in? The chauffeur's eating his head off."

"Let him," said Teresa. "I enjoy the bus ride."

She got off the bus at Brighton wishing that she had worn a cotton dress; though her suit was light, it was not light enough for the unexpected warmth of the day. The thought of walking in the heat to her godfather's house did not attract her; she crossed over to a taxi rank and, getting into the foremost vehicle, directed the driver to Lawrence's house.

The taxi drew up in front of the building. She got out and paid the driver and turned to open the gate—and as she did so, she saw immediately in front of the taxi a sports car, long and low and shabby. In it were two figures, one tall, one small.

Teresa stood still. Mark got out of his car and came towards her, his face almost lost behind the tall sheaf of roses he carried.

"Happy birthday." He took her hand, held it to his cheek and released it; then he stood smiling down at her. "Shall I sing it on this lovely day?" he asked, and raised his voice in a pleasing tenor. "Happy birthday to yooo; happy . . . David," he called, "come and say Happy Birthday to Teresa."

David, scrambling eagerly out of the car, ran up to Teresa and held out a small and sticky package.

"Happy birfday," he said. "That's from me. It's a surprise."

"It certainly is." Teresa took the parcel and smiled at the child. "Can I open it now?"

" 'Course; it's yours. It'll break if you drop it," warned David.

She unwrapped the paper; inside was a small, very small china goose. She held it gently in her hand and then looked down at the boy.

"It's simply lovely," she said. "Thank you, David. Has it got a name?"

"Not yet. You give it one," invited David. "Let's call it Smoochy."

"All right; Smoochy it is." Teresa looked up at Mark. "How did you get here?"

"Tck tck; silly question," reproved Mark. "There's the car, straight in front of you. We'll have to rechristen that goose Teresa."

"How did you know it was my birthday?"

"Intuition. And the rest was intuition, too. What, I asked David here, was a girl likely to do on a lovely birthday morning? Well, she'd like to see the sparkling sea, and if she could do it and see her godfather at the same time, why wouldn't she? The fact that we're here is of course pure coincidence; David and I thought it would be wonderful to drive down and get a breath of sea air. Didn't we, David?"

David, however, had gone back to the car and was seated in the driver's seat, his gaze straight ahead, hands on the wheel, driving along an imaginary road far from Brighton. Teresa looked at Mark.

"You shouldn't have come," she said. "But perhaps it's just as well that you did."

"I don't like that," he said. "It's got an under-current of——"

"You shouldn't have come," said Teresa again.

"You mean I mustn't bring David down here for sea air? Not even after his chill?" He took her hand and drew her gently towards the car. "Come on," he said. "We'll find a warm spot on the beach and then David can build castles while I . . . well, perhaps I'll build castles too, but not sand ones. Come on."

"I want to see my godfather."

"And so you shall. But there are things to be said first; you've got something serious to say to me, and you can't say it here. Perhaps you're going to dismiss me, and when I weep, I want to weep in some quiet spot and not on the busy street. Come."

He led her to the car; they got in and drove away from Brighton, following the coast road. David sat between them, kneeling up and pointing eagerly as the sea came now and then into view.

They found a quiet stretch of beach on which, later in the year, holiday makers would gather in their hundreds. Now it was empty save for one or two strollers exercising their dogs. Mark left the car by the roadside and the three—man, woman and child—walked down on to the sand. Mark spread a large groundsheet and over it a rug, and he and Teresa sat down. David, spade and bucket in hand, found a rock, and a small warm pool not far away, and began to dig energetically.

Teresa lay back and gave herself up to the stillness and the warmth of the day. She was here and so was Mark; it would be perhaps the last time they would meet before the storm clouds broke. For the moment they were alone on a stretch of golden sand, with blue-grey sea before them and a pale blue sky above. They were here, and it was quiet and infinitely peaceful, infinitely removed from hard words and difficult decisions. They would say what they had to say—in a little while.

Mark, however, was sitting upright beside her, alert and expectant.

"Well, go on," he urged at last. "Say it. You've spent the last days thinking—and now you want to tell me what you've thought about."

"Presently." Teresa's voice was dreamy. "Presently."

"No; now." He slipped a hand under her shoulders and lifted her gently to a sitting position. "We can't enjoy the nice sunshine if we've got any feeling of guilt about being here. For myself, I feel nothing but pleasure. More than pleasure—but we can come to that later. You, far from feeling happy, are rehearsing your big speech. Well, off you go."

"What's the use? You know it already."

"Of course. It isn't, if I may say so, a very original speech. It's been made before and it'll be made again. 'Sir, leave me, I beg; my betrothed e'en now cometh o'er the mountain, and he will slay thee.'—How did he say he'd do it?" he asked with interest. "Was he going to throw me to the lions, or was he going to seize my shirt-front as they do in Westerns, and draw me up to him and shake me until my teeth rattle, and then throw me to the ground? He could too; strong chap, is Neville. And in many ways, a decent chap; I don't for a moment blame you for allowing yourself to be talked into becoming engaged to him—any more than I blame him for thinking he could make you happy. But——"

"Please stop," broke in Teresa.

He smiled at her.

"All right. I've stopped. Now you go on."

She stared at the calm, still sea; it was some time before she spoke, and then her voice came calmly and slowly.

"I like you very much, Mark," she said. "I find you gay, and amusing and . . . and good company. I've enjoyed the few moments we've spent together. But I should never have let you say some of the things that you did say, and——"

"Half a moment." Mark held up a hand. "Let's deal with the points as they arise. How could you have prevented me from saying anything? Speech in this country is free; you've only to read some of the exchanges in the House of Commons. I spoke—and you had to listen. Proceed."

"I needn't have listened. Don't let's pretend about this; if a girl wants to get rid of a man, there are lots of ways in which she can do it."

"Not really," said Mark, and his voice was quiet. "Not really, Teresa my darling. And certainly not a girl like you. A man in love—and I'm in love—has a lot he wants to get off his chest, and if he's in earnest, it would take more than a gentle girl like yourself to stop him. He wants to have his say."

"And in other circumstances a girl would have to listen to him. But I'm engaged, Mark and——" She paused.

"And——?" prompted Mark.

"And my mother will soon be back, and—and I think that I shouldn't have allowed you to . . . to go so far."

"How far, exactly, have I gone?" inquired Mark. "I would have said I hadn't really been travelling; I've seen you once or twice when your fiancé wasn't around, and that's all."

"And I shouldn't have let you—and that's really all," said Teresa. "I'm engaged to him, and I owe it to him. You must see that?"

"What I see," said Mark, "is that Neville has done what a great many people do: come to a decision regarding a third party and taken it for granted that the third party will fall in with the findings of the Committee. He decides I must go—and doesn't bother to go beyond that."

"He said——"

"He said that if I didn't remove myself at once, he'd take over where you left off, and scrub me out of the picture. Well," mused Mark, "I'd have said the same in his place. The only thing he left out, and you left out of these deliberations, is my position. Because of course I've got a position. That in itself is a cheering thought—for me. If I hadn't gained a foothold, Neville wouldn't be so worried."

"Why should he be made to worry?" asked Teresa. "He's a thoroughly nice man and I promised to marry him, and when I gave him cause for uneasiness, I was being terribly disloyal."

"Look." Mark turned to face her. "Let me tell you what the real position is. You and a man make a bargain; you become engaged, and you say you'll marry—in due course. Between the putting on of the ring and the ceremony at the altar, there's usually a waiting period. And if, during that period, a third party

makes his appearance, he has to be—if he's in deadly earnest, as
I am—he has to be taken seriously. By which I mean that he has
to be regarded as a possible danger. If he's merely a nuisance, as
a rule he knows it—and he gives up trying. But if he thinks that
the girl he loves is unawakened, that she gave her word before
she knew what she was doing, that she drifted into an engagement because everybody round her seemed to expect it—then the
man constitutes a real threat. Why? Not because the girl is disloyal; not because she's a weak character who can be worked on
—but simply because deep down, she knows that her own feelings aren't secure—aren't sure." He put out a hand and gently
took one of Teresa's. "Do you think I haven't eyes? There's only
one thing wrong with Neville, and that's his insensitiveness. He
sees what's there, and he doesn't trouble to move it aside and see
what's underneath. He's so busy watching me that he hasn't
bothered to shift his glance and take a look at you—and that's
where I have an advantage, because I've looked at you all the
time. I've seen Neville—a man with whom you profess to be in
love—enter a room after three days' absence from you. You offer
your cheek—because strangers are present and a display of affection is not good form. He sees another man, and he thinks it a
good time to declare his position; he turns your lips to his and
puts his own on them. It's a declaration: This woman is mine.
And the woman? She remains as cool, as unmoved as though he
had merely touched her cheek. Affection? Yes. Love? My God,
no! After three days away from you, a man in love would have
drawn you out of the room and given himself—and you—a few
shaking seconds in his arms. Neville didn't move you—because
he couldn't. Because you don't love him. I can move you. How
do I know? Because I have eyes, and I read the signs. I know
the signs because I feel them in myself. When I take your hand
like this, I can see the pulse—there, in the wrist. Racing, just as
mine is racing. I hear your voice, and know it isn't steady, just
as mine isn't. And because I know these things, I know that you
feel—a little, just a little—of what I feel."

Teresa's voice trembled.

"You—you sound so . . . so sure."

"I am sure. I love you, Teresa."

"But . . . but you can't."

"Why not?"

"Because . . . in the first place, you don't know me. You don't know anything about me."

He laughed.

"What makes you think that?"

"You saw me for the first time—when? About a week ago."

"And I haven't got eyes? Ears? Senses?"

"They could mislead you."

"Never. Shall I tell you why? Because love isn't blind; love is entirely clear-eyed and clear-headed. When he shoots his arrows, he's blindfold because by that means everybody, high or low, rich or poor, fair or ugly, gets the same chance. The arrow is shot—and finds its mark. And at the tip, there's a heady, potent mixture that turns a man into a god. Love isn't blind, Teresa. Every blade of grass looks greener, every flower looks more beautiful. If that line's not very original, I'm sorry, but it's true. This beach . . . the sands are pure gold. The sky is blue—bluer than any sky has ever been. Is that seeing less—or seeing more?"

"Is it seeing too much?"

"No. It's the way life should look all the time—and doesn't. We accept without ever really seeing it—and then something like this happens and the mist of everyday dissolves—and I see . . . you. I see truth in your eyes, I see gentleness in your bearing. What else do I see? I see hands, here in my own, that are white and delicate. I see hair of spun gold—do you know that it's almost the same colour as this lovely sand? I see your skin, pale and clear—but healthy withal. I see your lips, soft and . . . Perhaps, I'd better not think about your lips. Teresa, Teresa, oh Teresa, I love you so much . . ."

He turned in a swift movement and lay on the sands, his head resting in her lap, her hand held to his cheek.

"I'm so glad," he said dreamily, "I'm so very, very glad I didn't meet you before. I used to wonder what was the matter with me—so many lovely girls, and no reaction from me. Was I normal? Yes. Oh yes, I was normal—but I was waiting. I was waiting for you. And I'm not sorry that I didn't meet you when I was twenty, or twenty-five or even thirty. At twenty, I was going to reform the world, and I think I would have bored you. At twenty-five I was certain that I knew everything there was to know about everything that was really important: food, wine, dealing with head waiters, getting the best tables and escorting the most photogenic blondes. That was a bad stage, Teresa, and I'm glad you didn't come in just then. And at thirty? I was rather lonely at thirty; I would have welcomed you—but you knew exactly when to appear. You waited until my inner vision had fashioned a replica of you—you, exactly as you are. And then you came—the model to the last exacting line—but you were alive, and warm, and soft . . . oh so soft, my darling, my darling, my darling . . . Teresa, marry me please, my darling—and soon. I'm not fit to touch you, but I'll love you—humbly—until I die. And I'll try to become anything you wish."

"I like you," said Teresa gently, "exactly as you are."

He rolled over and stared up at her.

"You mean that?"

She regarded him steadily.

"Yes, I mean that."

"You . . . how can you be sure?"

"How can you be sure?" she asked him, smiling.

"You . . . you love me? Me? This man before you, of whom you know nothing?"

"I love you—as you are. You said you saw truth in my eyes. I see truth in yours. And . . ."

"And?"

"I feel a kind of strength in you that I never felt before in anybody. With you, beside you, I feel completely safe."

"Bless you," said Mark, a little hoarsely. "Oh, bless you, Teresa."

"I feel safe—and happy. And in some curious way, awake. I don't see, as you seem to see, bluer skies or more beautiful flowers, but I seem to be looking back over my life—especially my recent life—and wondering whether I could have been mad —or asleep—or just stupid. It doesn't seem possible that I ever imagined I could marry anybody without feeling . . . this." She smiled at him. "Perhaps it's because I've . . . I've never met anybody like you before."

"Do you understand"—his voice was slow and of deadly seriousness—"do you understand that I will love you until I die? Do you, Teresa?"

She bent and put her lips briefly to his.

"I think I understand," she said gently, "because . . . because I know that nothing can ever make me forget you. Nothing, ever again. I don't know"—her voice trembled—"I don't know what will happen, or even whether we can marry—but I know that nothing like this moment has ever happened to me before, and never will again. Mark——"

"Yes?"

"I love you very much. But——"

Mark put a hand on her lips.

"Leave it at that—for the moment," he begged. "Just for this one day—please, my darling. I love you with all my heart—and you love me. What do we know about each other? A great deal. What do we feel about one another?" He leaned forward, his lips near her own. "You're beautiful," he said softly. "But I've met lovely girls before. You're good—but so are other girls I've known. Why should I feel about you what I've never felt for anybody before? Why? Why, Teresa? Why should you love me? We don't know. But we know that when we're together, time stands still. We know . . ."

His lips were on hers. The place, the time were alike forgotten. When his arms came round her, Teresa surrendered to them without thought, without reservation.

When he released her, she saw that things had not changed outwardly; the beach, the sea, the sunshine was there; David was still digging, a pile of sand testifying to the extent of his labours. The walkers with their dogs were going by, some with their gaze somewhat pointedly out to sea. Nothing was changed outwardly—and yet Teresa knew that for her, nothing would ever be the same again. She loved—for the first time. This man beside her had awakened in her a tumult of feeling greater than she had ever experienced. Shaken, giddy, she could yet feel a surge of pure happiness sweeping through her.

"You're twenty-four today," said Mark, out of a long silence, "and this is your first love—and your last. Are you happy?"

"Yes."

She was happy. The day went on and she did not think of time; she thought only of the man who had come into her life and changed it for ever. They spoke little, but their silences were easy, relaxed. They played with David; they ran races and built castles. They bought lunch and ate it on the beach. As the afternoon drew to a close, they drove slowly back to London, David's head drooping drowsily now on Teresa's, now on Mark's arm.

"This is the last time," said Mark, looking down at the boy, "that he'll be going to bed at your uncle's house."

Teresa turned to him in surprise.

"Why?"

"Because we're leaving."

"You didn't tell me."

He laughed.

"It wasn't as important—I thought—as all the other things I had to tell you. Did you think I'd settled down at Grosvenor Drive for ever?"

"No—but where are you going?"

"To a flat in Abbot Square, which I shall take you to see— but not this evening. This evening, I shall take you home—and then I'm going to talk to Lolly."

"Talk to Lolly?" There was apprehension in her voice.

"Yes. In the absence of your mother."

"My mother——"

The apprehension was more evident now, and Mark gave her a brief, but searching glance.

"You're very fond of her, aren't you?"

"Of course. She's my mother."

"That isn't always a sufficient reason for love. It's a difficult relationship, mother-daughter, and I congratulate you both on having made a success of it."

"She—she won't like this," said Teresa slowly.

"Because Neville was her candidate?"

"She met him first, and she thought—I think she felt——"

"—that he'd make a good husband for you? So he would have done, in many ways. But he wasn't the man for you—and I am." He threw her another glance, this time a smiling one. "There's so much about me that you don't know. I always imagined women were curious—and yet you ask so few questions."

"I've got a lot of time to ask them."

"I might be keeping all kinds of sinister knowledge from you."

"Are you?"

"No. Not sinister. There's one fact I've kept from you."

"An important one?"

"Yes and no. It's nothing that can affect what you feel or what I feel."

"Then it isn't important. Do you want to tell me?"

"Not yet. You'll have to know soon—but today is for . . . other things. Agreed?"

"Agreed."

Not until they had put David to bed and left him in Maxie's care did any thought of the future arise to disturb Teresa. But with one of Mark's hands holding her own closely, with Mark's voice soothing her fears, nothing seemed very difficult of accomplishment: she was sorry for Neville, sorry that her mother's plans should come to nothing, sorry that Lolly would be disappointed—but she was content to leave everything to Mark. He was strong in a way that Neville, she knew now, had never been strong; she could lean on him, she could have utter confidence in his ability to smooth matters out; she could leave everything safely in his hands.

Even the sight of her godfather's car standing in the drive of the cottage did not greatly disturb her newly-found confidence. Lawrence would understand.

They went inside. In the drawing-room they came face to face with Lolly and Sir Lawrence—and for some time there was a heavy silence in the room.

"I don't need to ask," said Lolly at last, "what's happened. One has only to look. I've had," she added bitterly, "hell's own day. I honestly don't understand, Teresa, how you could——"

"Won't you," put in Mark quietly, "say it all to me?"

"What is there to say? It's too late," said Lolly.

"It isn't too late at all." Sir Lawrence's voice, gruff, uncomfortable, went on hesitantly. "If you'll give me a few minutes alone with this young man, perhaps I can——"

"It really is too late, Lawrence darling," said Teresa. "I'm sorry it's happened this way, but . . . I love him very much."

"My dear"—Sir Lawrence's voice was heavy—"if you will allow me to speak to him——"

Mark walked to the door and opened it and smiled at Teresa.

"Please," he begged. "I'll explain to Sir Lawrence, and you can talk to Lolly. Only a few minutes."

He closed the door behind them and faced the old man.

"Go ahead, sir," he invited.

Sir Lawrence, hands clasped behind his back, head bent, was walking up and down the room restlessly. Presently he stopped and looked at the younger man. He seemed to be on the point of saying something, but instead, gazed at Mark's features with wonder growing slowly on his face.

"My God," he said slowly at last, "but you're like your mother."

Mark's eyebrows went up.

"You knew her?"

"I knew them all—all three girls. They were the prettiest trio in Sussex. And your mother was the loveliest of the three. She died, Lolly told me."

"Yes."

"Well, I'm sorry." Sir Lawrence stared unseeingly at a point beyond Mark. "I'm sorry. I was only thirty at the time, and she was seventeen—and it was winter. We used to go skating. I could skate, too, in those days. And so could she—magnificently. We used to glide over the ice . . ."

"Go on," said Mark softly.

"It was a close thing." Sir Lawrence spoke dreamily. "It was a very close thing. She was looking up at me, with her hands in mine, and she looked like an angel, and I opened my mouth and I was going to tell her so—tell her that and who knows how much more? And then ——"

"And then?"

"Then we both went down with an almighty crash—down on the ice. I was all right, but her wrist was broken. They took her away—and my leave was up. The next time we met, she had a husband and I had a wife. But it was a close thing; a very close thing. She never knew how close. They took her away—and I followed the, as you might say, cortege, feeling like a skunk, just as though I'd pushed her down on purpose. Everybody looked at me as though I were a great hulking brute—and then from nowhere up skated a little fair-haired bit of a girl, and she looked up at me and she said 'Oh, I do hope your friend isn't badly hurt'——"

Mark smiled.

"And it went on from there?"

"It did." Sir Lawrence's thoughts came back to the present. "Funny, isn't it, how things happen?"

"And you never gave my mother another thought?"

"Well . . . Let's say that when I made that speech I was on the brink of making, I made it to the little fair-haired skater. And we lived happily together until she died."

"And so instead of being my father, you turned out to be my future godfather," said Mark. "That being so, sir, you ought to be on my side in this little matter of Teresa's engagement."

Sir Lawrence stared at him, his expression slowly hardening.

"Little matter?" he repeated.

"Little matter," Mark spoke firmly. "She made a mistake. Girls have done it before. She loves me; I love her very dearly. I can look after her, and I think I can make her happy."

"I've no doubt you can. But you don't know what you're doing," said Sir Lawrence moodily. "There's going to be trouble."

"From Morley?"

"No. Neville's not really the trouble, though I don't suppose he's going to take this lying down. No. The real trouble is Teresa's mother."

Mark's voice was formal.

"I hope we shall be able to make her see that this is for Teresa's happiness."

Sir Lawrence did not reply for some time; he had turned and was gazing out of the window. When he faced Mark again, his face looked older and rather haggard.

"Lolly asked me to talk to you. She wanted to stop this before it went too far. She came to me and I agreed to speak to you; agreed to explain one or two things; agreed to——" he broke off. "Look," he said more abruptly. "It's no good my moralizing or catechizing. I'll give you a few facts and then you'll see how matters stand. Sit down."

"Do you mind if I stand?"

"As you like. Well, this begins a long way back. Teresa's father was my greatest friend and I knew him, I think, as well as anybody in the world. He was a good, a thoroughly good man, but—like Teresa—he was a bit too gentle, a bit too defenceless, a bit too soft, if you like, when it came to dealing with harsh realities. Well, he married. Teresa's mother had always lived with her brother Hubert, and their combined incomes——"

"I know," put in Mark quietly. "Four hundred to him, eight hundred to her."

Sir Lawrence stared at him.

"You know? How do you know? Oh—Teresa told you."

"No," said Mark. "I'll explain when you've finished. Please go on."

"Hubert couldn't get on on four hundred, and he came down to the cottage and put in a strong bid for all or part of his sister's share of the money. She refused. Her first refusal was abrupt enough to make her husband a bit unhappy; a little piece of the veil lifted—but not much. Then finally, Hubert saw it was no use and—whether to spite his sister, or to find somebody who'd look after him and make his money go further than he could make it go—he married the woman who cooked for him and who'd also been his mistress. Then he came down to the cottage and told his sister what he'd done. There was a scene in which she was transformed, before her husband's eyes, from a pretty little, clinging, devoted wife into an ugly, spiteful, incredibly vindictive creature, hardly recognizable. I came in for some of it, because I happened to be there at the time—otherwise I wouldn't expect to be able to make you understand what an appalling shock the sight was. It was no surprise to her brother; it was clear that they'd got used to scenes of that kind—but to her husband . . ." Sir Lawrence paused and looked unhappily at the younger man, and shook his head. "It's no use," he went on. "I was going to tell you that to her husband, it was a blow from which he never really recovered. It's true, but why should you believe it?"

"Was he so . . . unrealistic?"

"No." Sir Lawrence spoke almost fiercely. "No, that's not the word. He was vulnerable—too vulnerable by half. I'm not going to argue about whether a man—a strong, intelligent man —should have been as vulnerable as that. But he loved her, and he believed she was one thing—and under stress, she showed that she was another. And he couldn't get the picture out of his mind. And I've told you; Teresa's like him. Teresa——"

Mark broke in, his voice calm.

"Do you mean to tell me that Teresa has lived in this house with her mother for twenty-three years without——"

"—without knowing that her mother has a bad temper? No,

certainly not. But I do tell you that in all that time her mother
has never exhibited the incredibly ugly side she showed her
husband. You needn't try to tell me that it's impossible; it's true.
And it's true because Lolly has made it her life's work to stand
between Teresa and her mother; to act as a—as a buffer, to look
for the signs and to see that Coralie got enough of her own way
to prevent her from . . . from going over the edge again." He
took out a handkerchief and drew it across his brow. "Over
twenty years," he said slowly, "but I swear to you that I still
remember it." He saw Mark's frown, and gave a grim smile.
"You think I'm exaggerating, don't you?" he said. "You think
I'm a fussy old fool making a lot out of nothing. You don't
believe a damned word of this. You think I'm an old woman
making scares. Well . . . I assure you I'm not."

"Exhibitions of bad temper are never pleasant to watch. Why
should Lady Thurloe's be——"

"You've never seen Teresa's mother, have you?"

"No."

"Well, you can picture her pretty well as she was when she
was young, because she looked just as Teresa looks now—only
she was even more fragile-looking; even more delicate-looking;
even more gentle and graceful. With Teresa, all this comes from
—from within. She has her father's goodness, and it—it shines
out of her. Her looks go right through, if I can put it that way.
But her mother's . . . Coralie's appearance was purely an exterior.
There was nothing pretty below it. But because she was a vain
woman who placed a good deal of value on her looks, it was all
the more shocking to see her wavering for a few seconds between
. . . between preserving the illusion, and giving way to her fury.
Well, she gave way to it. She threw overboard all her beauty, all
her carefully practised tricks—she threw them all away, cleared
them all away to make room for the stream of vindictiveness she
wanted to release. You were right when you said that a display
of wicked temper is never pretty to watch—but there are degrees
of ugliness. The shocking part of Coralie's display was its swing
from all that's loveliest in a woman to all that's ugliest. I saw it,
and it didn't do me any good—and I wasn't her husband and I
wasn't deeply, trustingly in love with her. To Teresa's father it
was a . . . a shocking revelation, and it was to save his daughter
from a similar experience that he asked Lolly to come and live

here and—and keep the peace as far as possible. And that's what Lolly's done—and whether you agree with the arrangement or whether you don't, it's worked; it's come off. And if at this stage you turn up and upset the work of over twenty years . . ." He stopped and ended abruptly. "Well, there it is; I've told you."

"Thank you," said Mark.

Sir Lawrence stared at him fiercely.

"And you don't agree with a blasted word of it, I suppose—is that it?"

Before answering, Mark walked across to the window and stood staring out into the garden. Sir Lawrence waited.

"Well, come on," he urged at last. "Are you going to leave Teresa alone, or aren't you?"

"I'm going to marry her," said Mark slowly.

"And you fully understand what will happen when her mother learns that her plans have come to nothing? Four years of planning, remember: choosing a man—for she did choose him, and he's a good one. Bringing him here and working patiently, secretly—and successfully—to get Teresa to agree to marrying him."

"What did he have," asked Mark curiously, "that several other men couldn't have offered?"

"Everything Coralie thought important. Appearance—he's well-built and handsome; the kind of son-in-law to do her credit. A prospective title: he's heir to Lord Willard. Money: she's got plenty and Teresa'll have more, but his money comes from great estates; in other words, he's of better stock than she is: landed gentry. Pliability: he looks self-sufficient, but he gives in to her; she can get round him. That's a lot to find combined in one man. Can you offer anything like it in exchange?"

"No; there's myself, a good income, a good job, good health and I think a good brain. Come to think of it," said Mark thoughtfully, "that adds up to quite something."

"Not by Coralie's reckoning."

"And so she'll make another scene. She'll go over the edge again, and we'll be treated to the sight of a lovely woman transfigured with rage. And so," ended Mark with raised eyebrows, "what?"

Sir Lawrence stared at him.

"You take it very lightly." Anger sounded for the first time in the old man's voice. "But let me warn you that what I've said has been, if anything, an understatement. Do you want Teresa to go through what her father went through?"

"She won't," said Mark. "The circumstances are entirely different. Her father took it alone. Teresa'll have me with her. Her father was in a worse position altogether; he was watching something crumble—an image he'd built up in his own mind. In other words, his illusions were being swept to hell. But Teresa?"

"Is her father's daughter."

"And her mother's. Don't think I don't honour Lolly for what she's done—but children, you know, are very rarely fools; they don't live with people all their lives without getting a pretty sound idea of what they're like."

"Teresa has not the faintest idea——"

"—of the lengths to which her mother can go when thwarted; quite. But she knows—consciously or sub-consciously—that there's a lot of mud lying about and that Lolly has always been at pains not to let it get stirred up. And if this scene you dread should be repeated, then——"

"I know Teresa far better than you do, and I tell you that it will be a tremendous blow to her."

"She's not a child any longer, and there's a strong man—me—to help her to take knocks," pointed out Mark. "What possible good can come, at this stage, of keeping from her the knowledge that her mother can look and behave like a hellcat? When she was younger, it was necessary to stave off unpleasant revelations. It preserved the peace and happiness of the household, and it enabled her to grow up without shadows—and so a certain measure of protection was right and proper. But now? She's a grown woman, and not a weak one."

"And so you see no need to protect her?"

"I shall spend the rest of my life trying to make her happy— but I don't feel for a moment that she'll need to be walled off from real life. I'll protect her; I'll do all I can to keep her away from danger or from unpleasantness—but she can't go through life wearing blinkers, and she wouldn't want to. She's got to look —and see. Seeing, she's got to judge. The fact that her mother might turn into a fury—if that happened, Teresa wouldn't have to take it on her own, as her father did. I'm here, and although

I hope Lady Thurloe will like me and grow reconciled to the idea I'm not Mr. Morley and that the marriage isn't all her own unaided work, I shan't be unduly depressed if she shows any disapproval. In fact, I won't really mind if she screams the place down."

"You . . . you don't know what you're saying," said Sir Lawrence hopelessly.

"I think I do."

"You don't know Teresa—how can you? You don't know how deep it would go."

"I think—if you'll forgive me, sir—that you forget certain facts. First, it's over twenty years since——"

"We protected Teresa because Teresa's father asked us to. He sent for Lolly Hyde and Lolly came. She hated Coralie, but she agreed to stay with Teresa."

"And now," said Mark, "her work's done and I thank her with all my heart—but she has put Teresa on her feet, and Teresa can stay on them. If you were going to ask me to withdraw merely in order to let the tigress go on sleeping . . . I'm sorry."

"You won't see it from Teresa's point of view?"

"This is Teresa's point of view. She loves her mother. If you think she loves her only because she's seen her sugar-side up all these years, I respectfully submit that you're wrong. In any case, the need for protection is past."

"You're talking sense, but good sense doesn't cover every situation. Coralie won't stand aside and see her candidate defeated."

"If she wants her daughter to be happy——"

"She'll consider that Teresa will be happier with Neville."

"And Teresa will consider that she'll be happier with me. Please don't worry, sir; I'm certain we can work it out."

"If you'd seen Neville's face an hour ago, you wouldn't have thought so."

"Has he been here?"

"Been here? He rang up before leaving town, to speak to Teresa. She wasn't here. He came down. She wasn't here. He drove out to my house, passing me on the way. She wasn't there. He came back. She wasn't here."

"I must give him my address," said Mark coolly.

"He knows it."

"I'm leaving Grosvenor Drive tomorrow," said Mark.

"You are? Well, I'm glad to hear that." The door opened, and he went forward to meet Teresa and Lolly. "D'you hear that, Lolly? He's not living at Hubert's any more; that's one good thing, anyhow."

Lolly did not appear to be listening.

"There's a car," she said. "Neville's back. We came in here——"

She paused.

"Quite right," said Sir Lawrence. "We've got to have this out, I suppose, and this is as good a time as any other."

The four in the room waited and listened; a car door banged, and footsteps sounded on the steps, in the hall. Teresa made a restless movement and Mark, putting out a hand, took one of hers and held it in a firm grasp. She smiled at him—a rather tremulous smile—and then faced the door, ready to meet Neville.

The door opened—but it was not Neville who stood on the threshold. Coralie, in a neat suit, a fur across her shoulders, came with her graceful walk into the room. She had a smile for Lolly and Sir Lawrence, a faint puzzled up-lifting of the brows for Mark; then she had caught Teresa in a soft embrace.

"Darling," she said, "I came home—as a surprise. Happy birthday."

Chapter Ten

CORALIE THURLOE had in the past made a great many effective entrances, timed and carried out with great care and success. None of them, however, had had as shattering an effect as her appearance before the unprepared quartet in the drawing-room.

Teresa, muffled in her mother's furs, had the advantage of being able to conceal her first feelings of dismay; Lolly and Sir Lawrence were less fortunate, and Coralie, observing them, had time to draw some interesting conclusions from their confusion.

Mark alone remained unmoved. He had heard much of Coralie, and now she was before him. He let his gaze rest frankly upon her, and took in her beauty—so like Teresa's—her poise, her all-but-natural charm. Certain things about her surprised him: he had not expected the look of youth and freshness. Her air of indolence, too, took him unawares; he had expected her to have a look of alertness, even of sharpness.

Coralie was taking in some impressions in her turn: she noted Mark's height and ease of manner and quiet air of authority. She did not as yet know who he was or why he was in her drawing-room—but she saw that he had an air—unobtrusive but unmistakable—of being perfectly at home there.

In a few moments, Sir Lawrence had recovered his poise. With a fair appearance of ease, he greeted Coralie as she released Teresa.

"Nice to see you back, Coralie," he said. "Nice surprise for Teresa, too. Will you allow me to present a young friend of mine? Mark Tudor. Son of one of m'old flames—Mary Grant. You won't remember the Grants; they left Sussex before you came—but you must have heard of the three Grant sisters; they were local beauties."

"Indeed I have." Coralie extended a hand to Mark. "They lived near some friends of mine who used to mention them frequently. How d'you do?"

Mark bowed over her hand and awarded her full marks for

deportment; he was, he knew, going to come in for some scratching—but not until she was ready. For the moment, she was content to feel her way.

"Lily"—she had moved away and was bending to kiss Lolly's cheek—"it's lovely to be back. How have you all been?"

"So-so. What went wrong with the trip?" inquired Lolly. "You paid for two weeks and I don't suppose they'll give you your money back."

"I don't suppose so either." Coralie smiled. "But I kept thinking of Teresa's birthday, and wishing I could be here for it —and it rained and rained and the sea was rough and there was so much mist that we couldn't see any of the scenery, and so I decided suddenly that the next time we stopped, I'd come home. And I did. Where's Neville? Isn't he dining here?"

"Yes. He went to fetch Lawrence, and passed him on the way," lied Lolly stolidly. "He'll be back presently. Lawrence and Mr. Tudor," she added, "are leaving."

"Oh—no! Won't you both stay and dine?' said Coralie.

"No; very good of you, very good indeed," said Sir Lawrence hastily, "but got to get back. Mark, too. Come 'long, young feller; we've got to be going. 'Bye, Coralie; 'bye, Lolly my dear. Teresa, come and see us out."

He had ushered Mark and Teresa swiftly out of the door and shut it behind them. In the hall, he gave them no time for speech, but waved them on. Not until they were out of the house did he pause, and then he took out a large handkerchief and wiped his brow.

"Close thing," he remarked. "Now then, you two, I'll give you three minutes to make your farewells; no more."

Teresa reached up and dropped a light kiss on his cheek.

"I love you very much," she said softly.

"Nonsense. Now, don't just stand there; your mother'll be waiting to see you."

"Mark was going to——"

"—to ruin us all by rushing his fences; quite," said Sir Lawrence drily. "Well, I'll be waiting."

He strode away to his car, and they looked after him with a smile.

"Saved the day," said Mark. "But we've only got three minutes." He enfolded Teresa in his arms. "Darling Teresa," he murmured, "shall we go back now before Neville gets back, and have it out?"

"No. Not now," said Teresa. "Tomorrow. Neville will come back tonight and——"

"I don't want you to have to see him alone."

"I've got to, Mark. This is something I've got to do myself."

"Why? We could do it together. Why can't we go back to your mother now, and tell her how things are?"

"Because it wouldn't be fair—and it wouldn't be wise. You don't know Mother. She needs . . . well, a special approach."

Mark held her at arm's length and studied her for a few moments.

"If she takes it badly?" he asked slowly. "Sir Lawrence hinted that she might."

"She's fond of Neville, and she'll be disappointed but she'll come round. I'm not, as you pointed out this morning, a seventeen- or eighteen-year-old. She knows, I think, that I was never entirely sure about Neville."

"And you're sure—quite and quite and quite sure—about me?"

Teresa walked forward into his arms and laid her head on his chest.

"I love you," she said steadily. "I'm sorry it happened so— so fast and so suddenly, because it makes us look as though we . . . as though we lost our heads. But it's happened, Mark, my darling. I love you and I want to spend the rest of my life with you, and nothing matters any more—much—except you. I hope Mother will be happy, and I hope Lolly won't be disappointed— but it won't make any difference in the end. I love you." She raised her head. "Please listen carefully, Mark. I love you."

He did not speak. Gently, he put his lips on hers and held her close to his heart. Sir Lawrence, turning to urge them to hurry, changed his mind and remained silent; his eyes, resting on them, were full of affection, but there were creases of worry on his brow.

Teresa stood on the drive to watch them go, and then went slowly back into the house. She found her mother alone in the drawing-room, her hat, her fur and gloves thrown on a chair.

"Where's Lolly?" Teresa asked.

"Gone to see about an extra place at dinner. Darling, who was that man?"

"Mark Tudor."

"Why should Lawrence suddenly produce him? It was odd, I thought, to bring him on a birthday call. Unless, of course, he's staying with him."

"No, he isn't," said Teresa. "As a matter of fact——"

She paused. A car had driven up to the house, and it seemed reasonable to suppose that it contained Neville. Teresa, who had not looked forward to his coming, felt grateful at least for the timeliness of his arrival. She had felt herself, a moment ago, equal to explaining the situation to her mother—but with Mark's departure, something of her courage had evaporated. She felt tired, and a little more than apprehensive; something in her mother's voice had disturbed her; a note of hardness below the casual questions. It wasn't, thought Teresa, going to be too smooth.

She decided, suddenly, that she would put off explanations and recriminations until Mark could be with her. This was her birthday, and she had spent the greater part of it with him and she was grateful. She longed now for his presence or, lacking that, the opportunity to go up to her room and lie quietly on her bed reviewing the events of this eventful day—but instead she was committed to a difficult evening during which she must strive to make it appear that all was as it had been when her mother went away. She did not think that Neville would force the issue—not this evening.

She heard voices in the hall, and felt a surge of relief as Lolly's deep notes came to her ears. Lolly had waylaid Neville; Lolly would warn him to say nothing tonight.

When the door opened to admit Neville, however, she saw that whether he spoke or not, his demeanour would arouse at least uneasiness in the mind of her mother. He greeted Coralie with an obvious effort, and then his eyes, black with anger, rested on Teresa.

"I've been looking for you," he said. "Happy birthday—if it isn't too late."

"It isn't too late. Thank you," said Teresa.

His eyes were on her hand, and he saw that his ring was still on her finger—and he saw, too, from her look, that she would have taken it off—if she had remembered. The fact that it was there because she had forgotten it drew the blood from his face and left it deathly white, and for the first time, Teresa saw him with the eyes of her new understanding, and knew what he was feeling. Before she could stop herself, she had gone forward and put her hands in his.

"I'm sorry, Neville," she said gently. "I'm . . . I can only say I'm sorry."

He drew his hands away and stepped back, and she saw that he was suffering, at the moment at any rate, more anger than pain. Then Coralie was speaking in a distressed voice.

"Have you two quarrelled?"

"Not yet," said Neville, without taking his eyes from Teresa. "And when there's anything to be said, it won't be said between Teresa and myself. There's——"

"Please, Neville!" Coralie held up a slender hand. "This is Teresa's birthday, and tonight you're going to be friends. I don't know what sort of misunderstanding has arisen between you, but it can be talked over tomorrow and——"

"I'm not going to sit down to dinner pretending that everything's fine and rosy," broke in Neville abruptly. "I'm sorry; I'm not in a social mood. I've spent the last few hours chasing my tail and if I can't have it out now with Teresa, I'll come back tomorrow. You'll have to excuse me, I'm afraid."

He strode to the door, opened it and turned for a last look at Teresa. "Don't let yourself go quite overboard," he warned her. "There are a few things you ought to know about him first, and perhaps some of them will jerk you out of your dreams."

The door closed, Teresa and her mother stood unmoving as the sounds of the car died away. Then Coralie swung slowly round to face her daughter, and raised her hands helplessly.

"Have I gone mad?" she asked. "Or has everybody else? Teresa, what is all this about?"

Teresa raised calm eyes to her mother's.

"I'm not going to marry Neville," she said.

"But my darling"—Coralie's voice was blank—"but *why* not?"

"I don't love him. I'm sorry I found it out so late—but it isn't too late, Mother."

"But . . . but how and when did you find this out?" inquired Coralie. "I've been away a little over a week; when I went, you were talking quite happily of the house you and Neville were going to buy. Now you're talking wildly about not marrying him. Teresa, what has come over you? And who"—Coralie stopped and her eyes narrowed. "This man Lawrence brought —is he . . ."

"Yes," said Teresa, and waited.

Nothing came for some time, however. When at last her mother spoke, her tone was quiet.

"Are you telling me," she asked, "that in the mere few days that I was away, you met this man and decided to break your engagement to Neville?"

"Yes."

"You . . . you mean that you imagine you are in love with this entire stranger?"

"I don't imagine it. I am in love with him," said Teresa.

Coralie looked at her for some moments, and then walked slowly across the room to a table in the corner and poured herself out a drink.

"I'd better hear it all, hadn't I?" she asked.

"There isn't much," said Teresa, "and it all sounds . . . improbable. But this isn't infatuation, Mother."

"How do you know?"

"Because I feel so . . . so certain about it all. With Neville, I was never sure. I liked him, I felt he would make a good husband and I thought that my—my lack of feeling, strong feeling, for him was some kind of lack in myself. I thought that I was . . . well, cold; frigid. But when I met Mark—from the first moment, I felt something. Not love, at first; just curiosity, and then a sort of . . . I can't put it into words," she ended helplessly. "It doesn't go into words."

"Well, try." Coralie spoke coldly. "I've got to know the whole story, surely?"

Teresa faced her.

"Not necessarily, Mother," she said. "If you can just try to trust me—I mean trust me to know my own feelings."

"My dear Teresa,"—from coldness, Coralie's voice was now edged with contempt—"I've seen infatuated girls before."

"This is not infatuation."

"Then what is it? Love? For a man you met less than two weeks ago?"

"Why not?" Teresa asked. "It's happened before."

"If you let a man like Neville go for the sake of a total stranger who's been glib enough to sweep you off your feet, you'll be insane. Insane. Crazy. What sort of a man can he be, to come near you at all when you're engaged to someone else? Or didn't you tell him?"

"He knew."

"And he made love to you?"

"He told me he loved me."

"And you can admire, look up to, love a man who could do that?"

"Need we argue about it?"

"Argue? No, we needn't argue. But do you expect me to come home and see all my plans, all your plans in ruins, and simply offer my congratulations? Do you expect me to tell Neville that we're sorry, but you met a man last week you think you'd rather marry? Good Heavens, Teresa, people can't do these things! Nobody wants to force you into marrying Neville if you don't want to, but at least you can pay him the compliment of giving the matter some thought before you throw him over for an utter stranger! Who is this man? What do you know about him—except that Lawrence knew his mother? Where does he come from? What has he to offer you? What——"

She stopped. The door had opened, and Lolly had come into the room. Teresa had a curious feeling that she had been standing outside the door waiting for a suitable moment to interrupt, and her heart lifted in gratitude.

"I suppose you know what's been going on?" Coralie asked her as she entered.

"I don't know much," said Lolly. "Things haven't been going exactly slowly. If you're going to ask my opinion, I'll give it to you: I like him."

"Can you tell me anything at all about him?"

"Not much. Except the salient facts, of course. He wanted Teresa and he got her. Must be something in him, wouldn't you say?"

"Every plausible schemer since the world began," said Coralie, "has been able to work on women. Has it struck anybody that Teresa is rather a good match?"

"Well, it's always easy to check up on his motives," pointed out Lolly. "You can tell him you'll cut her off, and see how he reacts."

"And if he has gone to the trouble of finding out that I cannot, as you put it, cut her off?"

"I don't quite honestly think he's had time to cook up any dirty motives," said Lolly. "This is one of those cases you read about, when they take one look and go into a daze. It's the favourite theme for popular songs; if you like, I could quote you half a dozen this minute. The only exceptional thing about this case is that you wouldn't have said that Teresa was a likely girl to get bowled over first go off—and the fact that at twenty-four, she takes one look and capitulates. And if you ask me," she proceeded without pause, "the most sensible thing for you to do, Coralie, is to meet Mark Tudor and see what you think of him."

"I have seen Mark Tudor, and I think he looks a perfectly ordinary man without——"

"Well, what I mean is, talk to him."

"I have no wish to talk to him," said Coralie. "What I want to do is get Teresa back to her right senses."

"Perhaps Neville will do that," suggested Lolly. "For the moment, I've cooked a very fine birthday dinner and it isn't going to be improved by neglect—so hadn't we better think about eating?"

Coralie rose and gathered together her things.

"If you'll forgive me," she said, "I'd rather not pretend that this is a small matter which we can all ignore. I'm upset, and I haven't your trust in everything being put right in the morning. Will you have something sent up to my room?"

"If you prefer it," said Lolly. "But it's Teresa's birthday and——"

"—and I gave up my cruise and came home to see her—and she has made it clear that I might just as well have stayed away," said Coralie coldly. "She doesn't want to listen to advice, to reason or even to comments. So I may as well go to my room and think it over by myself. Good night."

Not until the door of the bedroom had closed did Lolly move, and then she drew a long breath of relief.

"Went off better than I thought," she said. "Mind you"—she turned to face Teresa—"mind you, she's behaved rather well;

it must have been a nasty pill. But I suppose you know that she hasn't said her last word on the subject?"

"I suppose not. Should I go up to her?"

"Holy Moses, no! Let her chew it over, for the Lord's sake. And we'll eat our dinner by our two selves and you can tell me what got into you today. Come along."

Teresa's story was lame enough: Mark had been waiting for her outside Lawrence's house; they had driven away, they had sat on a beach, they had played with David, they had gone up to London, they had returned. A stranger, listening, would have thought it a bald and almost cold narrative. Only Lolly, who knew Teresa so well, could see below the calm surface. Only Lolly could hear the tremulous notes in her voice and note the deep glow in her eyes. Watching Teresa across the table, she learned how much Mark Tudor had come to mean to her, and one by one her doubts, her regrets faded and only her joy in Teresa's happiness remained. There might be trouble, there would be trouble, for Coralie had no intention, she knew, of allowing matters to stand as they were. But beyond the trouble, beyond the storm was happiness for Teresa and for Mark. Coralie might strike, but she could not destroy what Mark had built. Through Teresa's hesitating words, Teresa's half-sentences and uncompleted explanations, shone the steadiness of her love. She could not give reasons, but within her was deep, quiet conviction, shining through and giving her beauty a depth that brought a pricking to Lolly's eyes. Teresa—in love. Teresa, who had throughout the past four years shown for Neville nothing approaching this steady, hidden fire.

She reached out a large hand suddenly and Teresa grasped it. "Lolly—are you glad?"

"If he never did anything else in his life," said Lolly, "I'd love him for that look he's brought into your eyes. But oh Moses, Teresa, I hope he's strong. You'll need all the strength you can call up for the next few days, lovey. Your mother's a good woman in many ways, I suppose, but she's up there now plotting—I can't use any other word."

"Don't be hard on her. It must be difficult for her to watch me behaving—she thinks—like a smitten girl. When she gets to know Mark——"

"I knew it was coming. As soon as I looked out and saw you

both in the car, I knew it. People don't look like that unless they've forgotten what's round them." She pushed her plate away and leaned forward. "When did you first really *know?* Tell me everything, right from the beginning; it's the last chance I'll get of hearing it. Tomorrow plenty of trouble, but tonight—well tonight let's think about you and Mark and nobody else. How were you first sure that you were sure?"

Teresa smiled.

"I don't know. Perhaps I began to know when I imagined, for a moment—by mistake—that David was his son."

"You didn't like that?"

"No. Lolly——"

"Well?"

"About Mother——" She paused.

"Upstairs, plotting; I told you."

"I want to say something, but I don't know how to put it," said Teresa slowly. "It's about Mother—and you."

Lolly said nothing for a few moments. Then, quietly:

"What about your mother—and myself?"

"When you told me that you were going away when I was married to Neville, I went away and thought about it, and it seemed . . . odd."

"What's odd about it? Your mother'll get older and she'll lean on me more and more. I don't want to prop anybody up, unless they can't find anybody else to do the propping. So I'm going while your mother's strong and sprightly and able to fill my place without difficulty. What's odd about all that?"

"I don't know." Teresa gave a gentle smile. "I was hoping you'd tell me."

"Tell you what?"

"The truth. You've often told me you know me better than anybody else in the world. Hasn't it ever struck you, Lolly, that I know you pretty well, too?"

"You think I'm lying?"

"Lying? No. But behind that reason, there's . . . something else."

"Rubbish."

Teresa sighed.

"All right; don't tell me," she said. "I'll work it out when my mind's clearer."

"Your mind will never be clearer. You've got Mark in it now and for ever—and I'm glad. I hope you'll be happy all your life with him."

"I'm happy now," said Teresa. "And you know something, Lolly? Mother took it for granted that I met Mark through Lawrence—and so Uncle Hubert's name didn't come up at all."

Lolly pushed back her chair and stood up.

"Thank God for that," she said fervently. "Shall we go back to the drawing-room?"

"No," said Teresa. "Let's go out in the garden and talk about Mark."

When she got into bed that night and settled herself against the pillows, she had not long to wait; the telephone gave a ring and then Mark's voice was sounding in her ears.

"Good timing?" he asked. "I pictured you just in bed."

"I love you," said Teresa.

"I know. I knew all the time. Has your mother loosed all her fury?"

"She won't loose any fury. She's disappointed, and I suppose she's angry, but——"

"Then the worst is to come. I'm glad. I want to be with you. Will you promise to head off any crisis until I come?"

"Yes—but why should you expect a crisis?"

"One of the most dangerous creatures in all Nature," said Mark, "is a mother going into action for her young. There's only one force more lethal, and that's a woman deprived of something she worked for and succeeded in not getting. Your mother will make trouble; will you believe that, my darling Teresa?"

"She might make a small scene. She does—sometimes—but when she knows that my mind is made up, she'll understand that she can't do anything."

"And that's the point at which the curtain will rise on the big scene. And now forget everything but the fact that I love you with all my heart and that in future, you're mine and not your mother's. Close your eyes; I'm going to kiss you."

Teresa closed her eyes.

Chapter Eleven

S HE slept late. When she went downstairs, her first stop was, as usual, Lolly's sitting-room, in which at this time every day Lolly was usually to be found doing accounts, sewing or planning menus. This morning, however, it was empty; it was also tidy, which was a sign that Lolly had not entered it. Surprised, Teresa passed on to the small, sunny room in which she and her mother always breakfasted.

She opened the door and paused for a moment on the threshold, her eyes taking in the pleasant picture within. It was a sight which was to remain for ever in her mind.

Nothing, at this first glance, was different: her mother sat on a high-backed chair drawn up to the oval table; she wore a pale pink housecoat with an immensely full skirt that billowed round her as she sat. Round her hair was the wide ribbon she wore in the mornings and which on her looked so neat and so suitable and which on other women of her age, Teresa had always thought, would have looked out of place. The table was agleam with silver—the tall coffee pot, the milk and cream jugs, the sugar bowl. The china was pale green, the tablecloth a green of a slightly darker shade. The sun shone in through the long open window; outside, the grass lay under a faint haze; the hum of a mowing machine sounded in the distance. At one end of the table lay a neat pile of morning papers and new magazines; as Teresa came in, Coralie folded the newspaper she had been reading, and tilted a cheek for Teresa to kiss.

"Did you sleep well, darling?" she asked.

"Beautifully, thank you, Mother. Where's Lolly? She hasn't been in her room this morning."

"She's shopping in Brighton."

"Oh!"

Teresa said no more for some moments; she helped herself to coffee and put two slices of bread into the toaster; she was outwardly calm, but within she was re-assessing her first impressions of the peaceful scene. This room, the breakfast, her mother, might look the same—but Lolly did not go shopping in Brighton at this time of the morning; she went—if she went at all—in the afternoon, when the household matters had been arranged. Her mother's words were casual, laconic, but the brief sentence was sufficient indication to Teresa that things were not as they had been.

"That's unusual, isn't it?" she asked.

"Unusual?" Her mother's glance, faintly surprised, met hers over a large and glossy magazine. "Lolly going shopping?"

"Going into Brighton at this time."

"My dear Teresa, the shops have been open for almost two hours."

"Yes—but if she wants to shop in the morning, she goes into the village. Why the rush into Brighton?"

"I imagine," said Coralie carelessly, "that she's gone in to see Lawrence."

"See Lawrence?" Teresa assembled the butter and honey by her plate and tried to guess what lay behind her mother's unruffled manner. "Lawrence was here yesterday—why does she want to see him again this morning?"

The question was put in Teresa's most direct manner, and Coralie lowered the magazine and raised her eyes to her daughter's for a moment.

"We had a slight argument," she said. "I imagine Lolly has gone carrying tales to her old friend."

The contempt in her tone brought the colour to Teresa's cheeks. Slow, unaccustomed anger rose in her, but she kept her voice steady.

"What was the argument about?" she asked.

"Don't try to be naïve, my pet," begged Coralie. "I go away for little more than a week, and during that time Lolly allows you to make a fool of yourself with a man nobody has ever heard of. Did you think I would let it pass without even mentioning it?"

"Lolly had nothing whatever to do with it."

Coralie closed the pages of the magazine and laid it aside. When she spoke, her voice was soft, but Teresa knew that the battle had begun.

"If I had been at home, do you imagine that this man would have been able to make any impression on you? Lolly means well, but I wouldn't call her a good judge of character."

"Lolly had nothing to do with it," repeated Teresa. "When she saw Mark, I think it was too late to do anything."

"You mean that you fell deeply in love with him after one glance?"

"I think so," said Teresa steadily.

"You met him, I understand"—Coralie's voice now held open contempt—"in your Uncle Hubert's house?"

Teresa hesitated; Lolly had obviously been under cross-examination.

"Yes."

"And I understand that your plan of making contact with your uncle after all these years came to nothing?"

"The visit wasn't very successful."

"I could have saved you the trouble of making it. Hubert chose to make his own life and to go his own way. I would never willingly meet him again, and I'm not surprised that you found the visit a waste of time. This man is living there as a boarder—a lodger; I don't know the term."

"Yes. At least, he was. He's not living there any more."

"He must feel his prospects are brighter."

"Mother"—Teresa sat down and faced her mother across the table—"quarrelling isn't going to do either of us any good. Won't you meet Mark, talk to him, try to get to know him?"

"No, Teresa, I will not. The trouble has only arisen because he wasn't investigated right at the beginning, and shown to be——"

"If I tell you that I love him, doesn't it make you want to know something about him?"

Coralie leaned back.

"Well, let's see how much you can tell me. He has a job?"

"Yes. He's—he's something in the City."

"What, exactly?"

"I don't know."

"He has an income? Prospects?"

"We didn't go into it."

"He saw you at your uncle's, knew who you were, knew from what he had heard previously in the house that you were certainly not poor. He set out to make an impression on you—and he succeeded."

"Yes, he succeeded."

"And as I see it, my duty lies not in throwing you into the

arms of a complete and probably fortune-hunting stranger, but in trying to find out something about who and what he is. And that is what I have done."

Teresa waited. The sounds of battle were nearer, louder and more threatening.

"I rang up Neville early this morning," proceeded Coralie, "and I asked him to go to your uncle's house and make inquiries about this man. They must know where he came from, and something about him. When we know a little, we can find out more."

"And if you don't find out anything discreditable?" asked Teresa.

"His behaviour all the way has been discreditable. Why do you think he was in so great a hurry to pursue you? Because I was away. Why was he so anxious to get away last night? Because he didn't want to be questioned too closely by me. Why isn't he here this morning to present his case?"

"He will be," said Teresa.

"And so will Neville. He's coming down as soon as he has been to your uncle's house."

Teresa sat unmoving, her hands clasped tightly on her lap, her toast untouched, her coffee untasted. Her mind was busy. She had expected some initial opposition from her mother, but she had not been prepared for this cool, swift action. Something in her mother's voice—a cold, hard undertone—brought to her heart for the first time a touch of fear, a faint realisation that this was not to be a short and trying period which would end in her mother's acceptance of Mark in place of Neville. There had been—there would be, Teresa began to understand—little talk of feeling; her mother was not even considering matching man against man and throwing her weight on the side of the one she considered the more suitable of the two; she was unreservedly, inflexibly on the side of Neville. She would not, as Teresa had hoped, feel drawn to Mark because her daughter loved him; she would not see him until she had sufficient evidence with which to confront and if possible convict him.

She tried to revive her sinking spirits by telling herself that she must try to see the matter from her mother's point of view. Her mother had returned to find her plans in ruins; some disappointment, some anger was to be expected and must be borne. But there had never, she remembered, been any talk of love in their discussions about Neville. To her own desire to delay the engagement until her own feelings had become warmer, her mother had unvaryingly put forward the view that liking would become affection, and affection love.

A picture of Neville rose in her mind. He had, she supposed, been in love with her—but she had at no time experienced in his company any of the warmth, the confidence, the trembling joy that had come when she had lain in Mark's arms. Neville had been affectionate, but nothing more. Now she seemed to hear her mother's advice to him: "Give her time; don't rush her." She saw her own early misgivings brushed aside, and knew that if there had been no Mark to appear at this late hour to save her, she would have married Neville and spent the rest of her life regretting it.

She brought Mark into her mind-picture and set him beside Neville. Two men: one broad and powerful, the other slight, tall, in his way as strong. Neville, dark and serious; Mark, fair and incurably light-hearted. Light of heart? Deep and generous of heart. He would not come up to her mother's material requirements; he had spoken little of his background or his prospects— but she knew that she herself was content to take him as he was, and she knew with a deep certainty that she would be safe with him all her life.

Her mother's voice brought her back to herself, and she understood from the sharpness of the tone that she had been addressed more than once.

"Did you hear me, Teresa? Neville is here."

"Neville?" Teresa stared at her mother.

"His car is outside, and I gave orders that he was to be shown into the drawing-room when he came. I'm going upstairs to dress; will you go and see him?"

It would have to be done, Teresa knew. She owed him something—an explanation, at least.

She went into the drawing-room; Neville was standing at the window, and turned to face her as she entered; he did not, however, advance to meet her. He spoke at once, and his voice was quiet.

"Your mother asked me to come down," he said. "I've one or two things to tell her—but I would have come in any case. I had to see you."

Teresa stood helplessly in the middle of the room. She had wronged him, she had hurt him, and she ought to say something —anything. But words were hard to find—suitable words. She wanted more than anything in the world to say that she did not love him, had never loved him, would never have loved him— and that she loved Mark with all her heart. But the words would wound him, and she had wounded him enough.

"I'm . . . sorry, Neville," she said. "I can't say any more than that. I know it's inadequate, but . . . I'm sorry. The truth is that I should never have become engaged to you." She slipped his ring off her finger and, as he made no move to take it, placed it gently on the table between them. "Please forgive me."

He stared miserably at the ring. Then he stepped forward, picked it up and put it into his pocket.

"Perhaps you'll put it on again—one day," he said. "This isn't the end of the story."

"It's the end of our story."

"So you think at the moment. I've no doubt that you're pretty well infatuated with this fellow—but he isn't exactly all you think he is, you know."

"I know that my mother asked you to go to my uncle's house and make inquiries about him. I hope you didn't do anything of the kind."

"Why not? Why shouldn't I? A man comes out of the blue and you hand me back my ring. If I didn't want to know who and what he was, I'd be a fool. And if those who've got your interests at heart didn't check up on him, they'd be even greater fools. I'm not surprised at a man falling in love with you; I'm not surprised at a man trying to get you away from me, even with my ring on your finger—but even you can't pretend that this fellow kept the rules."

"I met him and I fell in love with him. It isn't the way I would have chosen. I would have preferred to have met him——"

"—in the ordinary way, instead of picking him up. And if there'd been time, no doubt you would have preferred to know more about him—but you fell in love, or thought you did, and after that inquiries seemed superfluous. And that's why it was left to others to make the inquiries for you—to stop you going any further before you've got your eyes wide open."

"I'm not infatuated, Neville."

"My dear, you are—deeply and thoroughly. You're a decent, gentle, trusting girl, just the right material for these parasites to get a hold on. The wonder is that it never happened to you before —but I was around, and I like to think that that kept them off. Until this one put in an appearance."

"Do you think it's really any good talking like this, Neville? All you can do is make me angry, and——"

"That won't worry me—just so long as you hear what I've got to say. But I'll wait and say it to your mother."

"If it concerns Mark, you can say it to me."

"You shall hear it—but I'm making a report and——"

He paused. The door had opened to admit Coralie, but close behind her came Lolly and Sir Lawrence. Coralie, on the point of closing the door behind her, had no choice but to step aside and admit them. The cold look on her face told better than words her extreme reluctance to see them at this moment.

"Good morning, Coralie," began Sir Lawrence at once. "I came back to see if you and I could talk over certain things."

"Lolly brought you. I told Teresa," said Coralie, "that she had gone running to you—and I was right."

"Quite right," said Lolly.

She had turned to face Coralie—but before turning, her eyes had sought Teresa's and her lips had formed one word: outside.

It was enough. With a murmured excuse, Teresa opened the door and, with newborn cunning, left it open and went up the stairs—and then, as she heard Lolly close the door, turned and fled down again, across the hall and outside—out on to the drive to where Mark's car stood, and into the arms of Mark, who was waiting for her beside the car.

They said nothing for some time. He could feel her swiftly-beating heart, and his arms closed more tightly around her; his lips were on her hair.

"Losing your nerve?" he asked gently at last.

She freed herself and looked up at him.

"No—oh no! But . . . I thought Mother would be angry and then come round. Only . . . in an odd sort of way, she isn't angry. She's—she's just cold and . . . and she sent Neville to find out things about you."

"I know. I saw Zoë." He cupped his hands about her face and

smiled down at her. "And now you'll hear the whole, sinister story."

She laughed up at him, love in her eyes.

"Is there a sinister story?"

"If there were, would you still love me?"

"I love you because you're the sort of person who hasn't anything to hide. You're clean and upright and honest. Have you concealed anything from me."

"Yes; I told you. But I also told you that it was nothing important. Nothing that could affect us—you and me. But there are certain facts that Neville has brought to light, and you'd better come inside and let him throw them in my face."

Teresa looked up at him.

"We could go now—go away," she said. "Couldn't we, Mark? We're here—and here's your car, and there's the road. Nobody could stop us. We could go away and leave all the recriminations behind, and all the arguments and all the quarrelling."

"We could." Mark bent and kissed her. "We could—but it wouldn't solve anything, my darling. Bitterness now—or bitterness afterwards. I'd rather get it all over now. Are you frightened?"

"If you're with me—no."

"Then we'll go in and the music will strike up. Come on."

In the drawing-room they found an atmosphere heavy with tension. It was easy to place the opponents: Coralie stood on one side of the room with Neville beside her while on the other were Lolly and Sir Lawrence.

Coralie gave Mark a brief, contemptuous look as he entered.

"Here is Mr. Tudor," she said. "Now he can tell us, perhaps, that nothing of what Neville says is true." She swung round to face Teresa. "I'm sorry you got yourself into this position," she said, "but as I told you this morning, you formed your opinion of this man without having any knowledge of what he's really like. Neville made some inquiries about him from your uncle, and——"

"Not her uncle," corrected Mark quietly. "It was her aunt who gave him all the facts."

"And the facts are these," said Coralie. "If Mr. Tudor wishes to contradict any of them, we shall all be glad—and immensely relieved. The first fact—isn't it so, Mr. Tudor?—is that you were living at Grosvenor Drive in order to find out all you could about my brother's monetary affairs?"

"Absolutely correct," said Mark quietly.

"You went there, in fact, to spy on them all?"

"You put it very harshly."

"But it is, in fact, true?"

"Quite true."

"You found out—how, we don't yet know—that if you could prove certain suspicions you had concerning Mrs. Towers and the other people in the house, you could use the knowledge profitably?"

"Correct," said Mark.

"You found out what you went to find out—and then you told Mrs. Towers what you knew. But—for reasons of your own —you didn't go to the police. That's correct, isn't it?"

"Quite correct," said Mark, and put out a hand to take one of Teresa's. "Like I said," he told her sadly. "Sinister facts."

He released her hand and turned to her mother.

"Is that all?"

"All? A spy, an informer, and probably a blackmailer." Coralie's voice broke on an unpleasant laugh. "Should there be any more?"

"Yes." It was Neville speaking. "Just one thing more. I told you that he'd found out what he went to find out, but I didn't tell you what it was."

"Then for God's sake tell us now," said Sir Lawrence abruptly. "Don't hang it out—just tell us. If Mark's done anything discreditable, I'll eat all the furniture and fittings, piece by piece—but let's hear all you've got to say. Come on—get it out."

"I would have said it before if I hadn't thought that it would give pain to Lady Thurloe. It concerns her brother," said Neville.

"Nothing that concerns my brother will give me the slightest pain," said Coralie. "Not more pain than I would feel for a stranger. We became strangers to one another more than twenty years ago and I haven't seen him since. Is he ill?"

"No," Neville hesitated. "He's . . . he's dead. He's . . . he's been dead some time."

There was silence in the room. Then it was broken by Coralie's voice, slow and puzzled.

"But I don't understand. My brother can't be dead, or I should have been told of his death. The lawyers would have had to know."

"You would have been told," said Neville, "but . . . there were reasons why his wife didn't want anybody to know that he had died."

"But that was impossible." Coralie frowned. "On his death, his income was to go to me and then to . . . Oh!" She stopped abruptly. "The money! Of course . . . the money," she said in a slow, tense voice. "The money!"

"Yes." Mark's voice came quietly, almost gently. "The money!"

She had swung round on him.

"You knew!"

"Not at first," said Mark. "But it was fairly easy to guess."

"You knew—and you said nothing to Teresa."

"Nothing. Nothing on this subject," Mark corrected himself.

"You knew that he had died and that that woman was living on money that should have been mine?"

"Yes, I knew," said Mark.

There was a pause. Coralie drew a long, noisy breath.

"When did he die?" she demanded.

"Some time ago," he replied.

She came a step nearer, and her voice was vibrant with rage.

"That isn't an answer to my question. I asked you when my brother died. When? How long ago?"

Mark's eyes went slowly round the circle: to Coralie, her face white, her eyes burning with fury; to Neville, pale and expectant; to Sir Lawrence and Lolly and Teresa. Then his gaze came back to rest on Coralie.

"He died," he told her slowly, "fifteen years ago."

Chapter Twelve

IN the long, tense silence that hung over the room after Mark's revelation, Teresa found that all her doubts, all her hesitations had been resolved—and that her courage had returned. The storm was about to break—but there was something to be said first—said by her, and said clearly and finally.

She stepped to Neville's side; the words she said to him came easily and quietly, and carried absolute conviction.

"You told me I was infatuated," she said, "but you were wrong. Try to believe this, Neville: nothing that happens now or in the future will affect what I said to you this morning. I like you. I've always liked you—but I've never loved you. I think Mother knows this, and so does Lolly, and so does Lawrence. Whatever comes of this feeling between Mark and myself, I know one thing: I shall never marry anybody but him. It will be Mark—or nobody. Please, please, believe that."

Neville said nothing for a time; his eyes, in a face suddenly drawn with misery, rested on hers.

"I believe it," he said at last. "I don't know how you can bring yourself to care for him, or to trust him, or to place your future in his hands—but I know I'm washed up. And that"—he managed a smile—"doesn't leave me much to stay for."

"Don't go!" Coralie spoke sharply. "Neville, I forbid you to go! She's crazy; we're all crazy—but given time, we shall all grow sane again. Stay here—and be patient."

"No." Neville was at the door. "If Teresa ever wants me, she knows where to find me." He looked at Teresa. "Good-bye—and good luck."

He was gone; it was so swiftly done that for a moment nobody realized he was no longer in the room. Then Coralie had run to the door and had opened it and was calling:

"Neville! Neville—come back!"

His only answer was the spurt of gravel on the drive and the screech of tyres as he turned out of the gateway into the road. Slowly, she closed the door and, leaning against it, gave Mark

long look of utter hatred. Her words, however, were mild
enough.

"Please go away," she said.

"By all means," said Mark, "but there are one or two things
we must talk over first."

"I shall not talk to you about anything whatsoever," said
Coralie slowly. "You will please leave my house and not return
to it."

"I must make at least one more visit," pointed out Mark. "To
take Teresa away."

Coralie's face became ashen. Her mouth tightened until the
soft red lips hardened into a straight and ugly line. After one
glance, Lolly stepped forward and spoke in what she tried to
make a brisk, businesslike tone.

"There's no point in standing here and saying things we'll all
be sorry for later on," she suggested. "I think, Teresa, you ought
to send Mark home, and then we can——"

"Get him out," came from Coralie in a strangled voice.

"Yes. Mark"—Lolly turned to him—"you can see, can't you,
that it would be better if you went away at once?"

"No," said Mark quietly. "I can't."

"Look"—Sir Lawrence moved forward and addressed him in
a reasonable tone—"there's no point in precipitating a crisis now.
Go away and it can all be discussed later."

"We're all here now," pointed out Mark, addressing Coralie.
"This matter concerns Teresa, and here in this room are all the
people most closely connected with her; if you will be patient,
we can talk the whole thing over and——"

"Get out," came from Coralie in the same strangled voice.

"Not quite yet," said Mark. "You made certain inquiries about
me and you have put forward a number of accusations; if you
won't discuss Teresa's future, you must allow me, I think,
to——"

Coralie had taken a step towards Teresa, and was standing
before her looking at her with burning eyes.

"You got him in. Get him out," she ordered. "If you don't,
you'll be sorry. I'm warning you."

Teresa stood quite still, and looked at the almost unrecogniz-
able picture before her. She had seen her mother irritated, petu-
ant, angry; she had become used to the quick changes from

graciousness to querulousness; she had heard the soft tones become hard and even shrill. But the changes had been moment- ary; a word from herself or from Lolly had been sufficient to restore the smoothness to Coralie's brow, the sweetness to her demeanour. This woman with a drawn mouth and gleaming eyes was a stranger to her, and after the first moment of horror, Teresa's heart filled with compunction and pity.

"Don't worry, Mother," she said in a low, hurried voice. "Please don't worry. Mark will go. He'll go now." She turned to him. "Won't you, Mark?"

"No," said Mark gently.

"But"—Sir Lawrence spoke incredulously—"but good God, my dear fellow, can't you see that you're upsetting Lady Thurloe? This is no time to demand explanations or to——"

"I'm demanding nothing," said Mark in the same quiet voice. "Teresa has done me the honour of saying that she loves me and will marry me. All I want to do at this moment is to convince Lady Thurloe, in a few words, that I'm a man of good character and good background who can support Teresa adequately and make her happy—and love her all my life. The points that were brought up can be disposed of quickly and to everybody's satis- faction. I'm not presuming to ask liking or affection from Lady Thurloe; all I'm saying is that before leaving the house I should be allowed to clear my name and present my credentials. I shall then go away and return, if Lady Thurloe wishes, only once more: to claim Teresa. I would like Sir Lawrence to say whether he feels this to be a reasonable request or not."

Sir Lawrence looked miserably round at them all, avoiding only Coralie's gaze.

"I . . . Nobody can doubt that in the ordinary run of things, Mark would be quite right in . . . that is——" He stopped, squared his shoulders, cleared his throat and spoke firmly. "You're right, my dear Mark," he said, "but the circumstances are a little difficult. Lady Thurloe is upset, and——"

"I am nothing of the kind," said Coralie shrilly. "This is my house and I am ordering somebody out of it. You sneaked in," she told Mark, "behind my back. I was away, and you knew you had to act quickly. Nothing about you or your circumstances is of any interest to anybody here. You will never marry Teresa if I have anything to do with it—and I shall have a great deal to do with it, I refuse to listen to anything you want to say. Now get out."

Her last words were shouted, and Teresa's face slowly became chalk-white. She looked at Mark appealingly.

"You can't do any good by staying," she said. "Please go."

"In a moment," said Mark.

"Lolly"—Teresa's voice trembled—"make him go."

Lolly was staring at Mark with an odd expression. She spoke slowly.

"I—I can't make him," she said. "I warned him—and he knows. But he—he won't go."

"Warned him?" Teresa repeated the words softly, and her eyes went from her mother's ravaged face to the white but steadfast countenance of Mark. A shudder went through her, and she addressed him in a new voice of authority.

"You must go, Mark."

"I'll go," said Mark, "when I've said this. I love you and I mean to marry you. Nothing your mother can say or do will alter this fact. You are of age and you are free—and you love me." His voice softened. "You do love me, Teresa?"

"Yes. Yes, Mark, but——"

"Then nothing can harm either of us." He turned to Lady Thurloe. "Please understand that. Teresa's engagement was a mistake, and——"

"Damn you!" said Coralie in a low voice. "Oh, damn you."

"—and she is now in love with me. We shall marry as soon as——"

"I'll see you dead first," said Coralie.

"I don't think you will."

Sir Lawrence had begun a protest, and had fallen silent. Lolly was wringing her hands in a slow, helpless gesture so unlike her normal brisk manner that it shocked Teresa almost as much as her mother's appearance and speech. She gave a little sound of misery, but nobody heard it; the room might have been empty save for the two who now faced one another by the window— Coralie, tense with rage and hatred and looking like an animal about to spring—and Mark, tall, calm, his grey eyes held unmovingly on the distraught woman before him.

"Teresa is going to marry me—but that is not why you are

angry," he told her in a slow, deliberate tone. "You are angry because——"

"You knew he'd been dead all those years, didn't you?" she broke in fiercely. "You knew, didn't you? You found out."

"Not at first."

"But you guessed."

"It wasn't very difficult."

"And you knew that that woman was living on money that should have been mine?"

"Again it was a guess—but an easy one."

"And you didn't go to the police?"

"No."

"Why didn't you? Because you saw something for yourself in it?"

"I saw something for your brother's widow in it. She needed the money."

"She was a thief—and you knew it."

"She was poor—and you were rich. You had enough; she hadn't."

"You knew that for fifteen years she had been defrauding me —and you didn't expose her."

"I felt that she was using the money to better purpose than you would have done."

"Four hundred pounds a year—for fifteen years. Did you work that sum out?"

"Yes, I did. The total came to six thousand pounds."

"And you knew that it should have come to me?"

"Yes, I knew," said Mark. "But when I was certain that Mr. Towers had died—he died abroad, of a heart attack—I had to decide whether I should expose a woman who was using the money to good purpose, and make her give it up to a woman who would use it simply to add to the comfort she already enjoyed. I thought you had enough—and I knew she hadn't. It was a very easy choice."

"You wouldn't by any chance have thought of blackmailing her?"

Mark smiled; a brief, cold smile.

"No. My pleasure sprang from knowing how angry you would have been—if you had known. I knew that money meant a great deal to you; I knew that your quarrel with your brother had been caused by the fact that he wanted some of your money—and you refused to let him have it. You would have enjoyed taking the income from your brother's wife. If I had imagined that you would be generous, that you would have shared the income with her, that you would have given her all or part of it for her needs —I would have told you the truth, before I ever met Teresa. But I knew more about you than you realize—and I decided to leave the income where it was—being used to good purpose. What would you have done with it?"

For answer, Coralie raised a hand and laid it viciously across his cheek. There was a moment's dead silence, broken by a gasp of horror from Teresa.

She had never in her life seen anybody struck. Nobody had ever raised a hand to her; her childish chastisements had been in the form of tasks or penalties suited to the wrongdoing. She had seen violence on the stage and on the screen; she had read of cruelty or of brutality. But in her small, sheltered world there had been no voice raised in shrill abuse, no hand lifted to inflict injury. Wounds had come by accident and had been tenderly treated; nobody in her experience had ever deliberately injured another person.

Now before her was the spectacle of her mother—this morning an elegant woman seated before a breakfast table, quiet, infinitely gracious—now a harridan, hands curled like claws, a face twisted to incredible ugliness, eyes almost blind with fury.

She waited for Mark to turn and leave—but Mark stood unmoving.

"Please hear what I have to say." His voice was heavy with contempt, and tears, unfelt, unheeded, began to run down Teresa's cheeks. "I love Teresa and I am going to marry her. You cannot stop me and you cannot stop her. And you cannot hurt either of us any more."

For a moment Coralie's head went from side to side like someone seeking escape—then she had made a rush to a table and seized a heavy vase. For one appalled second, it seemed that she would hurl it at Mark—but she dashed it, instead, to the wall and it shattered into a dozen pieces. Before they had fallen to the ground, she had thrown a delicate china plate and two exquisite statuettes.

"Mother!"

Teresa started forward, but Lolly's strong arm barred her way.

"Leave this to me," she said firmly. "I told him that this would happen." She was beside Coralie, and had taken her arm. "Come with me," she said gently. "Come and lie down. Throwing things is healthy; gets it off your chest—but it's an expensive outlet and you'll be sorry later. Come along and I'll settle you down with a good hot cup of something, and then you can sleep for a bit. Come along."

There was a moment's uncertainty—and then Coralie had turned and was accompanying her to the door. She walked calmly, the traces of her rage falling from her as she went. Her dignity and her poise were returning; before she went out of the room, she looked almost as she had looked before the brief, furious interlude.

The door closed behind the two women. Teresa walked tremblingly to a window and stood with her back to it, staring across the room at Mark, her eyes wide and incredulous.

"You see"—Sir Lawrence drew a deep, struggling breath of relief and addressed Mark—"you see, it wasn't wise. I told you what would happen. It was a terrible mistake."

"No." Mark was looking at Teresa. "No, it wasn't a mistake."

Sir Lawrence glanced from one to the other and then, after a helpless pause, walked to the door and opened it. Neither Teresa nor Mark glanced at him. With a shrug, he went out and closed the door softly behind him.

There was silence. Mark took a step forward and then stopped.

"Teresa——"

Her expression did not change.

"You . . . you knew," she said slowly. "You knew that Mother would—would——"

"Yes, I knew."

"You could have gone away before . . . before she . . . But you stayed, deliberately."

"Yes."

"You . . . you baited her. You said what you did to—to make her . . . to make her lose control and . . . That's true, isn't it?"

"That's true," acknowledged Mark.

"You knew—and you didn't care how she looked, or how she

behaved—because you . . . because you wanted me to see her
. . . like that."

Mark's mouth suddenly twisted in pain.

"Yes," he said.

"You say you love me—and yet you could make my mother
. . . you could expose her——" her voice became strangled and
died away.

"Teresa——" began Mark again.

She swung swiftly round and gazed unseeing out of the
window.

"Please go away," she said in a low voice.

"Will you listen to me, Teresa?"

"No. No, I won't. What you did just now . . . it was horrible.
And you did it deliberately, and . . ." There was a pause, and
when she spoke again, her voice was inflexible. "Please go
away," she said. "I never want to see you again. Never. Never."

She did not know how long she stood there. She heard no
sound. But when at last she turned, she saw that there was
nobody in the room but herself.

She was alone. Mark had gone.

Chapter Thirteen

TERESA did not see her mother until the following day. Then, passing her room before lunch, she saw the door of Coralie's room open, and paused before it.

Coralie lay in bed, behind her shoulders a pile of snowy pillows. She wore a loose jacket of palest blue; her eyes, of a deeper shade of blue, looked out at Teresa calmly, even placidly. Of yesterday's storm there was not the smallest sign, unless it showed in the slightly heightened colour in her cheeks. She had never looked more lovely, more composed, more self-possessed.

She seemed about to speak, but Lolly, tray in hand, edged Teresa aside.

"Let your mother have her lunch in peace," she urged. "I want her to rest—and then you can come up and see her and talk as much as you please." She laid the tray before Coralie. "Chicken and mushroom," she said, "and the teeniest bottle of white wine to make you feel good. Teresa"—she spoke over her shoulder—"I'll join you downstairs; I'll be down to lunch in a moment."

When she came down, Teresa was standing by the sideboard looking listlessly at the food placed upon it. She looked up as Lolly entered, but for a time neither spoke. Yesterday they had said little to one another; Lolly had spent most of the day waiting on Coralie.

"Well"—Lolly pulled out a chair and sat heavily upon it— "it's over. It's over and done with. And if I were you, I wouldn't let it worry me. Yesterday was yesterday—and it's done with. And if I could go back a few years, I wouldn't have let it worry me so much." She put up a hand and pushed back her hair. "You know what, Teresa? I'm a fool and that old livery Lawrence is a fool, and we've both been acting wrongly. We wanted you to grow up thinking your mother was an angel—and that was wrong."

"No—you weren't wrong," said Teresa.

"Yes—we were," said Lolly. "I feel at this moment like a woman who's been holding her ears waiting for an explosion to

162

go off, only to find that there's no explosion and what's more, no bomb. Stupid people—Lawrence and myself, to give two examples—grab an idea and hang on to it. Everything changes —times, fashions, circumstances—but not their idea. No, not their idea. Oh no. That they hang on to. Well, we hung on to ours—and we were wasting our time. Any time during the past five years or more, you could have found out that your mother had hell's own temper—and it wouldn't have hurt you. But we were so busy nursing our early ideas of protecting you, that we didn't see you were grown up and not a baby any more. And when I say we, I don't mean we; I mean myself only, because Lawrence, weak in the head though he may be, knew better than I did, and told me I was wrong. And now you can go ahead and talk."

"Do we have to? I mean, do we have to talk about . . . about that?" asked Teresa.

"Yes, we do. Mark understood that. And Mark was right."

There was no reply. Teresa put food on to a plate, carried it to Lolly and went back to help herself, but said nothing.

"Well?" asked Lolly, after a time.

"Well what?"

"Well, don't you agree with me? I said Mark was right."

"Mark was wrong. Please Lolly, don't let's talk about it."

"If you don't want to, I won't. But now that everything's risen to the top, why not let it stay there? Why not give it all a good airing? What do you think I feel like now, sitting here knowing that never again so long as I live, and you live and your mother lives, I'll have to listen to the tones of her voice and take quick action when she looks like misliking anything too much? What do you think it feels like for me to know that something your father dreaded for you, something your father wanted to protect you from, has happened—is over, done with, finished with, and could have been over and done with years ago?"

Teresa, on the point of pulling out her chair, paused and looked down incredulously at Lolly.

"My father tried to . . . I don't understand," she said.

"Then sit down and I'll tell you."

Teresa sat down; food was before them both, but they made no pretence of eating. Lolly pushed her plate aside, put her elbows on the table and looked at the younger woman.

"When you first spoke of your plan of going to see your uncle Hubert," she said, "I was frightened. If your mother found out, I knew it would make trouble. I was afraid she might make a scene—the kind of scene she made yesterday, the kind of scene she made when your uncle came and told her he'd married Zoë. It was your father's first view of the other side of your mother— and I may say his last—but it had an effect on him that never wore off. And he was afraid it would affect you in the same way —and as it turned out, he was wrong. But I promised him I'd come and live here and do what I could to keep your mother contented enough to prevent her from doing—well, what she did yesterday."

"You mean that all these years, you've been giving in to Mother because you thought——"

"It wasn't a matter of giving in. You get to know how to handle certain people, after a time. You don't give in to them all the time, but you saw off all the rough edges before you let them touch anything. You come up on their right side. You put awkward matters before them in a nice smooth way. I did it to your mother first deliberately and then out of habit."

"When did you . . . when did you tell Mark that Mother might——"

"—make a scene? I didn't. I hinted—and then I got Lawrence to talk to him."

"He—he worked Mother up, deliberately and—callously."

"He wanted a showdown—and he got it," Lolly looked at Teresa's white, strained face. "You're worrying," she said gently.

"If you think I'm worrying about Mark, you're wrong."

"Then you're worrying because you want to know what your mother means to do about Zoë."

"Yes."

"Why don't you go upstairs and find out?"

Teresa looked at her, and pushed away her plate.

"I will," she said. "I'll go now."

Lolly, longing with all her heart to ask questions about Mark, let her go without a word. She had seen him drive away the day before—and Teresa had steadily refused to speak of him since.

She sighed. It was not Coralie, after all, who had hurt Teresa
—and it was not only Teresa who had been hurt.

Teresa—and Mark. And upstairs, Coralie lay in bed, comfortable in mind and body, her rage spent, the future filled with
plans of getting even with Zoë.

Teresa, tapping gently on her mother's door, went in to find
the tray still on her bed. Coralie had finished—had, Teresa noted,
eaten and drunk everything. She put the tray on a table and sat
on the edge of the bed, and Coralie studied her briefly.

"You look tired," she remarked.

"I am—a little."

But Coralie did not pursue the topic.

"How much," she went on without a pause, "did you know
about what was going on at your uncle's house?"

"Nothing whatsoever."

"You accepted, I suppose, the explanation you were given—
that your uncle was abroad?"

"Yes."

"Fifteen years . . ." Coralie spoke musingly. "Fifteen years.
She must have been laughing at me—for fifteen years. But I
don't think"—her voice did not lose its gentleness—"I don't
think she'll laugh much longer."

"I——" Teresa hesitated—"I liked her, Mother."

"Liked her?"

"I liked Zoë."

Coralie gave a slight smile—brief, kind. Her hand rested on
Teresa's for a moment in a protective gesture.

"Darling, you liked her because you had no means of knowing
what sort of woman she really was. Lying here, yesterday and
this morning, I've been thinking about you—and I realize, too
late perhaps, that it isn't really wise to provide too much shelter
for one's children. They should be taught what the world is
really like, what people are really like."

"Yes, they should," agreed Teresa.

"Going to that house at all was a hideous mistake, and one
that you wouldn't have made if I'd been at home—but having
met your uncle's wife, having seen all those people Neville
described to me, you would have seen, you would have felt, you
would have sensed how shady it all was. You would have seen
through them all. But you weren't equipped to judge them; you

were taken in—and now, I hope, you'll see how near you were to wrecking your life."

Teresa sat quietly, and appeared to listen—but her mind was only partly on her mother's words. She was doing some painful reassessing—so painful that she shrank from the picture that emerged from her musings. She was struggling to set her world straight once more, and she was aware that she could not arrange it exactly as it had been before her mother's outburst.

Her mother . . . Teresa looked at her. She saw the same lovely, languid woman she had loved and admired all her life. Nothing, she realized, had changed—except her own focus. The picture had sharpened, and the defects were visible—but they had been there always, and if she had allowed herself to get a closer view, she would have seen them before. Lolly and her godfather had decided that she should get only the distant, softened view—but at this moment she knew that all their protection would have been in vain if she had not lent herself to the deception. She had joined in the conspiracy; she had exercised all Lolly's care, and more, to keep her mother's most charming side uppermost. She had known that there was another, a darker, a far less pleasant side, and she could have explored it at any time in the past few years if she had wanted to. But she had preferred to keep the scene in all its lovely completeness: Folly Cottage in all its trim beauty, her mother in all her smoothness and elegance—and their lives a succession of pleasant, ordered days. It had been a façade —and she had been aware of it in the deep, deep recesses of her mind—and she had chosen to leave things as Lolly and Lawrence had arranged them.

But Mark. . . . Mark had been resolved to sweep away pretences. He wanted her to see her mother as she was—and he had shown her.

He had shown her. He had been right . . . but he had been cruel. He had glimpsed, before it was too late, the ugliness of what he was about to reveal—and he had torn aside the last shreds of pretence and left her mother naked under the white light of truth.

Mark. . . . She would think of Mark later. For the moment there were other things. Her mother, she knew, would have made up her mind to act in one way or another; she was here to learn exactly how.

She had not long to wait. Coralie had reached for the little book in which she kept telephone numbers, and was looking for a name.

"I'm going to ring up Walter Creed. I'm sorry I shan't be able to see his expression when he finds out that for fifteen years he's been paying my income to somebody who wasn't entitled to it."

Teresa thought of the lawyer's kind old face and wise, gentle ways. His judgments, she thought, would not be as harsh as her mother's.

"I shall tell him that I shall prosecute, of course," went on Coralie.

"Prosecute?"

"Naturally. Have you forgotten, Teresa? Fifteen years—four hundred a year. I don't know what Walter will call it. Misrepresentation? She must have been signing my brother's name for all those years. False pretences."

"Mother"—Teresa spoke gently, but urgently—"couldn't you just . . . let it go?"

Coralie's glance showed nothing but astonishment.

"Let it go? You mean *not* sue her?"

"Yes. Couldn't you at least wait and——"

"Wait another fifteen years?"

"No. Couldn't you perhaps see her or ask Walter Creed——"

"Teresa, would you leave this to me, please? It isn't you who's been defrauded—it's myself. It isn't your income this woman has been enjoying herself on for fifteen years—it's been mine. Do you think for one moment that I shall behave as though six thousand pounds meant nothing at all to me? After my brother's death, it was mine—and she stole it."

Teresa waited, but there was nothing more; no word of regret for Hubert's death, no curiosity regarding his end. Coralie had been wronged, and was in pursuit of those who had wronged her; no arguments, Teresa knew, would prevent her mother from giving the necessary instructions to her lawyers.

She rose and picked up the tray.

"I'll take this downstairs," she said. "I'll come back later."

"I shall ring up Walter, and then I shall sleep for a little while," said Coralie. "Or perhaps it would be better to sleep first; Walter must be out to lunch at this time."

Teresa took the tray downstairs, and then the habits of a lifetime led her to seek Lolly. When there was trouble or perplexity, she had always sought Lolly.

She found her after some difficulty. Lolly, who after lunch every day busied herself with a dozen routine tasks, today was doing none of them. After much searching, Teresa found her in the unlikeliest place of all; seated in the small summer house at the end of the garden, staring out with a blank and uninterested gaze at the little fish swimming in the pond near by. She had been crying; her square, ugly face was mottled and her eyes red-rimmed. As Teresa came up to her, she made a clumsy attempt to get rid of the traces of tears.

"Lolly"—Teresa sat on the wooden bench beside her and took her hand—"Lolly, I've never seen you cry."

"Yes, you have, heaps of times." Lolly, between sniffs, groped for a handkerchief. Teresa shook out the folds from her own and handed it to her. "You saw me crying at Maisie Thurloe's funeral."

"Only one tear."

"It was the organ playing all that sad music."

"And Cousin Maisie too—no?"

"Well, I wouldn't have said I missed her enough to cry over her. And you saw me crying when I went to see you after you'd had your appendix out."

"Only two tears. And there was no organ."

"No. But I couldn't bear the thought of somebody having sliced a piece out of you." She examined the moist rag in her hands. "This is one of the hankies I gave you at Christmas."

"Yes. You didn't think you'd cry into it, did you?"

"Cry. . . . Crying's no use," said Lolly heavily. "Except to make me uglier than I am. How's your mother?"

"She's going to sleep. Lolly——"

"Well?"

"Was it very difficult, all these years, keeping Mother happy?"

"No. It wasn't difficult at all. I told you—it became a sort of habit. If an argument developed, I had to let the thing slide and bring it up in a different way, that's all."

"I've been doing it, too, in my own way, haven't I?" said Teresa gently.

Lolly turned to look at her.

"I suppose . . . yes," she said slowly. "We think children are fools, but they're not. Certainly not you. And I've been sitting here thinking that after all, what we did was what people all over the world do when there's a difficult member in their household. They have to choose between a peaceful existence or a hellish one, and in nine cases out of ten, they choose to duck whenever they see a storm coming. You see husbands who discover their wives have fiendish tempers—and what do the majority of them do? They give in, to save appalling and ceaseless rows. One fight now and then is good and healthy—but a series can wear you out. What we really feared for you was that you would feel the horror your father did at finding out how ugly your mother could be when she was thwarted. If we'd stopped to think, we'd have known that his was a rather special case—he was too romantic, and so he'd invested her with a sort of unearthly beauty of character. He was too dreamy—like you—and so he never saw the signs that might have shown him that she was human after all. And he was too much in love with his dream to want to embrace the reality. Perhaps he didn't really love your mother; perhaps he only loved his own fancy portrait of her. You and he . . . the two cases were entirely different, but we didn't think of that."

"She's going to tell Walter Creed to—to——"

"Institute proceedings?"

"Yes."

"I'm not surprised, Are you?"

"No. But Lolly—I've got to do something."

"What can you do?"

"I can go and see Walter."

"What good would that do?"

"I could give him the true picture—I could explain that Zoë isn't really the criminal Mother's making her out. I can——"

"But all you know," pointed out Lolly, "is what you heard yesterday between Neville's version and Mark's version. You don't really know the whole story."

"No. But I thought that before going to Walter, I'd——" She hesitated.

"—see Mark?"

"No." Teresa rose and stood looking down at the older woman. "Lolly, I'm going to see Zoë."

"Now? This minute?"

"Why not?"

"If your mother wants to know where you are?"

"Tell her. Do you know something, Lolly?" she added thoughtfully.

"Yes, I know—but tell me."

"At this moment," said Teresa, "Mother isn't really interested in me, or in my future—or even in Mark. All her mind is on——"

"—getting her own back on Zoë. Well, she's waited for over twenty years," said Lolly. "Now's her big chance."

"And so," continued Teresa, "what I do won't interest her much."

"People like your mother," said Lolly, "only go after one thing at a time—and that's how trouble sets in. They concentrate all their forces in order to get something they want, or think they want—and then when they don't get it, there's nothing to fall back on; no balance, no perspective, no nothing. Do you want me to come with you to see Zoë?"

"No, thank you. I'd rather go alone."

"Well, give her my love, and tell her she'd better gird her loins, or whatever. And Teresa——"

She paused. Her tongue trembled with the urge to put questions about Mark—and then, with a mighty effort, she fought back the words.

"What were you going to say?" asked Teresa.

"Nothing. Nothing at all," said Lolly stoutly.

Chapter Fourteen

IT was Zoë who answered the door at Teresa's summons. For a moment, the two women stood looking at one another—and then Zoë stood aside and ushered the girl inside. And Teresa, entering, was at once aware of a change in the house. All was quiet; there were no trembling airs on the violin, no furious clacking of castanets, no whirr of a sewing machine—and no anxious heads peering from the landing.

"The Baron and his wife—they are out," said Zoë. "Maxie is in the kitchen, and Paloma is in her room shut up."

"Shut up?"

"She has shut herself up. She is . . . she is unhappy. Please—will you go in."

She was ushering Teresa into the room which Teresa had privately designated as a chapel. She paused with her hand on the door handle, and looked round at Teresa.

"You . . . know everything?"

"I know something. I came to find out the rest. I . . . I was worried about you."

Zoë followed Teresa into the room and closed the door and stood looking round at the holy symbols.

"In here . . . you thought, perhaps," she asked, "that there was too much of God and His saints and His angels?"

"I. . . . Well, I'm not a Catholic, and so——"

"It was because I was frightened," said Zoë quietly. "Each year, each half year when I received your uncle's money—I was frightened. Not frightened of the law, you understand? No; I was frightened because I knew that I was sinning. So I spent some of the money in putting these things in here each time, and I prayed that God would forgive me. Because I did not"—her dark eyes rested on Teresa—"I did not do it from greed."

She had indicated a chair, but Teresa remained standing.

"Zoë"—her voice was urgent—"I want to help you. My mother knows, and . . . and she's angry."

"She will send me to prison if she can—yes?"

"I'm afraid so."

171

Zoë shrugged.

"It had to be so; soon—or now," she said. "I did not hope that I could go on for so long. Fifteen years . . ." She fell into a reverie and then roused herself. "Please sit down. I would like to tell you everything."

They sat on stiff, high-backed chairs, face to face, intent, absorbed.

"He died in France," began Zoë quietly. "It was true what I told you—that he travelled all the time. He found this house, I think, very dull; when your mother went away to be married, there was not enough money for him, and to get more, he sold things—furniture, ornaments, carpets, even curtains. But even so, the money was not enough, and prices became higher and we became poorer. I wanted to let rooms, to make money—but he would not allow me to. He wished, he said, to have his home to himself, even if a great deal of the time he was not in it. He was always away, in France, Germany, Switzerland, and because he could not afford to pay for so much travelling, he began to make certain . . . arrangements."

She paused, her eyes on a small figure of the Virgin that she had picked up from a table by her side. Fingering it absently, she went on with her story.

"The arrangements were not honest; he received money—and other things—from people, but he did not pay them back. He arranged with the Baron that he would live in their house and that he would in his turn entertain them in England. House? No, theirs was not a house; it was a palace, a château I know, for I worked there when I was a girl. It was through me, through my descriptions, that he knew so much of the Baron and the Baronne and of their home. He made himself known to them— not as my husband—mon Dieu, no! As a rich traveller only. He lived with them; he could be charming like your mother, and they liked him. And then—war came. And the Baron, living in France, was not French—but German. He thought that if he could get to England, he could perhaps use this house, as your uncle had promised him. But . . . he had no papers. And your uncle, who wished to stay at the château, who did not wish to come back here—your uncle got papers for him. Not legal papers, you understand? They were forged—for the Baron, for the Baronne, and also for Maxie and Paloma. Maxie, who had

for many years been their servant, would not let them come alone
—and he would not leave Paloma. And so they came. It was
dangerous—but they came, and they found that the house was
not, after all, grand, and that I, their old servant, was mistress
here. And the money that your uncle owed them—how could I
pay them? But they stayed here, for they had nowhere else to go.
I had to keep them—feed them."

She paused, and Teresa put a question.

"My uncle?"

"The war did not go well over there at first, as you know. He
became anxious—and he tried to get out. When the Germans
came near, he tried to leave France—but he was too late. He
hid for some time—and he died in hiding. The news was sent,
by this one and by that one, to Maxie. And Maxie told me."

"And . . . and the authorities didn't——"

"Nobody knew—only those who had hidden him, and those
who had passed the news of how he had died. But I knew that if
I told the lawyers—Creed and Creed—I would have no more
of the money. I was keeping all four of them here—and I had
not a penny. The old people had given much—and had got
nothing in return. Maxie . . . he could not earn much. Paloma
was a child. And so——"

A long sigh came from her—a sigh almost, Teresa thought, of
relief.

"It is over," she said slowly. "And I think that I am glad. At
first—it was all right. For years, we felt safe, we were almost
happy. But then . . . people began to come. Walter Creed came.
His brother came—and I knew that it would not be long before
the police came. And we grew frightened, and it is not good to
live in fear, Teresa."

"No. But"—Teresa hesitated—"I'm sorry that my mother sent
Neville here."

"It did not matter. It was then already too late for us—for
Mark had guessed what we were hiding. But Mark did not
make accusations, as the other man did—your fiancé. When he
had gone, Mark came to see me again and I told him what had
happened."

"But Mark would never have—have told the police."

"No. So much he promised. But your fiancé would tell your
mother, and your mother. . . ." She stopped. "That is why you

have come—is it not so? Your mother—I think that she will try to send me to prison." Zoë gave a slow, mirthless smile. "She has waited a long time. Always she hated me. She thought that I tricked your uncle into marrying me——"

"Zoë"—Teresa broke in impulsively—"I'm going to see the lawyers. They're kind, and they're—they'll understand. Mother will only give them one side of the story, but I can give them the other. I can tell them what you've told me just now and they can——"

"What can they do?" asked Zoë gently. "Nothing. But you are kind, Teresa. You are like your father. He, too, would have liked to be kind, all those years ago—but your mother would not let him. The lawyers will perhaps wish to be kind—but they will have to do as your mother wishes. The money was hers—and I used it."

"Walter will talk to her. When I've been to see him," said Teresa, "he'll talk to Mother and he'll make her act reasonably. You didn't use the money for yourself—you used it to help people to whom my uncle owed something." Teresa rose and stood looking down at the older woman. "We're not going to sit down and let Mother have things all her own way, Zoë. I want to help you—and first I shall see Walter Creed and then I shall see my godfather, and then . . ."

"And then?"

"And then I shall go and find Mark."

"When did you see him?"

"He came to the cottage yesterday. He . . . there was a terrible scene."

"I know." Zoë's voice was calm. "Your mother makes them, isn't it so? Your uncle knew quite well; he was used to them."

"There was . . . yes, there was a scene. She was angry—but I can help you, Zoë. At least, I can try to."

"I shall be grateful." Zoë put out a hand and touched Teresa's. "You are very good, and I am glad that you came—and that we liked each other. But I am not afraid. I know what I did, and I know that there are penalties for doing it—and I am ready. I ask only that the old people should be looked after—and Maxie, and Paloma. It could not go on for ever. Fifteen years . . . for those I am grateful."

"My godfather has great influence—he can do something

about their papers—I know he can," said Teresa earnestly.
"Don't worry."

Zoë did not reply; the tears, long held back, were now flowing
freely. Teresa bent over her and kissed her gently on her wet
cheek.

"I'll come back, Zoë," she said. "Please, please don't worry.
Nothing terrible is going to happen—I'll see to that, I promise.
No"—she put out a hand—"don't get up. I'll let myself out.
Stay here, please."

Zoë did not move; as Teresa closed the door of the room
behind her, she knew that the older woman was praying.

She went through the hall, into the little outer hall, and opened
the door—and then stood rooted to the spot, fear flooding her
heart.

On the steps stood a policeman—and Teresa knew that she
had seen him before. She had seen him when he had tried to
detain Paloma in the street—and Paloma had broken away from
him and run to the house and had been admitted by her father
and given shelter.

There was silence for some moments; Teresa struggled to get
her fears under control, and then spoke coolly.

"Are you looking for anybody?"

"I am." The strong young face came closer as the man came
on to the topmost step. "Anybody in?"

"Nobody, I'm afraid," said Teresa. "Everybody is out. And
I'm just going out myself."

"Well, I'll have a word with you first," said the policeman.
"I'm looking for——"

A fear, black and shaking, welled up in Teresa. She broke
into the man's sentence with a trembling question.

"Who . . . who sent you here?" she asked.

"Mr. Mark Tudor sent me," he replied.

The street outside turned a circle and came to rest again
before Teresa's pain-filled eyes.

"He . . . he told you to come here?" she heard herself asking.

"He did. And now if you'll——"

But Teresa heard no more. With a swift movement, she had
pulled the front door shut behind her and had slid past the man
barring her way. She was running, heedless of his shout behind
her; she was running towards the taxi rank at the corner of the

street. She had reached it and was fumbling at the door of the foremost taxi. She was in and was giving a breathless direction.

"Pym's Court."

"City?"

"Yes. Hurry, please."

Walter would know what to do. Walter would hear the story in all its truth, and Lawrence would see that nothing was done to hurt Zoë. She, Teresa, had money; she would give it to make up the loss her mother had incurred throughout the years. Zoë. . . .

Mark.

Had Mark betrayed them? Mark, of clear grey eyes and the light manner that concealed—concealed what? The police at the house—sent by Mark.

A sob shook her, and she strained forward as though she could speed the taxi on its way. Kingsway . . . Aldwych . . . Fleet Street; they were coming nearer. They were turning down the narrow alley; they had come to a halt before the door with the series of small brass plates. She was paying the taxi; she had turned and was running swiftly up the dark, narrow stairs leading to Walter Creed's office.

And as she ran, her heart became lighter. She had known here nothing but kindness; Walter had known her all her life, and he knew her mother—and now he must prevent her mother from taking her revenge. And he must find Mark and find out why Mark changed his mind—why Mark had sent the police to Grosvenor Drive. He must. . . .

She saw the mild surprise on the old clerk's face as she came to a panting halt at his desk.

"Is Mr. Creed in? Mr. Walter Creed?"

"Yes, Miss Thurloe. He's expecting you."

"Expecting. . . . Oh, did Miss Hyde ring up?"

"Yes; she said that you would be coming to see us." The old man opened a door leading to a long corridor. "Will you come this way?"

Teresa followed him down the familiar passage. They skirted a workman who was busy painting a door, and edged their way past his pails and brushes. Then they were before the door on which was displayed Walter's name. The next moment, Teresa was in the room, facing the tall, white-haired man who was rising from his chair and who was coming round the desk to greet her.

"Teresa, my dear!" He took in her flushed, breathless air. "Did you run all the way from Brighton?"

"No." She managed a smile. "No. I just. . . . Oh, Walter," she burst out, "you've got to help me."

"Sit down, my dear." His voice was soothing. "Sit down and take several deep, long breaths and then you'll feel better. Would you like a drink, or a cup of something? Tea?"

"No. No, thank you. I just want to talk to you—and to ask your help."

"That is what we are here for. You want us to help your uncle Hubert's widow?"

Teresa gave a gasp of relief.

"Oh—has Lolly told you?"

"She told us a part. But"—he smiled at her—"may I say that it wasn't entirely a surprise?"

"You mean——"

"I mean that we may look a sleepy lot, but we have our wakeful moments. If we do not see a client for ten, twelve, fourteen or fifteen years, my Teresa, we begin to formulate certain theories." He leaned forward. "Why did you come here looking so panic-stricken?"

"My mother is going to prosecute, and——"

"She rang me up. What else?"

"I went to see my uncle's wife . . . widow . . . at Grosvenor Drive. The—the police are there."

"The police!"

"Yes. And I came here at once and. . . . Oh Walter, you must listen to me, and then you must—you must talk to Mother and stop her from doing anything that will hurt Zoë. I know the money wasn't hers to use—Zoë, I mean—and I know she had every right to it—Mother, I mean—but there was a good reason why she had to have it—I'm talking about Zoë. She's *good*, Walter, she's *good* and you've got to believe me when I tell you that——"

"Please!"

Teresa came to a breathless halt and gazed miserably at the man before her. Walter Creed waited for a moment and then spoke slowly and clearly.

"I told you just now, Teresa," he said, "that we are not fools."

"I know. Oh, I know! But——"

"And therefore," proceeded Walter, disregarding the interruption, "we—I'm speaking of my brother Hilary and myself—have been for some time past—I might almost say for some years past—uneasy about the situation at Grosvenor Drive. Almost two years ago, my brother paid a visit to the house specifically to inform himself whether all was or was not well with your uncle."

"Then if he saw Zoë, he must know that——"

"He saw your uncle's wife. He was not admitted to the house."

"You mean——"

"I mean that she would not, did not invite him to enter. But she set his mind at rest in certain particulars—that is, he thought that she was speaking the truth when she told him that your uncle was abroad. He was not sure, but he was almost sure. Later, we became uneasy again, and this time I myself called at the house. Like my brother, I failed to get inside."

"I know. She was . . . she was frightened because——"

"Please wait. I am trying to——"

"Wait!" Teresa stared at him in desperation. "Wait? Walter, Mother is there at home, planning to have her revenge on Zoë—and the police are at Zoë's door! And you tell me to wait!"

"I was merely trying," said Walter patiently, "to put before you our own version of the affair." He rose and walked round the desk. "You will have to add your knowledge to ours," he told her, "and then we shall be able to form a clear picture. We have a file on the subject, and you had better see it. Will you come with me?"

Teresa began to speak, thought better of it, and rose. She knew Walter and she knew Hilary; they went at their own pace, and it was a slow, steady tramp. She could not rush them; she could not even hurry them.

Some part of what Walter had said, however, brought her comfort. He had given no indication of which camp he and his brother were in—but they had both been to see Zoë, and they had both appeared to like or at least to trust her. She had only to be patient and wait until the moment when Walter was ready to advise her.

He opened the door for her and she stepped past his tall, trim figure, immaculate in its beautifully cut clothes. He was the City man to perfection: black coat, striped trousers and—in the street —bowler hat and neatly rolled umbrella.

They were out in the corridor, but this time there was not so far to walk. Walter led her past two doors and stopped at the third, and Teresa saw that it was the one on which the painter had been at work. He was collecting his pails and brushes, his task done; she saw on the glass panel the newly-painted letters of a name. Then Walter had opened the door and ushered her in.

But she did not go in. She did not see through the open door the desk, the filing cabinets, the swivel chair and, rising from it, a younger model of the City lawyer, black of coat and striped of trouser. Her eyes were on the letters and she was staring at the name they spelled. Motionless, speechless, she gazed at it. Walter, beside her, smiled gently.

"Our new junior partner," he purred, "will put you in touch with all that we know of the affairs of your uncle's wife. Will you go in?"

Teresa turned slowly, and the man at the desk waited for her.

"This is Miss Thurloe," said Walter. "Teresa, I think you know our Mr. Tudor?"

Without waiting for an answer, he went out and closed the door behind him.

Chapter Fifteen

OF that moment, all Teresa could remember later with any degree of clarity was the smell of paint in her nostrils. The rest was a haze—but an infinitely pleasant, an infinitely soothing one. She was in Mark's arms; there was nothing to say, nothing to plan, nothing to fret over. She was safe within a strong, warm circle; her own problems, her mother's, Zoë's—Mark would solve them all. In the long silence she stood quite still and felt his lips on her hair and his heart beating close to hers.

The aged clerk opened the door, closed it again after an appalled glance, stood in the corridor biting his nails for perplexed seconds, opened the door again to see if he had been dreaming, and closed it again without being sure. Within the room, Mark stirred and spoke gently.

"You were angry with me."

Teresa did not raise her head from its comfortable resting-place.

"Not for long."

"I had to hurt you. I had to——"

"I know. And you were right. But Lolly was right, too—before that."

"Yes. How is your mother?"

"Exactly as usual." She freed herself and looked at him. "Mark, Zoë——"

"I know. Your mother's after her blood. Well . . . that's what we all expected. We—Why are you staring at me?"

"I'm not staring. I'm just looking. I haven't seen you dressed like this before."

He looked down at his immaculate attire.

"You like?" he asked.

"It's devastating."

"I should have prepared you. But Walter would have his little joke."

"He knew . . . about us?"

"From the first moment. When I rang him up that first day and told him you'd come to your uncle's house, he wouldn't

180

believe it—until I described you, piece by beautiful piece. He agreed with me when I said that it was a miracle—and he wished me luck."

"Mark—begin at the beginning."

"My darling, that is the beginning."

"No, not quite. Why were you at Zoë's?"

"It's a long story, and this isn't the place to talk in," he said. "I'll take you home with me and you can ask all the questions you like on the way."

But Teresa asked no questions as they drove; she was content to sit back beside him and watch his long, lean hands on the wheel and remember the first time she had seen him outside her uncle's house.

They were not going to her uncle's house now. She roused herself and spoke for the first time since leaving the office.

"Where do you live? I mean, did you live at Abbott Square before you went to Zoë's?"

"Yes. It's a large house that's been chopped by its owner into flats. I chose the ground floor because there's a nice big garden and David could run in and out and so could his pets later on. No outlook—except lawn—but more freedom than being upstairs."

"Whereabouts is Abbott Square?"

"In the Dowager's district: Belgravia."

"Who looks after David?"

"A nice couple called Polly and Pete; married and doing this to give themselves a cheapish start in life.—Isn't it time you turned your mind from my affairs to Zoë's?"

He had turned into a quiet street and was turning again into a quieter one. He brought the car to a standstill before a large mansion, and sat looking at it for a moment.

"Well, there it is," he said. "I suppose you think this is a more suitable background for me than the house in Grosvenor Drive?"

"It's slightly smarter, isn't it?"

"David and I enjoyed being at Zoë's; in a way, we were both sorry to leave."

Teresa turned in her seat to face him.

"Walter sent you there, to—to find out things, didn't he?"

"He did. And so Neville was right; I was doing a nasty, low-down spying job. But it had to be done. We had to find out what had become of your uncle—because we were pretty certain something had happened to him. At one time, he was always dropping in to see Walter or Hilary—not in a friendly way; merely to pass the time of day and say some harsh things about your mother. Then he stopped coming. They were rather relieved —and then they began to wonder."

"For fifteen years?"

"For about two or three. We're lawyers and Trustees, remember, not sleuths. Our job was to pay your uncle's income into the Bank. He and Zoë had a joint account—so all she had to do was use the money. It was as easy as that. She might have gone on using it until she died—but Walter went a-looking and——"

"And didn't get in."

"Quite. And neither did Hilary. Zoë recognized the name. And so they thought it might be a good idea if I had a go—not as a member of the firm, but as a stranger looking for rooms. Well, I went. No go. I tried once more. Same result. I reported failure—but one day I took David for one of those wandering walks we both enjoy so much—and I found that we were close to Grosvenor Drive. I liked the look of Zoë, and on the purest impulse I took David along to see her—just to show him off; nothing more. But when she opened the door and saw us both standing there. . . ." He frowned. "It was almost too easy. She said she had no idea that a little boy was involved in my search for rooms—and she took us both in."

"And how soon did you——"

He laughed.

"Could I continue this story over a hot cup of tea? You can make it; Pete's at work, and Polly's out with David. Coming?"

In a dream, she stood in a small, spotless, primrose-and-black kitchen and made tea, and Mark prepared a tray and carried it into the large drawing-room that opened on to a long, half-tended, half-wild garden. She poured his tea and he took it from her and put it down again in order to take her in his arms. It was some time before she came back to her questioning, and then he sat beside her and finished the story.

"You were in the house—you saw them all," he said. "It didn't take a Sherlock Holmes to know that they were all as frightened as blazes every time strangers came to the door. And Paloma was causing trouble; it was merely a matter of time before she staged a one-woman revolution and blew the whole thing to blazes. But all those were secondary matters; the sub-plot, as it were. The real question was: where was Hubert? No letters came from him—Zoë used to read out bits from letters on days when I knew that the postman had passed the house without delivering anything. And the letter she read from was always the same one—and your uncle seemed to me to cover long distances in amazingly short times—and to take an astonishingly zig-zag route. But it was the dressing gown that made me certain, in the end, that your uncle was either dead—or would never return to the house."

"What dressing gown?"

"The one that was hanging behind your door. The one you wore on your way to and from the bathroom. It was a man's; it was—Zoë told me—your uncle's. But it had never hung there before; she had always worn it herself. A woman's entitled to wear her husband's dressing gown when he's away, but when she deliberately hangs it up and explains that it's there waiting for him to come back and wear it—you begin to wonder." He rose and walked to the open door leading out to the garden, and stood staring out thoughtfully. "I thought, once or twice, that Zoë would tell me the truth. She trusted me—but she always stopped just on the brink of bringing it all out."

"But . . . did you go out to work every day?"

"Yes, but not in this get-up. I used to take David to the nursery school and leave him there, and then go home and change—and in the evening, I changed again and went back to Grosvenor Drive."

"Did you tell Zoë who you were? In the end, I mean."

"Yes. I told her when I knew that it was certain your mother would make some inquiries about me. She would go—or send somebody—to the house, and I wanted to prepare Zoë. And I wanted to tell her what she was to say. Neville went to see her—and then went back to your mother with what he thought was the full story."

"But——"

"He told your mother—and from that moment, her mind swerved off your affairs and became centred on her own. The big blow-up was not, in the end, caused by the fact that you were going to marry me; it arose from her sudden realization that for fifteen years she'd been missing out on a pay-cheque. And that's why I kept hammering the fact at her. That . . . and to clear the air once and for all." He came back to Teresa and bent to kiss her gently. "There's nothing wrong with your mother that isn't wrong with a million other women," he said. "She's selfish—so what? She's apt to go off the handle if she finds herself in a corner without something she wants—who cares? You and I will love her when she'll let us, and duck when she starts throwing things—and either way, it won't matter much to either of us."

"Lolly did it because——"

"I know. But there always has to be a first time—and you'd been wrapped up long enough. My guess was that you didn't really imagine your mother was the twenty-two carat charmer you all made her out to be. But you didn't want a scene because it was easier, it was more comfortable, it was more in keeping with those pleasant surroundings to avoid jarring notes. In other words, you didn't want your sugar candy cottage to fall down. Am I right?"

"Yes. Were you always so bright?" asked Teresa, "or was it a late flowering?"

"You think I'm too clever?"

"I think you're wonderful."

"Good. In a way, so's your mother. And speaking of your mother, don't worry about Zoë. And speaking of Zoë, when you saw that policeman, why did you bolt straight to Walter? Why didn't you ask Zoë where you could find me, and come to me?"

"The policeman said you'd sent him. I thought. . . . No," she corrected herself. "No, I didn't really think you'd done anything like that." She went up to him and rested her cheek against his. "It's a funny thing, but when Mother was reading out that list of crimes, I didn't for one moment worry about you —I mean, I never for one moment lost confidence in your—in your——"

"Integrity is the word you want." His arms went round her. "Teresa, my darling, you're so . . . so . . ."

"So what?"

"It doesn't matter. Just stay like this, quietly. I love you."

"And I love you," said Teresa, "but we haven't settled anything."

"Anything about what?"

"Mother is determined to sue Zoë."

"And Lawrence will see that she doesn't."

"How? Mother won't listen to him."

"She won't have to—yet. His first job will be to inject a little legality into the positions of the old Baron and Baronne, and Maxie and Paloma."

"The policeman . . . Why did you——"

"—send him?"

"I'd seen him before. He . . . he was after Paloma."

"That must be what they call woman's intuition. Because that's just what he was—after Paloma. He loved her—and she loved him. He's been hanging round her, desperate with love and longing, for nearly four months. I don't suppose he's noticed one single criminal activity on his beat during all that time—he's just been in a daze, dreaming of Paloma and wondering how he could get past her papa. And so when I happened to drive past him this morning, I stopped the car and leaned out and said to him, 'Brother, the door's open; go in and get her.'"

"Little friend of all the world," said Teresa gently.

"Me? Yes." Mark grinned. "It's been a nice change from sitting in an office and taking dull clients out to lunch. I'm sorry it's over."

"But Mark, it isn't over. It's only just——"

"For us, beginning. But for Zoë and the others, for your mother—everything will be arranged. You wait and see. And now could we stop talking about other people and decide what names we shall give our children?"

"Mark, first of all," decided Teresa.

"Certainly—but the other eleven?"

"Eleven?"

"A dozen, if you insist," said Mark generously, and took her into his arms.

Chapter Sixteen

"WELL, if he doesn't like it," Lolly told the shopkeeper in Brighton, "he'll just have to come and change it, that's all. Wrap it up, will you?"

She waited impatiently as Lawrence's birthday present was wrapped and tied; then she hurried awkwardly out of the shop and walked to the bus stop. Once on the bus, she relaxed for the first time since leaving the cottage; there had been much to do before she left, and she was feeling breathless and irritable. Monday was laundry day, silver-cleaning day and baking day; it was just like Lawrence, she reflected, to have a birthday on a Monday and insist on her coming to lunch.

But she would see Teresa—and Mark. Her spirits rose. The house with Teresa out of it had been dull indeed; two days absence was not a long one, but she had become accustomed to having her at home, and the last day or two had reminded her unpleasantly of the long school terms when there had been nothing to do but wait for the holidays—and for Teresa to come home.

Her mind went back to Teresa's announcement that she was going to stay in London and shop—and to see Mark—for a couple of days. Just that; no more. And she, Lolly, had waited for Coralie to fall down dead with shock—and what had Coralie done? Coralie had looked up from the morning paper and said "Oh really, dear?"—and gone on reading. It had been as easy as that. No arguments, no recriminations—one might have added, no interest.

The house was the same, reflected Lolly—and not the same. They were all, inwardly, more at ease. Something had stretched, something had snapped—and no great damage had been done. And things would go on exactly as before. Coralie would be charming and she, Lolly, would try to keep her so. Teresa? Teresa would marry and go away and at this moment it was not possible to say whether she would go away for ever, or whether she would come home from time to time to stay at the cottage. It all depended upon Coralie—and for the moment, all Coralie's thoughts were fixed on when and how her brother's widow was to be made to pay for her wrongdoing.

A week. . . . It was a week, one week to the day since they had stood in the drawing-room and listened to Coralie—and looked at Coralie. One week. A dull week; one had waited for something to happen and nothing whatsoever had happened. Or if it had, it had happened somewhere else and nobody had brought news of it to the cottage. Perhaps Lawrence would know something; perhaps Teresa would know more than she had known when she returned from London.

She fell into a dream; it was all very confusing, but on the whole it was all very pleasant. Teresa—and Mark. Mark—and Teresa. And their children. They would live in London and—with luck—come down to the cottage for week-ends and holidays, and drive to the sea, and she would teach the children the breast stroke and show them how to float. Leave the cottage? No, she would never leave the cottage. Coralie would never ask her to stay, and would show no sign of wanting her to stay—but Coralie needed her, and knew it. There would be no more affection between them than there had been in the past—but there would be no more strife, either. She might leave and make a home for herself, but she needed work, and plenty of it, and here at the cottage she found a hundred outlets for her energy and usefulness. She was older than Coralie, but she would, she thought, outlive her; at least, she would never, if God knew His business, fail in health and have to go into one of those depressing places where people sat about waiting to end their days. And if Coralie ever turned her out, which she could and welcome, Teresa would give her something to do. The future wasn't so bad, on the whole, and——

A glimpse of unfamiliar roads made her realize that she had passed her bus stop. Springing to her feet, she put her finger on the Stop button and kept it there in spite of the conductor's protests.

She got off the bus flushed with the joy of having got the last word, and walked back towards Sir Lawrence's house. As she reached it, she saw Mark's car turn into the road, and stood waiting for it to draw up. Teresa and Mark got out and she greeted them affectionately.

"I missed you both. What's been happening?"

"We'll tell you inside," said Mark.

"I wouldn't have come on a Monday," said Lolly, lumbering up the steps, "if it hadn't been Lawrence's birthday and—Oh!" She stopped abruptly and turned to them with her jaw dropping in dismay. "His present!"

"Left it at home?" asked Mark sympathetically.

"Left it on the bus," said Lolly gloomily. "Now what?"

"Want me to chase it?"

"No. No, thank you. If nobody walks away with it, it'll go to the bus station and Lawrence can go and fetch it this evening. If a present's worth having"—she went on up the steps and gave a peal on the doorbell—"it's worth fetching."

Sir Lawrence came as usual to the door to let them in, but he led them not to the little study, but to the drawing-room. Lolly stood on the threshold looking round and clicking her tongue.

"How did you get the old she-bear to let you in here?" she asked. "Did you clean and tidy it yourself?"

"I certainly did not," said Sir Lawrence. "In future, I'm not going to live in two rooms; I'm going to spread myself out."

"What's this?" Lolly stared at him. "Aren't you frightened of her any more?"

"I am not."

"Then perhaps you'll grow into a man after all. Would there be any nice healthy tomato juice among those poisons on the table?"

Lawrence laughed and brought her a glass.

"Here," he said. "How's Coralie?"

"Plotting vengeance," said Lolly. Her face became anxious and she looked at Mark. "What's going to happen to Zoë?" she asked.

"Nothing," said Mark. "Nothing unpleasant. Sir Lawrence has seen to that."

"What did you do?" Lolly asked the old man. "People without papers—you may be a man with unlimited influence; who's questioning it?—but no papers are no papers."

"Maxie might be the difficult one, but I don't think so. For the others—something will be arranged." He turned to Teresa. "I suppose Mark told you that that isn't what's going to worry us?"

"I know. It's the money," said Teresa.

"Yes. The money." Sir Lawrence said no more until he had poured drinks. "The money," he repeated. "Your mother, Teresa will never let that go."

"I know. It's odd, isn't it?" said Teresa. "She's got so much."

"What makes people think," asked Lolly, "that only the poor know the value of money? The poor don't; half the time, that's why they're poor. It's people like Coralie who know exactly what money is and how much it can do—and who prize it above everything in the world. She was muttering in her sleep as I passed her room last night. I didn't stop to listen, but I'm willing to bet that she was murmuring six thousand pounds over and over again." She sighed. "She's going to have her pound of flesh."

"She isn't," said Mark quietly.

"But she will"—Sir Lawrence turned to Teresa—"have the money."

"Yes. Mark explained, and I agree with it all," said Teresa.

"Agree with what?" asked Lolly.

"We've arranged," Sir Lawrence told her, "to let Coralie have the six thousand pounds."

"Who's we?"

"Walter, Hilary, Mark and myself."

"You're giving her a quarter each?" Lolly's voice was squeaky with surprise.

"No. Teresa will pay the money out of the inheritance she got from her father. If Coralie doesn't spend it, it will come back to Teresa eventually. Walter will tell Coralie that Zoë has managed to raise the money—and she will never be told how."

"She won't care how," said Lolly. "But she'll still sue."

"She won't," said Mark. "Sueing means going into court and giving evidence—and listening to evidence. There are certain aspects of the case which Teresa's mother wouldn't care to have widely known."

"Such as?"

Sir Lawrence smiled grimly.

"Such as the fact that Hubert spent years on the Continent cheating people. The Baron can put us on to one or two of them and Zoë can put us in touch with the rest. Pure swindling. The picture of Zoë trying to make reparation for her husband's mis-

deeds isn't quite the one Coralie wants to paint for the jury. No"
—he raised his glass to Teresa and Mark—"God bless you both,
Coralie won't prosecute. Revenge is sweet, but six thousand
pounds is sweeter, and she'll settle for it. When are you two
going to be married?"

"Four weeks and two days from now," said Mark. "I'm going
to drive Lolly and Teresa home after lunch and see what Lady
Thurloe has to say about it. Somehow, I feel she'll be at the
wedding."

A gong, booming softly through the house, brought Lolly's
amazed eyes to rest on her host.

"In the name of Moses," she said slowly, "how did you get
that old crow to——"

"Lunch." Sir Lawrence offered her his arm. "My birthday
lunch and"—he led them to the dining-room—"my new and
most valued housekeeper."

The neat, smiling woman standing by the sideboard turned
for a moment, and Lolly, after a single glance, had given a cry
of amazement.

"Zoë!"

Zoë smiled.

"Please—sit. The food should not get cold."

But Lolly did not sit. She was wringing Zoë's hand and con-
gratulating Sir Lawrence and asking questions all at the same
time.

"Did Sir Lawrence import the whole household?" she asked.

Zoë smiled and shook her head.

"The others? No. I am here; I am cook; I am housekeeper."

"And the others?"

Zoë placed a bottle of wine by Sir Lawrence's plate; she
looked serious, absorbed, entirely professional.

"Please sit," she said once more. "Sir Lawrence will tell you
of the others."

She went out to bring in the food, and Teresa answered Lolly's
question.

"Maxie," she said, "stayed at Grosvenor Drive to look after
the old people. Lawrence is going to buy the house from me—
because it's mine and not mother's—and is going to let them
live there."

"And Paloma," said Mark, "is going to marry her policeman.
And Sir Lawrence is going to the bus station after lunch to get
his lovely, lovely present. And we're going to make Lolly our
first godmother. And"—he turned to drop a light kiss on Teresa's
cheek—"we are all going to live happily ever after."

"Amen," said Lolly.

OTHER ROMANTIC NOVELS BY
ELIZABETH CADELL

All these books are available at your bookshop or newsagent, or can be ordered direct from the publisher. Just tick the titles you want and fill in the form below.

....

CORONET BOOKS, Cash Sales Department, Kernick Industrial Estate, Penryn, Cornwall.

Please send cheque or postal order. No currency, and allow 5p per book (4p per book on orders of five copies and over) to cover the cost of postage and packing in U.K., 5p per copy overseas.

Name...

Address...

....